And Enjoy!

Phillip O. Otts

A STORM BEFORE THE WAR

by Phillip O. Otts

BYGONE ERA BOOKS

TABLE OF CONTENTS

1. Morning in Havana   1
2. A Young Man Corrupted   11
3. An Evening's Entertainment   27
4. S. S. Central America   43
5. A Storm at Sea   57
6. Into the Darkness   75
7. Survival   91
8. The Packer Trade   115
9. Island Intrigue   135
10. A Great Man's Secret   159
11. An Unexpected Offer   183
12. Liverpool Gaol   197
13. A Chance Encounter   211
14. St. George's Hall   227
15. The Spymater   237
16. Unexpected Developments   247
17. The Telegram   267
18. A Double Life   295
19. Homeward Bound   313
About the Author   353

"Without the firing of a gun, without drawing a sword, should they [Northerners] make war upon us [Southerners], we could bring the whole world to our feet. What would happen if no cotton was furnished for three years? ... England would topple headlong and carry the whole civilized world with her. No, you dare not make war on cotton! No power on earth dares make war upon it. Cotton is King."

Senator James Henry Hammond, South Carolina
1858

CHAPTER ONE:
MORNING IN HAVANA

John Harvey, a freed man of color still bound to his owner, sat outside the baggage terminal at the port of Havana, watching young Martin McCrary's property. A pair of heavy trunks was stacked nearby, waiting to be loaded on the *S.S. Central America*, a glorious mail steamer bound for the city of New York. Harvey wore a proper suit, a mended cast off made for Martin's father, Mr. Hank McCrary, who happened to be one of the wealthiest men in South Carolina. Some of the house slaves wondered why their master's old clothes seemed to fit Harvey so well, but the white folks didn't notice.

It was a hot, muggy afternoon in early September 1857. Towering thunderstorms lined the horizon, like ivory citadels on ebony bluffs, but the sky above was clear. Harvey stood, removed his jacket and shook it gently before folding it carefully on the rough bench beside him. As his eyes wandered, Harvey noticed a crumpled newspaper lying on the ground beneath the bench. He reached for the paper, ignoring the grease stains as a frightened mouse scurried for cover, leaving a tiny trail of crumbs in its wake. Normally cautious about public displays of literacy back home, Harvey had been traveling abroad with the younger McCrary for months, so he unfolded the paper without hesitation. He was pleased to find an edition of the Charleston Daily Courier dating back to March of that year.

The paper featured the usual advertisements, slave auctions and the like, but the lead article on the front page was different:

"The decision of the Supreme Court just pronounced, in the Dred-Scott case, that the Missouri Compromise is unconstitutional (an opinion we have always entertained and maintained) and that free negroes have no rights as citizens under the Constitution of the United States. The decision will, we confidently believe, settle these vexed questions forever, quiet the country, and relieve it of abolition agitation, and tend to greatly perpetuate our Union—our Constitutional Union—the greatest political boon ever vouchsafed by God to man."

"Free negroes have no rights as citizens," Harvey read the words out loud. He felt a familiar rage, an anger that could easily erupt into violence. He quickly regained control and glanced around to make sure no one was

2

watching, a survival instinct that had served him well during most of his 27 years.

"Well," Harvey thought to himself, as he took a deep breath. "I suppose I'll have to find some other place to live, when the time comes..."

This line of thinking caused Harvey to look around at the harbor and streets of Havana. He shook his head and laughed quietly to himself—he would never find a home in Cuba.

Harvey knew more about the Spanish colony than he should, given his station in life, but he had found other ways to exert a little influence in the world. Cuba was hell for a black man, no better than South Carolina. The most influential families lived off the sugar trade, which was made profitable by the slaves who worked the plantations and the insatiable markets of Europe and the United States. Some slaves and freedmen had rebelled over the years, but all of the rebellions were crushed. As he waited, Harvey recalled the story of the Ladder Conspiracy: Some years back, the Spanish colonial authorities lashed over 300 black men to ladders on the streets of Havana and whipped them until they confessed. Many of the confessions were false. Afterwards, the Spaniards executed all of the men, anyway. People don't forget that sort of thing, and some would try to do something about it.

"Speak of the Devil," Harvey thought to himself as a thin figure approached his location from an alley off the Desamparados, the main street running between the docks and warehouses lining the west side of the harbor.

3

Harvey stood politely as the man he knew only as "Placido" extended a hand in greeting.

"The last time we met," Harvey growled, while enveloping the Cuban's hand in his calloused fist , "you never told me what "Placido" meant." Harvey had hoped to elicit a laugh from the Cuban, a neatly dressed man of mixed race who could easily pass as an olive-skinned European from the Mediterranean, but a shadow moved across the man's face, and he pulled his hand back to his side.

Looking down at his feet and then up at Harvey again, Placido responded proudly, in fluent but heavily accented English. "Placido was the nickname of my father, Gabriel de la Concepción Valdés. He was murdered by the Spanish bastards when I was a boy. He was a poet and a great man."

"The Ladders?" Harvey asked, with a look of genuine surprise on his face. "You told me the story, the first time we met, in New Orleans. I didn't know your father was... "

"We should not speak of such things," Placido interrupted sharply. The Scotsman would be angry, as he expects the both of us to maintain our anonymity." The Cuban carefully pronounced the latter word, breaking it up into five distinct syllables.

Harvey responded by holding Placido's gaze for a moment, while nodding his head with regret and understanding.

"Speaking of the Scotsman, what gifts do you bring?" the American freedman asked the Cuban who hoped to free his people.

"A document of great value. You must pass it along as soon as you arrive in Liverpool. The thing is disguised as a commercial document, with lists of items to be ordered from the merchants of England for the wealthy families of Havana." Placido reached into his jacket and pulled out a tight bundle of papers, a collection of disguised and encoded reports on Spanish military deployments in Cuba, which he handed to Harvey without hesitation.

"And for me?" Placido asked in turn, while standing tall and fully composed.

"A gift from the Scotsman," Harvey responded, as he turned to open one of the trunks with a large key tied to a cord around his neck. After fishing around amongst his young master's clothes, he reached the bottom of the trunk and retrieved a rectangular package wrapped in brown paper.

"With compliments from our mutual friend," Harvey said with a smile as he handed the package to Placido. "It's a copy of the new Webster dictionary, along with a few instructions and some gold for your people. He said you should use the book as the key to lock and unlock your code, as you were taught."

"Yes, of course," Placido responded as his eyes scanned the area for potential enemies. "I should go," he concluded nervously. The two men stood silently for a moment before the Cuban turned to walk way, only to stop and face Harvey again.

"My name, it means the Peaceful One," Placido confessed, with an ironic smile.

Harvey's laugh echoed off the walls as the Cuban disappeared around the nearest corner. He knew the "Peaceful One" was a dangerous man, a killer when the need arises, just like him.

Some time later Harvey's attention was drawn to the noise of a mule cart led by a pair of Cuban dock workers, with a sweaty American shipping clerk perched on top of the cart.

"You must be Martin McCrary's nigger," the red-faced American exclaimed, as he climbed down with a great deal of help from one of the Cubans.

"I'm a freedman and no man's nigger," Harvey responded with a tight-lipped scowl, as he stood over the nervous clerk. "Harvey is my name—you best use it."

The clerk stuttered fearfully, speaking as quickly as he could: "I, ah, ah, meant no offense, Mr. Harvey, being a g-g-good Christian from b-b-Boston myself, but I spoke with Master Mc-Mc-Crary, and he told me I could find his, ah...MAN down here with the baggage, and...here I am!"

Harvey fixed his gaze on the fat clerk for a few moments, then turned to look at the Cubans, one a smaller man of mixed race and the other a larger black man, both of whom watched him carefully. Harvey winked at the Cubans before turning to face the clerk, responding in a friendlier tone:

"Well, young Martin did take it personally when his father freed me, since he believed he was gonna inherit my person. I suppose the boy likes to remind me where I come from."

Harvey had been fond of Martin as a boy, but he didn't care for the young man. He had served as Martin's shadow and protector from the time he was four years old until he went off to study at Davidson College in North Carolina. Things had changed since then, with Martin asserting his manhood and Harvey his freedom. Young Martin didn't know why his father had freed Harvey, nor why Harvey continued to serve his family, but that suited Harvey and Martin's father just fine, since both men shared a secret they had sworn to keep; in Harvey's case, under duress.

"W-w-well then," stuttered the clerk, who wasn't a bad sort and didn't take offense easily, "I have a copy of the b-b-baggage manifest and if you'll give Enrique a hand, we'll be on our way."

With a little effort, the trunks were loaded on the wagon. As Harvey waved goodbye to the grinning Cubans, a furtive movement caught the corner of his eye, some distance down the Desamparados to the south. Being careful to avoid making himself obvious, Harvey cast a glance down the street as he reached for his jacket and turned to throw it over his shoulder. Yes, he was right—a dark haired man with a pale face and a heavy mustache was lurking in the shadows of a building some 100 yards to the south, in a vain attempt to hide behind a narrow column at the end of a porch. Someone must have followed Placido to the meeting.

The Scotsman had trained Harvey well on the streets of Liverpool and he knew exactly what to do. The time immediately after a contact was the most dangerous, because your man may have brought a Watcher along, knowingly or not. Harvey walked casually along the edge of the harbor to the north until he reached a dense network of alleyways leading to a warehouse that was abandoned after a recent fire. He turned left into the first alley and stopped to listen until he heard the sharp report of footsteps on the cobblestones. Stepping lightly, Harvey continued for another 20 yards until he reached a doorway in the partially burned out building that offered concealment and a clear view back towards the harbor. While carefully controlling his breathing and allowing his perceptions to slow, Harvey used his strong left hand to pull a fine Italian stiletto from his right boot, and waited.

At first, Harvey heard nothing but the usual sounds of the harbor, and he began to wonder if he had been wrong about the Watcher. A few moments later, he heard footsteps again, just before a pale stranger turned the corner. He looked like a Spaniard, distinguishable from native Cubans in the way he carried himself, projecting an air of confidence that befitted his status as the representative of a colonial power. He wore a dingy brown bowler over coal black hair. After waiting patiently for his vision to adjust from the blinding sun of the harbor to the dark shadows of the alley, he began to move forward again. Moments later, he reached under his left arm and unholstered a small pistol, which he carried in his right hand, down by his side. Confident the man he was following must have continued down the main alley directly ahead of him, the Spaniard passed Harvey's doorway without looking to either side—a fatal mistake. In one fluid motion, Harvey leapt from the shadows, using his left hand to punch the stiletto between the Spaniard's ribs, while twisting the blade toward his victim's heart. A desperate gasp told Harvey he had found his mark. Using the stiletto to pin his prey against the wall, like an entomologist preparing a specimen for display, Harvey secured the pistol with his right hand. He was careful to press his palm over the hammer, to prevent the weapon from firing. Seconds later, Harvey allowed the Spaniard to fall to the ground. He stepped back carefully, leaving the blade in place to contain the blood, at least for a few moments.

With great effort, the dying man rolled over and stared up at Harvey with an astonished look on his face, whispering words the American didn't understand. Reaching for a brick, Harvey gave the Spaniard the only mercy he knew—by crushing his skull. Glancing around to make sure no one had witnessed the killing, Harvey seized the dead man by his ankles and dragged him into the abandoned warehouse. Wasting no time and feeling no regret, Harvey retrieved his blade and searched the Spaniard's pockets. He discovered a fat purse and a leather pouch containing several documents in Spanish, which he thought might be of use to the Scotsman, so he kept them. He also pocketed the pistol, one of those new-fangled cartridge revolvers he first encountered on the streets of New Orleans earlier that year.

Less than 15 minutes after he spotted the Spaniard, John Harvey emerged from a maze of tight alleyways and continued toward the hotel where his unwitting half-brother waited impatiently.

CHAPTER TWO:
A YOUNG MAN CORRUPTED

Martin McCrary was 20 years old, and looked it. He was handsome enough, with a bright smile that faded during rare moments of self-awareness, as he believed the world loved him and wanted him to be happy, a common sentiment among young man of good fortune. He was impeccably dressed, not exactly a dandy, but clearly a young man of means. He waited in the smoke-filled lobby of the Hotel Conquistador, just around the corner from Plaza Veja in central Havana, and stood on the strong legs of a healthy youth who could walk all day without losing his breath. Martin's classmates at Davidson College had observed his athleticism ended somewhere above the waist, where the thin chest and narrow shoulders of his mother's family marked him as a young man who had done more reading than sporting in a life that had been anything but extraordinary, until the Summer of 1857.

Martin began pacing again as he recalled his adventures over the past several months. Overriding the protests of his mother, a pastor's daughter, Martin's father had decided he wouldn't enter the Presbyterian Seminary in Columbia after all, but would earn his keep by learning the family business.

A worldly man of property, Henry aka "Hank" McCrary was determined to wean his only legitimate son away from his mother's kin, especially her father, a notorious abolitionist exiled to the mountains of North Carolina. Hank McCrary loathed his father in-law, the right Reverend Matthew Coulter, and was determined to correct the mistake he had made by allowing Martin to spend three summers under his Grandfather's influence. The senior McCrary had hoped the mountains would toughen the boy, who had been a sickly child, but he had not expected him to fall under the sway of the old man's heretical teachings. The solution: Send the virginal lad off to New Orleans, San Francisco, Havana, New York and on to England, where he could pick up the threads of his father's business empire and develop an interest in something more ambitious than a pulpit. Thus began the corruption of a quiet and studious young man who was surprised at the sense of gratitude he felt towards his cold-hearted father.

When he left South Carolina in late May, on a train bound for New Orleans, Martin believed he understood his father's intentions, but the generalities became specific when he reached the Crescent City, with Harvey behind him every step of the way. Martin flushed as he recalled his introduction to a type of women he had never known before, to include the colorful advice offered by his older, more experienced servant. He could never get enough of that first girl, Lucy, with her auburn hair, the shape of her neck and the curve of her ...

"Damn, where is that infernal Harvey!" Martin muttered under his breath, as he tried not to think about Lucy. He hated being dependent on a man he had taken for granted every day of his life, until he was sent off to Davidson college. He had been grateful for Harvey, when he was only a boy and the omnipresent house slave had taught him to fish, to hunt and to run like the wind, but that was a time when there was no question about their relative position in life, and their obligations needed no explanation. He couldn't understand why his father had freed Harvey, and he was furious when he first learned about the black man's change of status, after returning from his first year at Davidson. As a result, Martin didn't hesitate when his father suggested he should spend the rest of the summer with his grandfather in the mountains, while Harvey accompanied the senior McCrary on a long trip to England.

Martin adored his grandfather, the Reverend Coulter, but he grew angry and confused when his assumptions about the natural order of the Universe were gently but persistently challenged. The damned infernal question of slavery, the curse of his family, his state and his country! In his heart, Martin had accepted his grandfather's argument that slavery was an abomination, but what was he supposed to do about it? He stood to inherit a vast fortune, but would lose everything if slavery was abolished, or if he made his feelings known. The contradictions troubled Martin deeply and his conscience weighed heavily.

Unbidden, Martin recalled a passage from the Bible that had plagued him for years:

Matthew 19:16–24
"And, behold, one came and said unto him, 'Good Master, what good thing shall I do, that I may have eternal life?'

And he said unto him, 'Why callest thou me good? There is none good but one, that is, God: but if thou wilt enter into life, keep the commandments.'

He saith unto him, 'Which?' Jesus said, 'Thou shalt do no murder, Thou shalt not commit adultery, Thou shalt not steal, Thou shalt not bear false witness,

Honor thy father and thy mother: and, Thou shalt love thy neighbor as thyself.'

The young man saith unto him, 'All these things have I kept from my youth up: what lack I yet?'

Jesus said unto him, 'If thou wilt be perfect, go and sell that thou hast, and give to the poor, and thou shalt have treasure in heaven: and come and follow me.'

But when the young man heard that saying, he went away sorrowful: for he had great possessions.

Then said Jesus unto his disciples, 'Verily I say unto you, that a rich man shall hardly enter into the kingdom of heaven.

And again I say unto you, it is easier for a camel to go through the eye of a needle, than for a rich man to enter into the kingdom of God.'"

"To hell with that," Martin mumbled under his breath, just as Harvey walked into the hotel.

"Good morning, Mastah!" Harvey said, as he approached Martin in mock humility, with hat in hand: "Yo niggah has taken care of yo property. We best be heading over to the ship shortly." Harvey had an infuriating ability to get under Martin's skin, during their overseas adventure, but the young man wouldn't allow himself to be provoked, at least not today, because he needed Harvey's help—again.

"So you met the shipping clerk?" Martin asked. "I understand he's a kind-hearted Christian, like Papa Coulter—I hope you were gentle with him?"

"Don't you worry about a thing, Suh." Harvey responded, with an ironic emphasis on the honorific. "We're the best of friends, and I expect he'll keep me supplied with some good

15

American whiskey during the voyage. Not that I plan to share any with the likes of you. As a matter of fact, I'm not sure if I plan to share any of life's pleasures with a stoic, such as yourself."

Harvey enjoyed testing Martin, up to a point, and knew the younger man needed him, to get what he wanted, and to avoid getting robbed and perhaps killed in some dark alley. Havana was no place for a soft young man to go roaming about by himself, looking for a brothel. More than a few such men had disappeared in Havana over the years. Besides, Harvey knew he had to keep young Martin safe, if he wanted to free his own mother and sister in three years, assuming he could trust the word of a slave-owning father who would never acknowledge him as his bastard.

"There's no point in thinking about that," Harvey thought to himself, "you made a deal with the Devil, and the Devil's bastard better do his part!"

Whenever Harvey considered the possibility that Hank McCrary might renege on their deal, he was overcome with a burning desire to murder the son of a bitch, patricide or not, and take has chances by fleeing with his mother and sister to the mountains. A huge smile erupted on his face when Harvey recalled another secret he kept from Martin—the fact that his own Grandfather, Reverend Coulter, was a critical cog in the Underground Railroad, helping runaway slaves on the road to freedom.

"Well," Martin said, misunderstanding the smile on Harvey's face. "I can see you're as eager as I am. We only have four or five hours before we have to board the ship, so we'd best make the most of it!" The two men had an arrangement: Harvey would find the women, and Martin would pay for them. In any event, Harvey saw no reason to share the Spanish silver in his pocket with a rich white boy.

Harvey had been quick to sort out the bordellos of Havana, because they were remarkably similar to New Orleans, a city he knew very well. The higher class establishments catered to the Spanish landed aristocracy and their wealthy business partners, although they offered girls of every color. The cheaper venues were best avoided, suitable for sailors, longshoremen and the like. The best whore house in town accepted any customer who could afford its rates, as long as he agreed to take a hot bath, first—a service included in the fee, of course.

It took Harvey and Martin less than 10 minutes to reach La Casa de Venus, a three story brick townhouse with a stone foundation located a few blocks off Plaza Veja. A pair of black carriages, protected by drivers in colorful livery, was waiting out front. Being careful to avoid the horse apples that seemed to fill every gap in the cobblestones, the Americans approached a huge mahogany door, which featured a stained glass transom with topless mermaids in green and gold and a bronze knocker shaped like a dolphin. Martin glanced around nervously as Harvey rapped the knocker three times. The door opened immediately and both men stepped in, to be greeted by a pair of Spanish soldiers, still in uniform but serving as private doormen when they were off duty.

"Sargento Alvarez," Harvey began, looking at the shorter of the two Spaniards. "I see you're back on duty this evening. Have you earned enough to take a woman for yourself?"

Sargent Alvarez was very pleased with his part-time job at La Casa de Venus, which had its perks, so he wasn't offended by Harvey's jibe. He stood proudly in a pair of light blue trousers and a dark blue waist coat, with three enormous pink stripes on each sleeve and a matching pink collar that looked uncomfortably stiff.

"Welcome to La Casa de Venus—I remember you promised to return, with someone who could afford to pay. Madam Isabella will be happy to see the young man," he continued, while nodding at Martin, "and may allow you some privileges, if you behave yourself!"

Sargent Alvarez was a practical man with an unofficial wife and children of mixed race, willing to take everyone as he found them. He had learned to speak English while serving as a guard at the Spanish consulate in New Orleans and had followed his former Consul-General when he returned to Havana. Not coincidentally, the Consul-General was one of Madam Isabella's most avid admirers.

The sergeant opened a pair of inner doors, also decorated with glass panels of voluptuous mermaids, and escorted the Americans into a spacious lobby with an ornate ceiling, supported by bronze busts of Atlas in each corner. An elaborate crystal chandelier hung in the middle of the room. The walls were flocked with red paper and the mahogany furniture was upholstered in burgundy fabric. As soon as the sergeant shut the heavy door behind them, an elegant and breathtakingly beautiful mulatto woman emerged from a smaller door to the left. The former mistress of a filthy rich scion of New Orleans, she had been bundled off to Havana by her generous patron when he married into one of the first families of Louisiana. Isabella had been eager to accommodate her patron's desires, and still maintained a productive relationship with him, to include an occasional dalliance when he visited Havana each winter. Since arriving in Cuba, she had been her own master in all things, for the first time in her life.

To suggest that Harvey and young Martin were speechless would be saying too much. Both men were star-struck and Harvey swallowed nervously as Isabella approached with a confident smile. She was tall for a woman, over 5 feet 9 inches in her stockings, with a willowy grace accentuated by the whispering rush of silk brushing across the floor. Her eyes were huge, almond shaped and knowing, placed in a face of exquisite perfection, like a queen of Egypt carved from a marble of coffee and cream.

"Good evening, gentlemen." She began, with a nod toward Martin and a quick glance at Harvey. "Welcome to La Casa de Venus. You must be the young American Sergeant Alvarez told me about. Please, make yourselves comfortable while the baths are prepared. Shall we assume both of you plan to enjoy yourselves?"

19

she asked, while smiling at Martin and nodding toward Harvey.

Her voice was rich and musical, with the intonations of her Cajun heritage and the clarity and crispness of a governess. Martin was so mesmerized, he failed to respond, so Harvey came to the rescue.

"Yes, Lady of the House," Harvey responded, "I am the young man's guide and companion, a freedman, so I will accompany him."

Isabella considered Harvey carefully, admiring a handsome man who was only a shade darker than herself and who carried himself with a rare confidence, for a man of his station. His was a story she wanted to hear, perhaps in private—perhaps not.

"Of course!" She responded, with a brilliant smile revealing snow white teeth that matched the string of pearls around her neck. Turning quickly, she snapped her fingers and a wiry old Cuban appeared instantly, carrying white towels and robes over his left arm.

"Follow me, Señors!" He requested in a respectful tone, before turning to lead them down a set of marble steps to an elaborate series of pools and baths on the ground floor. When they reached the landing at the bottom of the staircase, they could hear a murmur of quiet voices and the sound of moving water behind paneled walls that didn't reach to the top of the tall ceiling, where wisps of steam circulated between brass windows shaped like portholes. A small bird popped out one of the windows, just as they stepped on the landing, which featured an elaborate tile mosaic with a blue and white compass rose.

"Your baths are here, to the left," the Cuban suggested helpfully, opening a small door leading to a paneled dressing area, which offered a glimpse of the hot and cold pools awaiting them.

"They say Madame Isabella offers the finest Roman baths in Havana," Harvey began, unbuttoning his collar as the wiry Cuban hung the towels and Turkish robes on a beautifully paneled wall. "The Spaniards say the baths are a pretense that protects La Casa de Venus from meddling by the Bishop. Sergeant Alvarez tells me the old devil is one of their most faithful customers."

Martin had grown up with Harvey and the older man had taught him to swim in the rivers bordering his father's plantations in South Carolina, and he hadn't been shy during their adventures over the Summer, but the thought of sharing a pool that may have been inhabited by an aging Papist was almost enough to curdle the young Presbyterian's enthusiasm. He quickly shed his clothes and his reluctance.

"A bath is just what I need, after the heat of Havana," Martin admitted. "Let's imagine I'm Julius Cesar and you're a Nubian slave, a prize captured in Egypt." An insecure young man at times, Martin enjoyed showing off his classical education in front of Harvey, because he had long since learned his servant was at least as clever as him, with the added benefit of age and the experience.

"Oh, you mean the handsome Nubian warrior who brought slave girls to Cesar, or was it Cesar he brought to the slave girls?" Harvey enjoyed little contests of wit with Martin and had recently surprised the young man when he learned the former slave had read nearly all of the books in his father's library, with a voracious thirst for knowledge that matched his other appetites.

"Generally, the man with no purse serves the needs of the man who carries one," Martin responded coolly. "Be content with my gratitude."

"Who would argue with such generosity?" Harvey asked, as he slipped into the hot pool with a sigh. "Someday I'll open an establishment of my own. Girls like Miss Lucy are eager to rise up in the world—like Madame Isabella. She could be my partner!" Harvey allowed himself to laugh as Martin slipped into the pool, shaking his head at the reference to Lucy.

"I don't know how you'll adjust to life back in South Carolina," Martin exclaimed. "Even Daddy won't tolerate your impertinence.'

"Don't you worry about that," Harvey responded. "Your Daddy told me he plans to keep the two of us on the road for a couple of years, until you learn enough about his business to earn some money for your people, instead of just spending what he's already made."

Martin looked over at Harvey and nodded his head as he settled into the pool, with his neck resting in a soft curve and his arms draped along the edge. He had to admit he was having the time of his life. He was in no hurry to go back to Charleston, much less settle on one of his father's plantations in the country, where he would be surrounded by pretentious dandies and ruthless matrons sizing him up for marriage to one of their daughters. All the girls he knew back home were infuriatingly false, offering smiles and good manners but no sense of a real woman beneath the facade.

The two men soaked in silence for a while, enjoying the hot pool, followed by brief plunges into the cold pool and back again. After several rotations, just as they were feeling perfectly relaxed but before they began to worry about their waiting ship, Isabella returned leading a line of six women of various colors and sizes, all beautiful in their own way and all wearing gauzy robes that revealed much but not all. The matron of the house smiled briefly as she sensed Martin and Harvey's discomfort until they glanced down at the water to confirm their dignity was protected by the shimmering pool.

"It's time to choose your pleasure, gentlemen." Isabella began. "Sergeant Alvarez tells me you are familiar with the rules of my House, so the choice is yours and the price is the same for all."

Martin carefully considered all of the girls and nodded toward the youngest and most petite, a mulatto of even lighter complexion than her mistress, with hints of auburn in her luxurious hair and beautiful green eyes. "That one should do," he exclaimed, before ducking under the

23

water to rinse his head, emerging on the far side of the pool, closer to the girls.

"A fine choice for a young man," Isabella responded, "but some might suggest a woman of greater experience would bring greater pleasure." She made a point of smiling and glancing directly at Harvey as she spoke the words. "Dalmatia," she continued. "Please go upstairs to the Green Room" and make yourself ready for this fine-looking young man." The green eyed beauty nodded demurely and curtsied before turning and walking up a narrow set of marble stairs on the far side of the pool.

"Now, it's your companion's turn." Isabella remarked, while nodding toward Harvey, who had not taken his eyes off of her from the moment she had emerged with her line of girls, although she was the only one of them who remained fully clothed.

"You know what I want." Harvey responded quietly, while keeping his eyes locked on hers, even as they flashed with anger as two of her girls giggled and whispered behind her.

"I see." Isabella responded, looking down at her hands briefly before raising her head higher and continuing: "If you come back some day with your own purse and your own prospects, we may talk. In the meantime, you must choose another."

Harvey nodded in response and was tempted to show off the dead Spaniard's silver, but quickly dismissed the idea, suppressing his wounded pride. After holding Isabella's gaze for a moment longer, he stood up in the pool so the

24

water reached his waist, revealing a splendid physique. He turned to face the remaining women and spoke: "I choose that one, the tall girl standing closest to you. She could be your sister." The remaining girls giggled as the chosen one examined Harvey silently.

"A brave choice," Isabella declared, "Serena is very strong and has been known to break the backs of weaker men."

The latter remark elicited an appreciative laugh from Martin, who swam back to the opposite side of the pool, to better observe the conversation while sipping the glass of whiskey he had left behind.

"Serena," Isabella continued, "you may go upstairs to the Blue Room and prepare yourself. The rest of you return to your rooms and relax, our next group of gentlemen will arrive in an hour. Gentlemen, Anton will take you upstairs when you are ready. If you like, you may wear these Turkish robes, so my servants can brush your clothes and set everything out for you."

Isabella spun on her heels with a flourish and followed the last of the women as they disappeared up the staircase behind Dalmatia and Serena. Martin and Harvey grinned as they pulled themselves out of the hot pool, dripping with water as they reached for the towels and robes offered by the wiry Cuban, who stared off into the distance as if had had never been in the room at all.

CHAPTER THREE:
AN EVENING'S ENTERTAINMENT

Harvey lay back in bed, admiring Serena as she rose gracefully and covered herself, standing before a man who surprised her with his gentleness.

"*Espero que esté satisfecho?*" She asked with mock seriousness, holding her head high.

"*Satisfecho?* You're damn right I'm satisfied, Serena—*muy satisfecho...*" Harvey settled back into the mattress, with his arms behind his head as the young prostitute smiled briefly and nodded before quietly steeping through the doorway into the hall, carrying a small brass lantern.

"No substitute for Isabella," Harvey thought to himself, "but close enough."

Thinking about the mistress of the house soured Harvey's mood, not because he didn't admire her, but because he knew he couldn't have her. To the rest of the world, he was just a servant, a black man in a white man's world, with no prospects of his own. Reality rankled, causing him to shift uncomfortably. He wanted to tell Isabella about his secret relationship with the Scotsman, Sir Ian McDonald, and his promise to resettle him up in the Bahamas with a small business of his own. His pride stung, Harvey played out the scene in his head, imagining how impressed Isabella would be, if she knew his patron was a powerful British spymaster. He indulged the fantasy for a moment, enjoying images of harmony and ecstasy as Isabella agreed to share her life with him...

It was all too much. A quiet but persuasive voice brought Harvey back to earth, as it always did. He had his dreams and was willing to work for them. Patience and discretion were required, if he wanted to survive long enough to build a new life for himself. His relationship with the Scotsman was both simple and complicated. Simple, because he had entrusted McDonald with his life, and never had cause to complain. The Scotsman always spoke the truth and kept every promise he ever made. Complicated, because it was hard for Harvey to trust anyone, hard for him to believe his patron would keep his word, when the time came to claim his final reward. He had little experience with trustworthy white men and worried he would be abandoned, in the end.

Harvey first met the Scotsman in the summer of 1854, during one of his trips to Liverpool with Hank McCrary. His bastard father and former owner maintained a significant interest in the cotton trade and visited England frequently, to look after his business. During their first private meeting, the Scotsman made his offer—a new home and a new life on British territory, in exchange for 10 years of good service, as his eyes and ears in the home of one of the wealthiest and most powerful men in America. Over the past three years, Harvey had learned to embrace his life as a British spy, and he wondered if he would ever be able to give it up.

As he lay in a comfortable bed with his arms behinds head, Harvey dreamed of becoming his own man some day, truly free, with his mother and sister beside him. His thoughts were interrupted by loud voices. He jumped out of bed and moved quickly across the room to stand near a window overlooking the street in front of the house. Glancing over the edge of the window sill, he could see the backs of two men in black suits and bowler hats, speaking to the drivers out front, in a lisping Spanish accent:

"Estamos buscando a dos estadounidenses un hombre negro grande y un hombre blanco más pequeño. ¿Los has visto?"

Harvey spoke very little Spanish, but he understood *"hombre negro"* and *"hombre blanco."* The two Spaniards where looking for a black man and a white man. They were looking for him. Wasting no time, Harvey pulled on his clothes and dashed across the hall to the Green room, where Martin was sharing a laugh and other pleasures with Dalmatia. Finding the door unlocked, he barged in without a warning.

"Get dressed, we have to go NOW!"

Harvey had Martin's attention, as he had never seen his companion in such an agitated state unless they were in serious trouble. Dalmatia seemed to understand and donned her flimsy robe as she fled the room, her bare feet slapping on the staircase.

"What the Hell is going on?" Martin asked, afraid to hear the answer.

Harvey lied without hesitation.

"I beat two Spaniards in a vicious card game earlier today. One of them accused me of cheating, so I knocked him down and left. They're out front, looking for me right now."

Before Martin could question Harvey further, Isabella appeared at the door, just as Martin was buttoning his trousers. She looked directly at Harvey, with harsh questions in her eyes, because Sergeant Alverez had recognized the strangers as agents of the Spanish Secret Police.

"I don't know what the two of you up to, but you must leave my house immediately." Calculating her interests carefully, she decided:

"Lucky for you, Sergeant Alverez is loyal to the discretion of this house. My clients include important men, so the Spaniards are reluctant to enter without my permission. As your presence was observed by others, he could not deny your arrival, but he convinced them you have already departed, and gave them reason to fear any further intrusion by revealing the name of a prominent landowner who is also my guest this evening."

"Thank you, Miss Isabella, it seems Harvey got himself involved in the wrong card game. I apologize for the trouble..."

Martin fumbled around in his leather purse and retrieved several coins. He moved toward Isabella with an embarrassed shrug of his shoulders.

Before the money changed hands, Harvey interrupted:

"Please, Suh, let me pay the bill!"

Martin looked on with amazement as Harvey reached into his pocket and produced the money he had taken off the unfortunate "Watcher," whose corpse had yet to be found.

"This is the silver I took off those Spaniards. Sore losers, both of 'em!"

Harvey lied with his usual ease, but lowered his gaze as he extended his hand, hoping to regain some respect from a lady he admired.

"A card game, of course." Isabella responded sardonically, as she weighed the coins in her hand. "I took you for a reckless gambler of some type, Mr. Harvey." Frowning, she paused for a moment before continuing: "No harm done, but you must leave now and never come back. Follow me."

Harvey and Martin trailed behind as Isabella led them down a narrow service staircase to the basement. Rather than turning towards the baths, she opened a small door leading to a short stone staircase. The trio emerged in a lush garden surrounded by high walls. The air was thick and humid, sweetened by the aroma of bananas ripe for the picking. The trio moved across the garden to a spacious carriage house with a door leading to a quiet alley. As he stepped into the darkness , Harvey struggled to devise a story that might limit the damage without revealing anything of value to Martin. Before shutting the door behind them, Isabella fixed Harvey with a cold but curious eye, leaving the two men standing in a muddy rut with little ambient light to show the way.

"Father told me to be generous, Harvey, but this is too much!" Martin was furious.

"Shush, now—no time to talk!" Harvey whispered. "We'll be safe when we reach the ship. Believe me, Suh, you don't wanna mess with the two of them! They may be armed, and we are not."

With so many secrets to keep, Harvey didn't tell Martin about his stiletto or the dead Spaniard's pistol. He hoped he wouldn't have to use them.

Martin flushed with anger but held his tongue. Based on their experiences in New Orleans and San Francisco, he knew Harvey was his master on the streets of any city, especially after dark, and his companion had saved him from a beating or worse in the past.

"Well, Harvey" Martin resigned himself, "You have the eyes of a panther, so lead on!"

Instinctively, Harvey moved in the opposite direction of the threat, keeping his back to the wall and listening carefully before scooting from one alley to another. He hoped to gain some distance from La Casa de Venus before emerging on a busy street, but he didn't know the neighborhood as well as he might. As Harvey paused to consider their options, Martin stumbled against a pair of barrels in the dark, sending one crashing to the ground. The jarring noise provoked a pair of dogs, somewhere behind them. The animals snarled furiously. With no way to know if the dogs were restrained in a yard or being used to hunt them, Harvey decided it was time to run.

"Come on" Harvey urged, "Move!"

It was 50 yards to the next corner. The sound of two men running brought the voices of the dogs to a crescendo. Harvey recognized the tone immediately when the dogs were released, the distinctive sound of a hound on the hunt. Much to his relief, the baying was not accompanied by an angry staccato of iron-shod horses. If the hunters were on foot, they might have a chance.

"You better run like you did when we stole that bottle of whiskey from Old Man Tate!" Harvey barked between breaths, as he sprinted toward the harbor. That was the first and only time Martin had beaten Harvey on a flat-out run, because he knew they would both get a whipping if the old man caught them. The shared memory seemed to inspire Martin, who moved up beside him.

The dogs were gaining ground, followed at some unknown distance by the Spaniards. Harvey knew they had to lose the dogs, or else he would have to stop and shoot them. That would be a shame and a terrible crime that could lead to even worse trouble. With no cover in sight, Harvey was about to stop and fight when he spotted a long wooden ladder leading up to a rooftop just ahead. A new warehouse was under construction, empty for the evening but possibly offering a safe avenue of escape.

"Sometimes a man has to take what's offered, Lord!" Harvey mumbled to himself, as he reached the ladder before Martin, bracing it with his right foot.

"Up you go!" Harvey ordered, in a tone that brooked no disagreement. Eager to avoid a mauling, Martin scrambled up the ladder and steadied the top as Harvey followed. Martin stepped back quickly, catching himself as he stumbled to his knees, amazed at Harvey's strength as he hauled the ladder up behind them. As soon as the ladder was up, the dogs rounded the corner. The tone of their voices changed again as they struggled to find the scent.

"That was close!" Martin whispered. "What do we do now?"

"Shush!" Harvey whispered. "Watch and wait!"

Harvey was surprised to see the hunters were not the same men who had inquired at La Casa de Venus. They were dressed differently, in working clothes. Where were the other two? Did he have four Spaniards to deal with?

Never mind that. From experience, Harvey knew he needed to focus on the task at hand, when the odds were looking grim.

34

One of the dogs, a young male, seemed confused. He sniffed in a tight circle and stopped barking, seeking reassurance from his handler as he rounded the corner. The second dog, an older bitch, was more experienced and settled on the exact spot where Harvey had stood when he steadied the ladder for Martin. Both Spaniards reached the spot and looked around, peering inside an open window into the empty warehouse. Working together, they hoisted the bitch up and over the windowsill, watching as she circled the room in frustration. The scent was lost, and there was noting they could do about it.

Unwilling to give up the hunt, one of the Spaniards pulled a hunting knife from a sheath on his belt and ran down to the next corner. Seeing nothing in either direction, he removed his hat and scratched his head, mumbling curses at the sky. Turning in a circle, the balding Spaniard tilted his head back just far enough to see a pair of bright eyes staring down at him from the edge of the rooftop, two stories up. Transfixed by Harvey's predatory gaze, the hunter turned hunted watched silently as an African Zeus stood tall, holding a bolt of lightening over his head. The man screamed, but it was too late: The ladder came crashing down, crushing his scull and knocking his companion unconscious.

Martin was shocked.

"You killed them!" He shouted, pointing down at the street.

"Knocked out, more likely, but killing is nothing more than they would have done to us."

Harvey responded casually. "You've seen enough of the world to know there's dangerous men everywhere you turn." The former slave spoke directly to his would-be master, with a confident tone that revealed a glimpse of the true-self he kept hidden from a white man's world. "They lost their silver in a game of cards and planned to take it back, by force. That's robbery, and robbers get what they deserve. Your father has killed men, or had them killed, for less than that. Maybe he'll tell you about it some day."

Looking down at the street again, Martin was reminded of the truth behind Harvey's words: A large knife was lying beside one of the Spaniards, and the dog looked even more ferocious than he had imagined. Although the words rang true, Martin was stung by Harvey's insolence. He decided to change the subject:

"What the hell are we supposed to do now? You've lost our ladder, and we're stuck up here on the roof!"

Eager to change the subject himself, Harvey pointed to the north.

"We'll just have to figure that out for ourselves," he offered, with a shrug of his shoulders. "Best work our way across this roof to the next alley, so we can find a quiet place to climb down."

That was easier said than done, as they soon discovered. The roof of the warehouse was only partially completed. With the dog still barking in the alley behind, they had to find a way to move forward. When they reached the peak of the roof, the shingles ended. The darkness ahead was punctuated by a row of rafters reaching toward the far side of the building.

"Those rafters are too narrow to walk." Harvey stated the obvious. "We'll have to climb down. Follow me."

Working his way to the point where the peak of the roof met the side of the warehouse, Harvey lowered himself from a rafter and dangled precariously until his feet found the cross-beam below. He was just tall enough to keep his fingertips on top of the rafter, while shuffling along toward the narrower end of the triangle. He stopped after a few yards and turned to face Martin.

"Come on, you can do it! I've seen you climb trees worse than this!" Harvey said, while beckoning with one hand. The words of encouragement only served to irritate Martin, who was still immature enough to resent reminders of his boyhood.

"That's easy enough for you to say!" The young graduate retorted in a harsh whisper. "You're a lot taller than me, so my feet aren't gonna reach that cross beam over here by the peak!"

The dog continued to bark behind them and some wagons could be heard moving north along the Desamparados. Harvey wanted to move quickly, as someone might stumble across the bloody scene in the alley. Despite the earlier denial, he knew at least one of the Spaniards was dead: The sound of a smashed skull is distinctive and he'd heard that music before.

"You're gonna have to dangle by your hands for a bit, until your feet reach the crossbeam. I'll be right here to catch you if you stumble." With those words, Harvey shuffled back toward the peak of the roof, to the point where his right hand still had a firm grip on the rafter. He extended his left hand toward Martin, who would only need to climb for 10 feet or so before his toes could reach the rafter.

"I can't believe this shit!" Martin hissed sharply, as he tied his jacket around his waist. "You're supposed to keep me out of trouble, not break my neck!"

Gathering his courage, Martin swung down on the rafter, gaining confidence as he realized his grip would hold. Carefully, he shuttled along like the gibbons he had seen at the Zoo in New Orleans, until the toe of his right shoe found the cross beam. As he slid his hands toward Harvey to close the final gap, a splinter pierced the palm of his left hand. The pain was excruciating. Instinctively, he pulled his injured hand away from the rafter, before his feet were secure. He wobbled precariously for a moment, until Harvey reached out and steadied him.

"Son of a bitch!" Martin hissed, sucking at his hand. "That smarts!"

Having had a few splinters in his day, Martin knew what to do. He used his teeth to remove the offending object and spit over his left shoulder.

"All right then, Harvey, let's get this over!"

Relieved to have his weight supported by the sturdy cross beam, Martin followed his companion until they reached the northern edge of the roof. Peering over the side of the building, neither man could see a way down. Looking over into the warehouse, Martin spotted a scaffold set against the wall below, toward the middle of the wall, some 20 rafters away.

"Look!" He whispered. "We can climb down over there!"

"I see it!" Harvey responded with a grin, his teeth shining brightly in the moonlight. "Just what we need. Come on now, you can lead the way!"

Pleased to have an opportunity to demonstrate his competence, Martin climbed from rafter to rafter, from crossbeam to crossbeam, until he stood over the scaffold. Estimating the distance, he realized he would have to drop a bit to reach the platform. Lowering himself carefully, he dangled for a moment, while trying to ignore the throbbing pain in his left hand, and released his grip. He landed on his feet, with his hands resting on the inside surface of the brick wall. The scaffold rocked gently but held. Harvey followed silently and the scaffold remained steady.

Feeling confident, Martin climbed down the side of the scaffold until his feet reached the floor, near an open window. Listening carefully to see if someone might be waiting outside in the alley, he sensed something wasn't right, behind him in the warehouse. A peculiar chill ran down his spine and he turned, just in time to see the furious bitch charging silently in Harvey's direction, before he had lowered himself all the way to the ground. Acting purely on instinct, Martin reached down and grabbed the handle of a heavy metal bucket. Moving faster than he ever had in his life, he swung the bucket over his head and smashed it against the hound, breaking her back. She twitched for a few moments before lying still.

Harvey stood over the dog with an astonished look on his face as Martin dropped to the ground and leaned against the wall, gasping for breath.

"Looks like I owe you one." Harvey admitted, as he sat down next to Martin.

"Why, why didn't she go for me? Why wasn't she making any noise?" Martin was glad the dog hadn't mauled Harvey, but he was even more relieved to have avoided the same fate.

"Who knows? One things for sure, she was a killer. She was probably trained to hunt runaway slaves, black men like me. Maybe she didn't like the way I smell?"

Harvey glanced over at Martin and offered an ironic smile.

Although it didn't come easy, having been raised in the expectation of privilege, Martin was touched by a moment of empathy and understanding, having seen what the dogs did to runaway slaves on his father's plantations back home. He thought about some of the things his Grandfather said during his prayers, as he asked God for the power to see the suffering of other people through the eyes of Jesus. The moment of insight was too much to bear, so he shoved it aside. Martin didn't know it yet, but the cracks in his world of false assumptions were getting deeper.

CHAPTER FOUR:
S.S. CENTRAL AMERICA

The *S.S. Central America* was a modern side-wheel steamer, a 280 foot miracle of oak and iron. She was bound for the city of New York with 476 passengers and 102 crew, on a regular run from Panama. The tall ship dominated the docks of Havana, creating a spectacle that attracted casual observers from all over the city, adding to the excitement. Small boys ran through the crowds as the last pallets of personal effects were hoisted aboard. Smoke rose from a black funnel secured to the top of a large rectangular cabin by a web of sturdy wires, clearly visible above the broad arch of a beautifully decorated wheel house. A sturdy ramp led up to a boarding deck in the gap between the wheel house and a ship's boat dangling from a pair of iron davits, where an officer and several stewards attended the

43

remaining first-class passengers. The prominent and prosperous were directed to their comfortable accommodations, while the anonymous and less affluent loitered in small groups at dockside, awaiting their turn for steerage, and trying to ignore a reminder of their lesser status.

Harvey and Martin first made their acquaintance with the steamer in the port of Aspinwall, on the Caribbean coast of Panama. They began their journey in San Francisco, changing ships after crossing the narrow isthmus on a railroad built by American investors, during the height of the Gold Rush. The big ship was carefully guarded by Pinkerton's detectives, for she carried a valuable cargo: Several tons of gold from the mines of California. Some of that gold belonged to Martin's father, who had invested in the provision of sugar, tobacco, tarps, tents and other goods to the miners and shopkeepers, earning substantial profits in return. In this way, at least, Hank McCrary differed from most of his kind, the landed aristocracy of the South who viewed commerce as beneath the dignity of a gentleman.

The two Americans reached the ship without incident and boarded with the last of the cabin passengers. After slipping back into his role as the personal servant of a wealthy young American, with a bag in each hand, Harvey carefully scanned the crowd at dockside. For a brief moment, he thought he might have recognized one of the Spaniards who had inquired at La Casa de Venus, but he couldn't be sure, even with the advantage of elevation offered by the boarding ramp. The thought was worrisome as it seemed clear the dog handlers must have been working on their behalf.

By law, only a commissioned naval officer could serve as the captain of an American mail ship, even if the vessel was privately owned and operated under contract with the Postal Service. Commander William Lewis Herndon stood on top of the cabin, to one side of the wheel house, and watched silently as his passengers moved up the ramp. The sober Virginian took his responsibilities seriously, which included hundreds of passengers and crew and 38,000 pieces of U.S. mail. The gold weighed heavily on his mind, and he was outraged by the presence of a half dozen private detectives, as if he couldn't be trusted with the cargo. Commander Herndon had met Allan Pinkerton himself during his last trip to New York City and had found the man to be insufferable, the arrogant guard dog of grasping Yankee businessmen. The Captain's initial impression was confirmed when Pinkerton suggested one of his patrons, a powerful senator from New York, would revoke Herndon's naval commission if anything happened to the gold. As a proud veteran of the Mexican-American War, with many years of service, that was a slight the Commander would never forgive or forget. His mood spoiled by the memory, he looked down the ramp and his eyes fell on Martin McCrary, the South Carolinian he encountered during the voyage from Panama. He reminded himself to

45

conceal his contempt for spoiled young men who never served anyone but themselves.

Having developed a sixth sense when under observation, Harvey glanced up and noticed Captain Herndon assessing Martin.

Unable to resist, Harvey whispered: "Suh, you better look sharp, yo' Daddy is watching!"

Confused, Martin looked back over his shoulder and stumbled a bit before recovering and catching the amused smile on Herndon's face, just before the Captain turned and disappeared from view. Stung by Harvey's remark, and well aware of his discomfort around older men with positions of authority, he pretended not to notice and held himself erect as they approached the duty officer on the boarding deck:

"Take those bags to my cabin, Boy. You can make yourself busy cleaning my shoes while I have a drink in the smoking room."

"Yes Suh, Mr. McCrary, right away Suh!" Harvey chuckled to himself quietly as he walked toward the ladder leading down to their cabin. Not for the first or the last time, he was grateful for the strength derived from his secret life, which sometimes enabled him to ignore the petty humiliations that marked his days. Besides, there were few things in the world he liked as much as a voyage at sea.

Begging his pardon as he worked his way down a busy service ladder with the grace of a boxer, Harvey ducked his head to catch a better view of the Grand Saloon. The space was illuminated by brass lanterns and several skylights, some fitted with stained glass panels. A lantern hanging from the main mast above decks projected colorful fireflies across the room, spinning and dancing with the breeze.

The first class berths were accessible from the Grand Saloon and a matching Dining Saloon further forward on the same deck, both paneled in quilted Cuban mahogany. The floors in the Grand Salon were topped with fine woolen rugs and six seating areas were populated by heavy leather sofas, an assortment of shaded lamps and tables and the kind of armchairs that belonged in a fine men's club. Brass lanterns mounted on gimbals hung beside the doors leading to each first class accommodation, with a total of 24 berths lining the main saloon.

Harvey strolled across the saloon to reach berth number 12, ignored by the white men who gathered in a cluster, enjoying their comfortable surroundings. He overheard two men talking:

"I regret to inform you, gentlemen," proclaimed a fair-haired man with a heavy mustache and a Northern accent, "there are no pirates left in the Caribbean. Otherwise we would be properly entertained as they acquainted themselves with the Pinkerton's!"

"That's true enough, Mr. Farlington," responded an older gentleman with a bulbous nose and a heavy black beard, "it's difficult even for the most enterprising man to acquire a substantial sum these days, as the mines are panning out; the price of gold is bound to go up next year!"

Harvey had heard enough of that kind of speculation during the trip to San Francisco, so he ignored the rest of the banter as he passed by, respectfully avoiding eye contact.

After shifting both of Martin's travel bags to his right hand, he opened the door with his left and slipped inside, closing the door behind him. Quickly hanging the young man's clothes in a standing cedar closet, he stowed the leather bags on an upper shelf behind a sturdy brass rail. Removing his own jacket and draping it over a chair, he removed Placido's documents from his left breast pocket and the dead Spaniard's pouch from the right. Although tempted to examine the papers, he knew it wasn't safe, and he couldn't read Spanish, besides. Resolving to correct that deficiency, Harvey used his stiletto to pry up a board in a narrow corner of the berth, where the curvature of the hull met a paneled bulkhead secured to an iron rib, and secreted the documents in a tight space under the deck. Harvey recalled with amusement a training session organized by the Scotsman, who quickly discovered even a spymaster could learn a thing or two from a former American slave, when it comes to concealing cherished items.

Harvey sat down with a smile that quickly dissolved into a frown as he contemplated the voyage ahead. Nominally a free man, he wasn't free to roam the ship. He had to cover every movement as a service to his "master"—a younger man with whom he shared the same father, but little else—not even the truth of their brotherhood. Harvey tried not to dwell on things he couldn't control, but certain thoughts wore deep trenches in his mind—and they would have their say, whether he liked it or not. He might have hated all white men, if not for the two who had shown him a way to channel his anger.

Martin's grandfather, Reverend Coulter, was a Godly man—a true Christian, if there was such a thing, who set an example with his words and his actions. Harvey wasn't much of a believer, but he was afraid to abandon all faith, or hope; he supposed that was his mother's influence. Coulter had recruited Harvey to help with the Underground Railroad, when the Reverend was exiled to the mountains for his abolitionist views, and Harvey had moved a total of 23 men, women and children along the road to freedom, using Mr. McCrary's business to cover his activities.

Harvey smiled when he recalled Martin's last trip to the mountains, after his junior year at Davidson College. Harvey had been charged with escorting the young man up to western North Carolina, where the aging Reverend Coulter served as the pastor for a small but energetic congregation in Waynesville. They were accompanied by one of the Reverend's accomplices, a white man named Bo Johnson, who posed as the son of a licensed slave trader. In fact, Johnson was an abolitionist from Kentucky who carried official looking documents forged by Grandpa Coulter. Martin had accepted the story without question when they met "by accident" along the road and had agreed to allow

49

Johnson, his mule wagon and six runaway slaves to tag along on a road to freedom known only to Harvey. That trip had been one of the most satisfying weeks of Harvey's life and he still cherished the memory.

His resolve strengthened by the accomplishments of a secret life, Harvey swore he would bear the burden of continued servitude with all the grace he could muster, for the sake of his mother and sister. Burying the rage he felt at their continued enslavement by his bastard of a father, Harvey resolved to fight his war one battle at a time, by focusing on what he could do at that moment. Right now, the only thing he could do was to further his education, so he rummaged around in Martin's things until he found the book he was looking for: "A Christmas Carol," by Charles Dickens. He had read the novella once before, but couldn't get enough of the dark humor. He opened the book, enjoying the title page and the first illustrations, before turning to Stave One:

"Marley was dead: to begin with. There is no doubt whatever about that. The register of his burial was signed by the clergyman, the clerk, the undertaker, and the chief mourner. Scrooge signed it: and Scrooge's name was good upon 'Change, for anything he chose to put his hand to. Old Marley was as dead as a door-nail."

Harvey read for a couple of hours, until he nodded off in his chair, only to be awakened shortly afterwards by a loud noise as the ship pulled away from the dock and the paddle wheels started to turn, first slowly and unevenly, then more rapidly.

"Might as well get some fresh air," Harvey decided as he rummaged around in the closet to retrieve Martin's spare shoes and a polishing kit. Once the ship was safely underway in good weather, steerage passengers and the servants of first class passengers were allowed to take their leave on deck, as long as they avoided areas reserved for their betters and the crew. Martin set himself up on the bow, near the traditional "head"—where sailors used to drop their drawers before the invention of cast iron plumbing and ceramic toilets. He sat down next to an elderly black man with short grey hair and large sideburns, who was polishing a set of silver cups.

"Good evening, Pappy!" Harvey exclaimed with a smile as he shoved a hand into one of Martin's shoes and began buffing with a vengeance.

"Why do you have to be so cheerful all the time, Boy?" Asked Jimmy Dew Drop, as he was known, taking up where they left off during the voyage from Panama to Cuba. "You must be the most spoiled black man I ever met, as pleased as a rooster on a hen! Don't tell me you got yourself laid again, now did you? Come on now, tell me some more of those lies!" Old Jimmy had given up on women, but he enjoyed reliving his youth by listening to stories. Lies or not made no difference to him.

"Let me tell you about the one I didn't get," Harvey responded in a conspiratorial tone. "A woman from New Orleans, by the name of

Isabella, the finest creature you've ever seen. Taller than most men, graceful and willowy like a tree leaning over your favorite pond, with eyes like a doe gone to heaven. She wouldn't have nothing to do with me, though, 'cause she's got her hooks into some rich white men and owns her own whorehouse right here in Havana."

A refreshing breeze picked up as the *Central America* steamed its way through the entrance of the harbor past a pair of brick and stone fortresses. Jimmy nodded and listened carefully as Harvey told the story of La Casa de Venus, leaving out the part about his final dash to safety. Just when he was getting to a detailed description of the girls working for Isabella, as they stood by the pool, Harvey sensed a shadow off to one side and turned his head to see one of the Spaniards he had neglected to mention, approaching with a smile as he casually smoked a cigar. That was unexpected.

The Spaniard walked up to Harvey casually, putting his right foot forward next to the younger black man's knee. He stared down quietly at Harvey before speaking:

"My shoes could use a nice polish," he began, surveying one side of his shoe and then the other. "If you do a good job, slave, I'll give you a tip."

Harvey stood up slowly, towering over the rotund Spaniard, who didn't flinch an inch.

"I am no man's slave and only work for the McCrary family," Harvey responded, while sizing up the Spaniard for a coffin.

"Hum, not a slave, you work for the McCrary family. That's very interesting, thank you."

The Spaniard chuckled as he turned and walked away, pleased with himself for having elicited the information from the big black man so easily. Harvey was puzzled and a bit embarrassed at first, but figured he hadn't given away anything important. He decided to ask a question himself:

"What's your name, Señor?" Harvey asked as the Spaniard turned away.

"Whatever you like," he responded with a flare, a dramatic pause and a flick of his cigar. "You can call me Señor Cazador, if you change your mind and want to earn a little silver..." The Spaniard wasn't sure what role Harvey was playing in the game he was investigating, but he would be neglecting his duties if he didn't consider the possibility that the big black man might be recruited to work for him, to spy on his former American masters.

Cazador—the Hunter. Harvey first heard that word when accompanying Martin's father on a boar hunt in Texas some years back. Shit. What else did the Spaniard know? Was he suspected in the disappearance of the Watcher? Did he know about the dog handlers in the alley? No, that seemed unlikely; otherwise he wouldn't have been allowed to board the ship. He would have to watch himself carefully: A member of the Spanish Secret Service could be dangerous, even on an American vessel.

"Now that wasn't right, Harvey. You best tell me what you've gotten yourself into," whispered Jimmy Dew Drop.

"Oh, nothing to worry about. I beat some Spaniards in a game of cards this morning and they took offense. Señor Cazador must be a friend of theirs." Harvey tried to avoid eye contact as he renewed his focus on Martin's shoes.

Harvey was a good liar, but Jimmy was an even better listener.

"Uh, huh. Well you best look out for that one 'cause he smells like trouble." Jimmy squinted his rheumy eyes and stared straight at Harvey, waiting for a response.

"Can he swim?" The younger man asked, causing Jimmy to cackle with laughter: During the previous voyage from Panama, the two men had indulged in a game, as they took turns identifying which of the first class passengers most deserved to be thrown overboard.

"Rats can swim!" Jimmy continued.

"A water moccasin, more like!" Harvey concluded, as they silently agreed to drop the subject.

As the two men continued to work, the ship made its way north and east through the Straits of Florida. Moonlight illuminated phosphorescent plankton at the base of the paddle wheels, which left long white streamers trailing in their wake. Silent lightening offered brief glimpses of dark clouds towering over the distant Bahamas, to the east. It was a breathtakingly beautiful scene, interrupted only by the thumping of the steam engines and the slapping of the paddle wheels, until the breeze picked up. After that, the crew passed the order for all passengers to go below, so they could raise sail without interference and proceed with good speed in a more economical fashion that didn't rely solely on large amounts of coal.

Harvey discovered the berth was still empty when he returned below decks. He placed Martin's shoes on the deck near the cedar closet and removed his own boots and jacket before reclining on a makeshift pallet, as the bed was reserved for the young gentleman. He read for an hour or too but soon grew tired and fell sound asleep.

Floating off in a dream, Harvey was adrift in a skiff on a river at night, lying on his back as he gazed up at the moon and the stars. He watched himself from above, like an owl drifting gently on the breeze, still able to feel the dip and sway of the water as the boat slid downstream. A feeling of peace and contentment swept over him, sweeter than anything he had known in his waking life. Harvey struggled to hold on to that feeling, but a dark corner of his mind told him it couldn't be real. Suddenly, through the eyes and ears of the owl, he sensed danger ahead. His dreaming self sat up in the boat and saw roaring water ahead, illuminated by a brilliant moon in a clear night sky. In his dream, Harvey scrambled madly about the boat, looking for an oar or a paddle, finding nothing but an empty wine bottle, which he tossed overboard. A feeling of dread overwhelmed Harvey as he gripped the gunnels and stared straight ahead. His emotions evolved as the boat raced through the rapids and suddenly his heart was filled with the joy of a young man galloping across a green field on a fine horse. Somehow the boat became a winged stallion, riding bravely through the waves with its head held high, defying death and embracing life. When he saw the waterfall ahead, Harvey gripped the horse's mane without fear. His soul soared as they took flight, with the sound of roaring water fading fast as they rose toward the moon.

Harvey woke with a start and floated back to earth, his heart still racing. Martin was snoring loudly on the other side of the cabin, his clothes smelling of whiskey and tobacco.

CHAPTER FIVE:
A STORM AT SEA

When John Harvey awoke on the morning of Friday the 11th of September, his head ached from a tumble he took during the first squall on Thursday, but at least he didn't suffer from sea sickness, like most of the other passengers. He glanced over at Martin, sleeping lightly in his bunk and looking paler than usual, with his left hand pointing in the general direction of a bucket. Although no one was allowed above decks in the storm, Harvey could stretch his legs long enough to empty the pail in the men's head, as long as he watched his step and didn't disturb any of the ill-tempered first-class passengers.

As he emerged from the berth, wind-driven rain lashed against the skylights above. Already dim, the spacious saloon darkened further as members of the crew slid wooden storm covers over the vulnerable glass. The space was devoid of people but full of sounds, to include the steady thump of the engines and the wailing of miserable children hiding with their mothers in berths further forward off the dining saloon. Stepping lightly, with his knees bent to lower his center of gravity, Harvey working his way gingerly over to the men's head, bracing himself along the way. When he opened the door, he heard a loud ripping noise as another sail shredded in the gale up above, followed by muffled shouts and the rhythmic slapping of bare feet on a wet deck. The ship shuddered and swayed and Harvey barely managed to avoid a spill as he poured the contents of Martin's suffering into the commode and pulled the chain. The narrow space was rank, a repository for multiple miseries during a long and stormy night.

Harvey had some experience with storms at sea, particularly during his first trip to England with Martin's father, but he had never experienced a real Atlantic cyclone. He was beginning to worry. All of the passengers knew they might encounter such a storm in late summer or early fall, but most assumed it wouldn't happen to them. The ship's chaplain led the passengers in prayer when the storm began; afterwards, the Reverend was confined to his bunk, too sick to stand. Harvey recalled with a brief chuckle the impertinence of a cynical passenger from Rhode Island who had asked where he could find the passage that declared "God helps those who help themselves," since he knew full well that familiar Protestant principle and the basis of the pastor's sermon couldn't be found in the Bible.

Harvey's revere was interrupted by the sound of a hatch opening and slamming shut, followed by shouts from Lieutenant James Frazer, the second mate, as he gave orders to a pair of sailors wearing waxed cotton jackets, with wide-brimmed hats tied under their chins.

"Pass the word to all of the passengers on this deck: Every able bodied man is needed down below. Tell them their lives depend on it, if need be, but try not to panic the women and children. Send the strongest men down to the coal bunkers. Bring the rest to the chief engineer— he's waiting by the starboard pump." A serious professional from a family of New England mariners, Frazer recognized a true emergency when he saw one.

"Sir!" Both sailors touched their hats and nodded before working their way down both sides of the Grand Saloon, knocking on doors and relaying their instructions.

As he moved forward toward the dining saloon, Lt. Frazer noticed a dark figure standing to one side. He stopped abruptly.

After pausing for a moment to remember his name, the Lieutenant asked:

"You're Harvey, right?"

"Yes Sir, that's right!" Harvey wasn't sure what to expect, as the sober-looking officer faced him.

"We need a strong man like you—I remember how you handled the crew's best wrestler during that friendly match back in

Aspinwall. Roust your master and tell him you're needed down in the coal bunker. He'll get his orders soon enough: We'll tolerate no slackers on this ship, not today!"

Surprised to be treated with any respect by a white man, and amused by the fact that his "master" would also have to get his hands dirty, Harvey responded enthusiastically:

"Yes Suh, I'll get down to those bunkers right away, Suh!"

"Good man. Best leave your jacket behind!" Frazer smiled grimly before moving off towards the wheel house, where Captain Herndon waited.

Harvey was grateful he didn't have to wake Martin himself, as one of the sailors was already pounding on his door, so he stood behind the sailor as he relayed the news. Martin seemed confused at first but accepted his instructions— and Harvey's jacket, as his companion moved toward the nearest ladder leading down to the bowels of the ship, where the hungry engines waited.

Harvey was familiar with the layout of the steamer, having accompanied Martin on a guided tour during the short voyage from Panama. He worked his way down two levels and then followed the sound of shouts further forward until he entered a nightmarish world of boilers, bulkheads and cast iron pipes. As soon as he approached the first boiler, Henry Kiefer, the second assistant engineer, shouted in his ear:

"Every sail we've set has been shredded by the gale. Water is flooding the coal bunkers and the men can no longer use their wheel-barrows. We've moving the coal in buckets over there," he said as he pointed to a narrow passageway on the port side. "If we don't keep the fires going, the ship can't make headway. If we can't make headway, the ship will founder. If the ship founders, we're all going to drown. If you help me keep the fires going, you may survive. Get to work!"

Harvey nodded his understanding and moved toward the bucket line. A weary sailor told him to squeeze past the others to reach the coal bunker, where the hardest work was underway and the need for a fresh man was greatest. As he moved down the narrow companionway, Harvey was thrown to the deck as the ship was pounded by an enormous wave. Further along, the water got deeper, reaching up to his knees at the entrance to the bunker. It could have been a cave, for all he could tell. The nose of the engines was deafening and the fumes were noxious.

The crewman at the end of the line was dead on his feet, having shoveled coal for over an hour. He looked like a miner: His entire body was covered in dust and the filthy kerchief tied around his neck was long past any useful purpose. Resting his right hand on his knee, while gasping for air, the crewman handed his shovel to Harvey and nodded with appreciation as he began moving toward the back of the line. An exchange of words would have been a waste of precious breath.

Although his hands were not as callused as they used to be, given the soft life he had enjoyed over the past several months, Harvey knew how to work and he took pride in his strength. Quickly establishing a rhythm, the bastard son of an African slave and her white master filled each bucket as soon as it was presented. He was careful to drain the water from each shovel-full, as best he could, before dropping the coal. His world became incredibly small, a tiny corner of Hades featuring endless mounds of coal rising from a pool of black water.

Meanwhile, Martin got lost on his way to the starboard pump. After wandering aimlessly in dark passageways, he stumbled upon a trio of Pinkerton's detective's arguing with John Black, the ship's boatswain. He was a large and intimidating man supported by two dangerous looking sailors. Instinctively, Martin backed around a corner to avoid being seen by the others.

"The orders come direct from the Capt'n!" Said Black, "Move your asses down to the coal bunkers, or my boys will carry you!"

Detective Brendan Smith, the senior Pinkerton on duty, reached inside his tailored jacket, out of habit, before he remembered Captain Herndon had forbidden his men to carry firearms. His pistol was secured in the arms locker, and the First Mate had the key. Smith's response was proud and defiant:

"I don't take orders from you or your Captain. My orders come from Mr. Pinkerton himself—and my orders are to guard the gold in this hold until we reach New York City!"

Boatswain Black's eyes narrowed when Smith's hand moved inside his jacket, followed by a thin smile. He would relish an opportunity to humiliate the arrogant detective, who had treated the crew with contempt during their initial voyage from Aspinwall. Casually resting his right hand on a large revolver strapped to his belt, Black hissed a final warning:

"Every man on this ship answers to the Capt'n. That includes you and your men. You have two choices: Do as you're told, or I'll shoot you dead and throw your carcass overboard!"

Clearly out of options, Smith nodded his head and submitted, but he couldn't resist a parting shot:

"All right, Mr. Black—but know this—you and the Captain are going to answer when Mr. Pinkerton hears about this!"

In a flash, Boatswain Black seized Smith by his lapels and pressed his back against the bulkhead. With a knee gently nudging the Pinkerton in his groin, he hissed a final warning:

"At sea, the Captain's word is law—and no man can protect you!"

The two junior detectives glanced nervously at each other before the wiser one spoke up:

"That's enough, Mr. Black—we'll do our share. And Smith, it's time to shut that mouth of yours, because none of the gold is going to make it to New York if the ship sinks, right? And besides, McKinnon and I will make sure Mr.

Pinkerton knows you had no choice in the matter!"

Brendan Smith was red with shame and humiliation. Having little experience with either sensation, he dropped his gaze for a moment and nodded his head in agreement.

"All right, all right—we have to save the ship to save the gold—I get it. Just give me a moment to secure the locks on this hold and we'll be ready to work."

"That'll do, then." The boatswain responded, as he released Smith and stepped back a pace or two. "These seamen will show you to the coal bunkers as soon as you're done." With those words, Black turned his back and his attention to other matters.

The heavy door securing several tons of gold was located in one of the deepest holds on the ship, with the extra weight serving as ballast while the steamer was underway. The water was rising, so even a hard-headed copper like Smith could see the ship was in danger. He checked all three locks on the sliding door, which was mounted on a pair of iron rails, before hanging the keys on a leather lanyard around his neck. A sixth sense developed during his years as a policeman in Chicago caused Smith to pause as he glanced at one of Black's men. The sailor's name was Broussard, a nasty piece of work who smiled like a fox waiting for a farmer to leave his chickens unattended.

"All right then," said Broussard. "It's time for the three of you to get to work—follow me!"

The group of three detectives and two sailors was surprised when they bumped into Martin lurking just around the corner.

"What do we have here?" Broussard asked. "A young gentleman trying to shirk his duty?" The ferocious looking sailor stood a few inches from Martin as the spittle flew. The younger, smaller man found himself staring at a huge, hairy mole on the sailor's cleft chin, unable to look him in the eye. He recognized the sailor as the same man Harvey had defeated in a wrestling match, back in Panama, and rightly assumed the sailor held a grudge.

"Not at all—Lt. Frazer told me I should report to the starboard pumps, but I got lost along the way." Martin tried to stand erect, but the strain showed in his narrow shoulders.

"A likely story. Let me see your hands!" Broussard was a bully at heart and embraced every opportunity to express his natural inclinations:

"Look at that, Stallworth" Broussard continued as he held Martin's right hand up in an awkward position, "this boy hasn't worked a day in his life. Can't imagine what the Lieutenant thinks he can do, but you best show him to the pumps, while I take these Pinkertons down to the coal!"

Wanting to prove his manhood, Martin was tempted to display the small wound on his left palm, but knew that would only invite more ridicule. Broussard sensed his discomfort and laughed contemptuously as he turned and waked away.

65

Broussard grew up in the city of New Orleans, a wharf rat and the son of a whore. Stallworth was a different sort. He grew up in Mississippi cotton country, where opportunities for working men grew out of their allegiances to the landed aristocracy. When Broussard looked at Martin, he was blinded by hate. When Stallworth looked at Martin, he saw opportunity:

"Pay him no mind, Sir—he's an ignorant brute." Stallworth whispered as he led Martin up a wooden ladder to a higher deck, adopting a friendly but subservient tone. "But know this: The ship is in real trouble. I'll do my best to look out for you, if worst comes to worst."

Back on familiar turf, Martin responded the way his father would have done:

"You're a good man, Stallworth, and I'll remember you when we get to port." Martin was careful to keep both hands on the rails as he scrambled up the ladder.

"Well, Sir, let's pray we make it to port!" Stallworth responded grimly as he lead the way down a corridor, bracing himself on the bulkheads.

"Now, listen up: If the ship begins to founder, you'll find me up on the main deck, on the port side, by the boat nearest the stern. I'm the crew chief for that boat, understand?"

"Will it really come to that?" Martin was feeling a bit overwhelmed. His breath caught in his throat as he considered the implications.

"It's best to think about these things before they happen, Mr. McCrary, so you'll know what to do when the time comes." The sailor

66

paused to think before continuing: "Regret there won't be room for your nigger, but that'll be no great loss to your family, as he's a freeman."

Stallworth stopped for a moment, in reaction to an unexpected look of surprise and disappointment on Martin's face. For his part, Martin was tempted to explain that he had known Harvey all his life and couldn't imagine losing him, but realized he would be wasting his breath with a man like Stallworth.

"Enough of that for now—the officers won't like that kind of talk, people might panic!" The sailor lowered his voice in a conspiratorial manner to emphasize his point.

The two men passed several members of the crew moving up the last ladder leading to the starboard pump, which had failed during the night.

"I best return to my duties, Mr. McCrary—just tell the tall fellow over there you're here to volunteer, he's the chief engineer. I'll seek you out the next chance I get!"

Before Martin could respond, seaman Stallworth disappeared down a ladder as quick as you please, using his hands to slide along the iron railings, with his feet floating a few inches above the risers.

Martin moved up to stand with a group of 6 civilians facing George Ashby, an engineer who joined the ship when she set sail from New York for the current round trip to Aspinwall. Ashby knew a great deal about steam engines, having worked on the development and production of locomotives, but had little experience at sea. He had been selected as chief engineer due to his connections with the Native American Party, or "Know-Nothings." The owner of the ship, George Law, was a wealthy and influential man who had run for Vice President with the American Party's presidential nominee, Millard Fillmore. Despite the bitter loss and third place finish in the the fall of 1856, Law had compensated many of his supporters and their families with appointments in various aspects of his business empire.

Ashby had to shout, to be heard above the noise, "We've just managed to get this pump working again—at least for now," Ashby began, with a solemn look on his narrow face. "But there's still plenty of work that needs doing. The ship is taking on water. The seal around the shaft driving the paddle wheel on this side of the ship is leaking, though we've tried our best to slow it down. Mr. Foster here," Ashby pointed to a sturdy looking sailor with a short black beard, "is going to need your help rigging up a whip. Using a system of ropes and pulleys, wooden tubs will be lowered into the hold and raised above decks, to be dumped into the sea. Now, don't worry, you won't be asked to work above decks during the storm, the seamen will handle that, but we do need you men to fill the tubs and haul the ropes. The same work is being carried out by other men just like you at several locations around the ship, so we're all in this together."

The civilians facing Ashby were a disparate group, with one younger man like Martin but mostly older men of business, with soft hands and stout torsos. Some faces looked willing, but others looked resentful; all were fearful.

"Mr. Foster, I'll leave it to you—I'm off to check the boilers." The engineer wasted no time as he set off, secretly relieved to return to his area of competency. He had no idea what to do about the leaks or the rising water in the hold, but he would do his best to keep the engines running.

Daniel Foster was a practical man who enjoyed solving problems. He spoke to the group of "volunteers" in a calm, reassuring voice.

"All right then. Here's what we're going to do. You men here," Foster pointed at Martin and three others. "We'll need you to pull the ropes. We've rigged up a system of pulleys, so you'll have plenty of leverage—but whatever you do, don't let go of the ropes, or you might drop a full tub on one of the other men and crush him. The rest of you will fill the tubs, which will be a wet but simple job, as the weight of the tubs will be carried by the ropes, see?"

The circle of men tightened around Foster and several shifted on their feet, but no one spoke.

"Follow me, then, and we'll get to work." With those simple instructions, the 6 men filed behind Foster as he moved up one deck and then forward to a pair of open hatches, with rain falling down from the deck above and a pair of ropes leading down into a lower hold. The ship continued to bob and sway, so most of the men gripped the iron railing encircling the hatch before they looked down; the one man who didn't almost fell into the hold before catching himself at the last moment. What they saw shocked them: A large wooden tub was floating in waist-high water. Looking up, Martin saw the ropes led to a heavy wooden spar above decks, with the leverage multiplied by a set of pulleys.

"We'd better get moving; the water is rising fast." Foster pointed to Martin's group, "The four of you need to seize these ropes, two men on each rope. When I give you a shout, pull the ropes steadily, until the tub makes its way all the way through that hatch above and the slack gives out. When the sailors up on deck give us a shout, we'll lower the tub back into the hold and repeat the process until we bail as much water as we can out of the hold. Understand?" Foster looked encouragingly at the rope-men and put a hand on Martin's shoulder before turning toward the others.

"Now, the two of you will need to climb down that ladder into the hold. You're going to get wetter than the rest of us, but all you have to do is to tip one side of the tub into the water until it fills up. Just give us a shout, and we'll do the hauling." Foster put his hands on both of the older men and walked them over to the narrow service ladder. "All right then, let's get to work!"

It took a couple of minutes for the men to get set in the hold, and one of them took a full dunking when he slipped at the bottom, but in no time the large tub was filled and Martin's team began to haul on the lines. The weight was tolerable, although the men had to sit on the deck to hold the tub steady when it reached the upper deck. With the third load, Martin's palms began to smart and he rubbed his hands on his trousers. Seaman Foster nodded his head in understanding and quickly distributed strips of sail cloth to the landlubbers, showing then how to wrap the cloth around their hands, to reduce the friction. That seemed to help, and the volunteers settled into an unending rhythm, broken only by the shouts of the sailors above. Martin's mind began to wander as he indulged a sense of hope that his efforts might make a difference. His musings were interrupted by the clunk and crash of the tubs as they bounced against every possible obstruction on their way up and down the hold.

Above decks, Captain Herndon was methodically deploying every tool and every hard-earned skill at his disposal, in an effort to maintain control over the ship. Broaching was the greatest danger, a likely fate if they were unable to keep the ship pointed into the wind. The steam engines couldn't provide enough power to maintain headway in a gale. He had ordered the crew to raise a variety of storm sails, but all attempts had ended in failure. During their last attempt, the storm sail had shredded when it was only three feet above the deck. Herndon secretly wished he was commanding a traditional sailing vessel, without the extra weight of the steam engines, the need to shovel coal or the awkwardness of the huge paddle wheels interrupting the sleekness of her hull. A man of great discipline, Captain Herndon set those useless thoughts aside and turned his attention to the matter at hand.

"Charles, it's time to rig a drag, least we broach." Lieutenant Charles Van Rensellaer, the First Mate, nodded his head. "Use the kedge anchor; we need this trick to work the first time." The two men stood in the wheel house, just forward of the main cabin. Four experienced sailors manned the wheel, trying as best they could to point the ship into the wind. Their valiant efforts were frustrated by the limited power of the steam engines driving the paddle wheels. The sailors exchanged glances when the Captain gave his orders. They knew the officers were running out of options.

"Sir," the First Mate responded, "we'll bend a 9 inch hawser to the middle of a yard and secure that to the stump when we cut away the foremast."

"Aye, Charles, there's no better solution. See it done."

As there was nothing left to say and no time for a silent prayer, Van Rensellaer left the refuge of the wheel house and found Lieutenant Frazer and Boatswain Black on the foredeck, supervising the clean up after the last effort to raise a storm sail had failed.

"All right, James" the First Mate shouted above the gale, "it's time to rig a drag. Use Black and the foredeck crew: There's no room for error."

Wasting no time, Lt. Frazer and Boatswain Black shouted orders to the experienced sailors on the foredeck. All of them cursed their luck, trapped on a heavy and cumbersome paddle-wheel steamer in an Atlantic cyclone. Practical men who knew their individual survival depended on a collective effort, the crew set to work immediately. First, they secured the ships heaviest kedge anchor to a 9 inch hawser line and made that fast to the middle of a sturdy wooden yard. Next, in a brutal but delicate operation that required perfect timing, they cut away the foremast, allowing it to drop into the sea in a break between the waves, while simultaneously dropping the kedge anchor and paying out 100 fathoms of hawser, in hopes the whole mess would serve as a drag, pulling the ship's head into the wind.

Down below, both Martin and Harvey lost their footing as the weight of the drag caused the ship to buck and slide. As soon as he picked himself up, Martin was showered with spray as the top of a wave washed into the hatch above. Down below, Harvey braced himself as the black water sloshed to and fro.

The drag failed and the ship was in grave danger.

CHAPTER 6:
INTO THE DARKNESS

After finishing his shift shoveling coal, Harvey asked around until he found Martin at the forward bailing position. Sizing up the situation, Harvey told Seaman Foster he would be willing to take a turn in the hold, filling the tub, so he could wash the coal dust off his body. Having stashed his shirt and boots, and wearing nothing but a pair of rolled up trousers, Harvey glanced over at Martin and winked before sliding down the ladder into the hold. The two miserable men wading in the saltwater pool at the bottom of the ladder were pleased to be relieved, but they refused to acknowledge Harvey.

"Why did they make us work if this nigger could 'a done it?" The surlier of the two men asked, making no effort to hide his contempt as he climbed up the ladder.

With a smile and a strange sense of exhilaration, Harvey ignored the insult and dunked himself in the cool water, while the tub was being emptied up above. When the tub slid back down, he had no trouble filling it by himself, doing the work of two white men. Oddly enough, he enjoyed the rolling of the ship and savored the breaks between loads, which seemed like an easy job after shoveling all that coal.

After some time had passed, Harvey's thoughts turned inward and he asked himself:

"Why ain't I afraid? It looks like this ship is gonna sink—how come I don't give a flip?"

Harvey had to admit, if not for the concern he felt for his mother and sister back home, he wasn't worried about his own fate. He mulled things over and decided he must be a low enough creature to enjoy the looks of fear and misery in the eyes of so many men who imaged they were better than him.

"Hell, I might drown, but so will those bastards!"

A storm at sea was a great equalizer, he decided. Nothing wrong with that!

Harvey lost track of time until Seaman Foster shouted down and told him to climb back up, which was no easy trick, as the ship was pitching and yawing in every possible direction. He was more than a bit surprised when he reached the top of the ladder and found no one waiting to replace him—just Martin, who was sitting on the rolling deck, nursing his rope-burned hands.

"What happened to the rest of 'em?" Harvey asked, looking down at Martin like a fire-blackened statue of of a Greek god, a glistening ebony Atlas with bright eyes and broad shoulders.

"Foster and the others men left." Martin began, while rubbing his hands over his eyes. "We were told to give up the bailing, 'cause it's hopeless." He paused and looked up at Harvey before continuing: "I suppose they'll be loading the women and children on the boats soon. Too bad about all that gold, sitting down there in that hold, with no Pinkerton's to watch over it."

Harvey sat down next to Martin and glanced over with a curious look on his face.

"What are you going on about?" Harvey asked, rubbing the water out of his eyes.

Martin told Harvey about his encounter with the Pinkertons, and remarked:

"I suppose it's foolish to think about the gold when there's so many innocents aboard, not to mention the not so innocent, like us. Stallworth is probably getting his lifeboat ready."

"Why, you're full of surprises today— worried about the women and children and all. Why don't you tell me about this man Stallworth and his boat." Harvey asked.

"I met him down in the hold, when I got lost on my way to the pumps." Martin responded. "He's the crew chief for one of the lifeboats, back on the left side of the boat—that's the port side, right? He promised to look after me, if the order comes to abandon ship."

Martin looked over at Harvey again, not sure what he should say next. After thinking things over, he decided it was best to be honest, rather than leave his man with any illusions:

"Stallworth said there won't be any room for you on his boat, Harvey. I'm truly sorry about that." Martin couldn't bring himself to look Harvey in the eye.

The black man nodded his head quietly. He hadn't expected to be a priority, when it came to abandoning ship, but there wasn't any reason to blame Martin for his fate, or the bad luck of being born a slave. In that moment, Harvey's thoughts crystalized: If he had enough money, he could buy his mother and sister's freedom. If he drowned, there was nothing he could do. The trick was finding a way to get his hands on some of that gold, without drowning in the process. First things first, he decided.

"Suh, I think you should hurry an up and find mister Stallworth, right away. You can help him with the women and children, and then you might get your chance. You go on ahead now, while I look around and find what I need to make a raft, before it's too late. Some empty barrels ought to do the trick. You know men like me are the last ones the crew are gonna worry about."

Harvey really did plan to make himself a raft, but not until he found some of that gold. His lie was a sin of omission that came easily.

"You're right, Harvey, that's our best chance. If I see you floating about on a raft, I'll do my best to have Stallworth pull you aboard his boat. You best make your raft big enough for two, in case there's no room for me on the boat. Likely as not, I'll drown and you'll float up on a beach outside Charleston, healthy as a mule, with no sunburn to spoil the celebration!"

Harvey laughed heartily in response, recalling a time 10 years back when he had taken Martin floating down the river near his father's plantation on a hand-made raft, on a hot summer's day. Martin had taken off his shirt, despite his mother's warnings, so he ended the day with a fearsome sunburn, while marveling at Harvey's natural immunity.

"That's the spirit, Suh. You best get moving!" Harvey stood up quickly, bracing himself with one hand and hoisting Martin up with the other.

"Think I know where I can find some empty barrels, down in that hold, and there's plenty of rope right here!" Harvey shouted, as he scrambled back down the ladder with a grin on his face.

Feeling lost and empty, but determined to survive, Martin turned to work his way up a level or two until he found himself in the Dining Saloon. Once a decorative showpiece, the space was now empty: All of the furniture had been broken up and tossed in the boilers, in a vain attempt to keep the engines running, after the water rose too high in the coal bunkers. The ship was listing badly as Martin worked his way along the bulkhead toward his cabin in the rear of the ship. Along the way, he noticed all of the doors to the private cabins had been ripped off their hinges, and all the inhabitants were missing.

With some difficulty, Martin reached his own cabin, on the up-hill side of the Grand Saloon, only to discover his belongings had been rifled, looted and scattered across the floor. One of his finest dress shirts was laid out in the doorway, with a boot print on the back. On impulse, he quickly donned a woolen jumper given to him by his grandfather, with the following advice:

"Wool will keep you warm, boy, even when you're wet, and it can save your life when you're cold and shivering in the mountains."

Steadying himself with both hands as he surveyed the the scene, Martin realized he was the only man left standing in the Grand Saloon. Looking around, he noticed a pair of drunken old bastards collapsed in a corner, mumbling to themselves as they cradled matching bottles of bourbon. Hearing other voices above the din of the storm, Martin glanced around and saw a cluster of feet, some bare and some not, standing at the top of a large staircase leading to the upper deck, and the boats. With a push, a stumble and a scramble, Martin reached the bottom of the stairs, momentarily blinded by a flash of lightning. The crowd at the top of the stairs was exclusively male, some clutching heavy leather bags stuffed with their most valuable possessions. Most would sooner drown than lose their gold.

With the advantage of youth and agility, Martin seized the opportunity and hoisted himself up until he was able to scoot along on the top of a handrail, shouting warnings to the older men to watch their fingers as he slipped by. Two of the old men reacted angrily: One punched Martin on the back of his thighs and another made an effort to drag him back into the scrum. Holding on to a large pad eye with all his might, Martin lashed out with his right foot, catching one of his assailants on the forehead and knocking him out cold. The melee caught the attention of two sailors armed with clubs, who were charged with keeping the men under control while the women and children were loaded. One of the sailors began to move toward the disorderly civilians, with the intention of cracking them on the skull. At that moment, Martin recognized the man in charge and shouted as loud as he could:

"Stallworth, Stallworth, over here!"

The friendly sailor from Mississippi looked over, moments before Martin's head was about to explode, and barked an order to his crew:

"Stand down, Iverson! I know that man; he can help us load the last of 'em!" Stallworth motioned for Martin to make his way over to the gunnels, where he immediately went to work assisting two older women as they climbed into the boat. The rig seemed remarkably steady, under the circumstances, as a team of sailors held fast to a set of ropes, which in turn were secured to a pair of iron davits. Peering over the rail, Martin saw a group of women and children huddled in the bottom of the boat, with looks of sheer terror on their faces. He tried to smile as he locked eyes with one little boy, whose head was pressed against his mother's breast. He wanted to comfort the child, but had nothing to offer.

When the *Central America* began her journey, she had a full complement of six boats, which wasn't enough for all of the passengers and crew. She had four large boats mounted on iron davits, two on either side of the ship, another sturdy wooden boat mounted on top of the main cabin, and a smaller, newfangled skiff made of metal, which was despised by most of the crew.

Lowering a boat alongside a foundering ship in an Atlantic cyclone was no easy feat. The boat hanging on the starboard side of the ship, nearest the bow, had been washed away by the storm well before Captain Herndon gave the order to abandon ship. The matching forward boat on the port side was crushed when she was lowered into water, as the ship was rolling unpredictably and the crew timed their actions poorly. The two stern boats and a third boat stored on top of the cabin were lowered successfully, immediately after the crew spotted a small brig to windward.

It was sheer luck when Hiram Burt, Captain of the brig Marine, spotted the *S.S. Central America*. He shouted out to his crew and shook his head sadly as his instincts were confirmed: The big steamer was flying the universal distress signal, an upside-down flag secured to the mizzen. Hiram Burt had been a sailor all his life: He would do what he could, although he believed the passengers and crew had tempted fate by trusting their lives to such devilish technology. His humble brig had no trouble making headway in the gale, as her stubby but streamlined hull offered no obstructions to waves or water. Her sails were not shredded by the mass of the steam engines, and her fine figure was not spoiled by heavy paddle wheels, hanging like saddlebags on a downtrodden mule. His crew was too small to lower their boats, while maintaining control of their ship, so Burt would stand by as long as he could, rescuing anyone who reached his little ship on their own initiative.

While Martin worked to earn a spot on a lifeboat, Harvey searched for the gold. Several times he lost his way and had to move quickly to avoid being trapped in the bowels of the ship. When he was beginning to lose hope, assuming the gold was now below the level of the rising water, Harvey heard the sound of metal beating against metal, just ahead and down one last ladder. As he crawled on his belly to take a better look, two bodies bumped against the ladder below, floating in several feet of water. He recognized one of the dead men, a Pinkerton named Smith, his throat a gaping wound that spread from ear to ear. Lowering his head a bit further, Harvey saw the bare back of a burly sailor, using a crowbar to bust the locks on a door that concealed something worth killing for. That man was Broussard, the sailor from New Orleans—the same man Harvey had defeated in a wrestling match back in Panama. Harvey decided to watch and wait, to let Broussard do the work, just as he had done when they wrestled.

Moments later, Harvey heard a loud snap as the last lock was removed, followed by a grinding sound as Broussard pulled the heavy door back on its rails, then a slopping noise as water washed into the hold. Harvey worked his way slowly down the ladder and crept up to the door, which was held in the open position by a metal latch mounted on the upper rail.

Harvey observed the distracted sailor discreetly, as he opened several wooden crates. The first two boxes were stuffed with gold double eagles, stamped by the mint in San Francisco. The third crate protected a single gold ingot, cast by the assayers Kellogg and Humbert in California. Broussard tossed his crowbar aside, picked up the ingot and cradled it like a baby.

Harvey stepped into the hold and spoke:

"It looks like there's plenty of prize money to go around, this time," Harvey suggested. He was prepared to fight, if necessary, but time was short and he was unarmed.

"Well lookey here, it's a dead nigger!" Broussard snarled, as he carefully placed the ingot back in its crate and reached for his crowbar.

"You've already lost one fight, Broussard—why don't you take what you want and leave the rest?" Harvey wanted to be reasonable, but didn't expect a peaceful response.

"There ain't much time left." Harvey continued. "Best fill your pockets and move on, no one the wiser, while you still have time to find a boat."

With crossbar in hand, Broussard waded a few steps closer and spoke his mind:

"Well, I reckon you're gonna drown, anyway, like the black dog you are, but I suppose I'll take my pleasure right here. As you already seen, I ain't planning to leave no witnesses, especially no trumped up nigger like you!"

The big Cajun charged directly at Harvey, swinging the crowbar in a vicious arc. Harvey dodged the blow and met Broussard's charge with a head-butt to his chest, quickly immobilizing the crowbar as he seized the sailor's wrist and twisted until the iron dropped in the water. Broussard responded with a knee to Harvey's head, which hadn't been allowed during their wrestling match but should have been expected. Dazed for a moment, Harvey stumbled and slipped down on one knee. He was quickly overcome as Broussard spun behind him, locking an arm around his neck, with the intention of choking him to death.

Harvey knew he was in serious trouble. He struggled to free himself by standing up and shoving Broussard backwards against the bulkhead, as hard as he could. The sailor lost his footing, and his chokehold on Harvey, as the ship pitched sharply, causing the door to shift an inch or too. In a moment of inspiration, Harvey reached up behind Broussard's head to unlatch the metal toggle holding the door open, and

85

twisted his body until he had the upper position, with both hands around the sailor's neck as they both gasped for air. Suddenly the ship pitched forward, allowing Harvey to shove his enemy's head against the lower rail, just as the heavy door slid shut, crushing Broussard's skull like a ripe melon.

The victor stood up quickly, catching his breath, and turned to face the gold. The crates of double eagles were too heavy to carry and, if broken, would spill their contents. He slipped a few eagles into a hidden pocket lining the inside of the waist band, a gift from the Scotsman. The trousers were made to keep secrets, but served well enough for this purpose. Looking over at the ingot, Harvey was seized with an idea: He could hide the gold in a barrel tied to his raft. Harvey grabbed the ingot with one hand and steadied himself with the other. He felt no shame or pity as he stepped over the Cajun's carcass, but grimaced as he waded past detective Smith, with his gaping neck wound shaped like a smile.

The water was rising fast. Harvey knew he had to move quickly. He struggled to reach the forward hold, which offered unimpeded access to the upper deck. After a missed turn or two, he reached his destination. Unceremoniously, he dropped the gold ingot into the flooded hold and waded to a hatch on the other side. Earlier he had discovered a hoard of ships stores, with some empty barrels and others filled with drinking water. Looking around, he found a cooper's wooden mallet hanging from a leather strap. He checked four of the barrels to make sure the lids were tapped shut before heaving them into the hold, where they banged against one another as the ship pitched back and forth. Next, he selected a small barrel of fresh water, which he dropped carefully into the hold. He nodded with satisfaction as it floated a bit lower in the salt water than the four empty barrels.

Digging around in the stores on either side of the hold, Harvey found a cargo net, some stout boards a little longer than himself and a large coil of hemp rope. He tossed the cargo net and rope in with the barrels before climbing back into the rising water at the bottom of the hold. And old hand at building rafts back back home in South Carolina, Harvey assembled a makeshift contraption by securing boards to the empty barrels, in a rectangular fashion, with the cargo net serving as a makeshift platform that wouldn't keep him dry, but might keep him from drowning.

Rummaging around with his feet, Harvey found the gold ingot and ducked under the water to retrieve it. He carefully removed the lid on the barrel of fresh water, dropped the ingot inside and secured the lid with the mallet. Moving quickly, Harvey wrapped the barrel of fresh water in some of the netting and tied it to a corner of the raft. With time running out, he cut the ropes fixed to the abandoned bailing tub and tied them to the raft, then scrambled up two ladders to the main deck, where the hoist remained intact. By this time, the water in the hold was rising fast and the ship was beginning to settle by the stern.

Scanning the waves, Harvey saw desperate men clinging to bits of debris. Just enough moonlight broke through the clouds to illuminate the scene in shades of silver and black. He watched in horror as the steamer's broad hull rolled with the waves and crushed the last of the lifeboats, just as she was trying to push off. It may have been his imagination, but Harvey swore he saw Martin clinging to the remnants of the lifeboat as she spilled a dozen men into the sea. He knew most of them couldn't swim.

Gathering his resolve, Harvey seized the ropes leading to his raft and pulled as hard as he could, hoisting his contraption up through the hatch. He almost lost his grip as the ship rolled and settled by the stern, raising the bow slowly but irrevocably towards the heavens. In a final, desperate move, Harvey kicked the raft as hard as he could, as it dangled from the hoist, and allowed the whole mess to drop into the sea. Suddenly, the bow of the ship pushed skyward. Just before he dove into the sea, Harvey caught a brief glimpse of Captain Herndon, still at his post in the wheelhouse, as the waves consumed him.

Harvey dove deeply and swam back to the surface, his head still aching from its acquaintance with Broussard's knee. Swirling his hands and feet, to keep his eyes as high above the water as possible, Harvey spied a barrel as it crested a wave downwind. Was that his raft? It must be! His options exhausted, Harvey swam as hard as he could, until his fingers touched something solid. The raft was hard to distinguish from the circle of debris surrounding a hole in the ocean where the steamship had foundered, but the cargo net was distinctive. Totally spent, Harvey hoisted himself up, taking refuge in a hammock-like hollow between the barrels, with his back immersed in the water.

The night was black, the wind howled, and Harvey was alone.

When the *S.S. Central America* left Havana, she was carrying nearly 500 passengers and a crew of 102. The brig Marine rescued 153 men, women and children. The little ship was so small most of the survivors had to take refuge on deck, exposed to the weather. This included some members of the crew who refused to row back to their ship, cutting their lifeboats loose rather than risk another crossing. Soon afterwards, the Norwegian bark Ellen pulled another 50 men from the sea. Hundreds perished.

When the news reached New York and London, the loss of the Ship of Gold sparked a run on the banks, as many were overextended and some could no longer pay their creditors. Pumped up by reckless speculation and the great fortunes of the Gold Rush, stock markets crashed. Among the wealthiest Americans, Southern planters were hurt the least, as the demand for cotton continued to grow. Filled with disdain for the commercial North, confident in the superiority of their society, some Southerners began to speak more openly of secession.

CHAPTER 7:
SURVIVAL

The wind howled and the ocean surged. Martin was left in a state of shock when his lifeboat was crushed against the side of the steamship. He clung to a gunnel and a section of lap strake boards that were just large enough to keep his torso above water. He heard desperate voices in the darkness, but they faded like fireflies in autumn, as the lives that animated them were lost.

Martin coughed and spat in an effort to expel the water from his lungs. As his mind cleared, the thought of being completely alone was too much to bear, so he shouted into the wind like a man possessed. A few moments later, above the howling wind, he heard a faint response. Driven by a desire to reach another person, any person, Martin spread his body on top of the remnants of his lifeboat and used both arms to paddle in the direction of the voice he heard, or imagined. A rising swell upset his balance and nearly carried him away, if not for the tight grip he maintained on a bronze oarlock. In the space between swells, Martin continued to paddle until he saw the head of a man clinging to an oar, shouting hoarsely in his direction. It was Stallworth.

"Come on, man!" Martin shouted, "Over here."

The sailor disappeared for a moment as a wave swept over him. He was still clinging to the oar when his head bobbed back to the surface.

"I can't swim!" He gurgled and choked, while reaching toward Martin with one hand.

Try as he might, Martin couldn't maneuver his sorry excuse for a raft any closer to the sailor, because the wreckage of the lifeboat offered more resistance to the wind than Stallworth's oar. Looking around, Martin found a bit of canvas and some rope trailing behind the boards as he paddled. Somehow, he knew what needed to be done. Lowering himself into the water, Martin grabbed the loose end of the line and swam towards Stallworth. Using a well-practiced stroke, he approached the sailor quickly. Before Martin could offer any instructions, Stallworth reached out in terror and tried to climb up, as if Martin were a tiny island surrounded by sharks. Struggling to keep his head above water, Martin remembered a warning and a bit of wisdom offered by Harvey when he was a boy:

"Now remember, a drowning man is dangerous!" Harvey intoned. "He'll loose his wits and crawl on top of you, even if that means you'll both both go down together. You have to cheat a drowning man by diving beneath him, so you can separate yourself. Then give him something else to cling to, anything you can use to pull him behind you at a safe distance."

That warning had been followed by a demonstration, with 10 year old Martin playing the part of the drowning man and Harvey his rescuer. A sense of guilt seized Martin as he tried not to imagine what might have happened to the man he had known and taken for granted all of his life.

Coolly and calmly, Martin pushed off against Stallworth. Simultaneously, he took a deep breath, tightened his grip on the line, thrust his legs into the air and propelled himself downwards. When he was safely beneath Stallworth's thrashing feet, Martin swam toward the oar, which he reached a few seconds later. When he surfaced, Martin pulled the line tight, causing it to bump against Stallworth's flailing arms. The sailor seized the line immediately. After wrapping the line around the middle of the oar, Martin pulled both men toward the remnants of the boat. Moments later, Stallworth bumped against the gunnel and shifted his weight over to his new refuge, coughing and gasping for breath. Martin used the rope to secure the oar to the wreckage, adding some additional flotation.

Clinging to either side of the makeshift raft, with their heads and shoulders above water, the two men stared at each other for several minutes as the storm continued to rage.

Gathering his wits and swallowing his shame, Stallworth spoke first.

"I almost kilt us both, didn't I?" He croaked, with eyes as wide as saucers.

"Guess I'll have to teach you how to swim!" Martin replied, shouting over the wind.

"Won't do me much good, but thanks anyway!" The sailor answered with a grin that faded to a grimace. "You know what the old timers say? Swimming only prolongs the misery!"

Stallworth wasn't joking.

"Speaking for myself," Martin retorted, "I plan to prolong the misery as long as I can. And besides, I'd be dead already if you hadn't gotten me on your boat!"

"All right then," Stallworth nodded, shuddering as he recovered from the shock and shame. "Suppose I'll keep you company for a while!"

The two men clung to the wreckage in silence as their thoughts turned to loved ones back home. Both of them wondered if they would ever see their families again.

"What's your given name, Stallworth?" Martin finally asked. "It wouldn't be right for us to drown without getting better acquainted." His attempt at humor may have fallen flat, but it was appreciated.

"Richard," the sailor responded, as he pushed a flock of wet hair out of his eyes. "That's

94

my son's name, too, except we call him Little Dicky. He'll be six in the spring. Promised I'd be home for his birthday, over in Mobile."

"Well, Richard," Martin said, "we're not gonna disappoint Little Dicky, are we?"

As they spoke, the two men were lifted high above their surroundings by an enormous swell, which sprayed them with salt water as razor-sharp wind shaved the summit. When they breached the top of the watery mountain, Stallworth spotted a dim light downwind, which could only be a ship's lantern.

"That must be that little brig that took on the women and children!" Stallworth shouted, "She's close, but the wind's gonna carry her away!"

Both men strained to catch another glimpse, but neither man knew if their minds were playing tricks on them as they searched for light on the sea.

"Hell, if we're gonna to drown," the sailor decided, "We might as well do it with style! Here, give me a hand with this oar!"

Knowing it was useless to explain, Stallworth went to work. First, he laid the oar cross-wise on top of the shattered boat, forming a shape that might look like a cross from above. Second, he retrieved his knife, which was secured to his person by a lanyard, as a matter of habit. Next, he cut a piece of sailcloth into a triangle. Using his skills with a rope, he tied two corners of the sailcloth to the oar, about four feet apart, then secured the middle of the oar to the bronze oarlock, in a manner that allowed the oar to be turned like a minute hand on the face of the ocean. Finally, he used the remaining length of rope to fashion a sheet, a control line he secured to the last corner of the triangle.

In no time at all, the sailor had fashioned an improvised sail. On his first attempt, the sheet slipped out of his hand, as the wind gripped the tiny storm sail. On his second attempt, he was able to keep the canvas low over the water, just high enough to offer some resistance to the wind, by twisting the rope around the oarlock. Unbelievably, the rig worked as Stallworth intended, and both men could feel their legs beginning to trail behind them. They clung to the gunnel and oar, on either side of the contraption, in an attempt to improve its balance. The curve of the gunnel and lap strake boards worked in their favor, skimming over the water like the prow of a ship rather than diving beneath it.

"Woooohoooo!" Cried the ecstatic sailor. "We've got ourselves a sleigh ride!"

For a few minutes at a time, the rig moved smoothly with the ocean swells, but the tail kept swinging around, crossways to the wind. This caused the unwieldy pile of debris to roll precariously, until Stallworth released the sheet. It took time and energy to retrieve the sail and paddle the improvised raft back into position for another try. After a number of short rides and longer disappointments, neither man was fit to continue. They floated in silence for what seemed like an eternity.

"We did our best, boy, but there's no use." Stallworth proclaimed, as he shivered from shock, exposure and exhaustion. "Nobody is gonna find us out here, and we'll never catch that brig!"

The sailor's last words were lost to the wind as a ferocious squall drove over them, blinding Martin as the rain lashed his face. He held on to the remnants of the boat, refusing to give up. When he opened his eyes, Stallworth was gone.

As a young man who had never known hardship, Martin had always been cold blooded. He never found it difficult to control his emotions, if not his selfish impulses. In fact, there were times when Martin wondered why his emotions never seemed to range beyond petty pleasure or mild irritation. Something changed, out there on the ocean. He wanted to live. His soul ached and his heart burst. Waves of grief and anguish flowed over him, racking his body, until he finally felt a sense of peace.

"I'm gonna tie myself to this wreckage," he declared to himself. "That way, if I pass out, I'm less likely to drown, and if I die, someone will find my body and wonder who I might have been!"

Scanning the wreckage, Martin noticed the ship's name carved in the wood, where the bow of the lifeboat used to be. That inspired him to wriggle a bronze fastener loose from the debris, which he used to scratch his name in the wood, to prove his existence to the world. Exhausted, Martin summoned his last reserves of energy and lashed himself to the raft. Cradling his head in his arms, he drifted in and out of consciousness, as the storm passed over him. During long periods of loneliness between the dreams and nightmares, Martin imagined what his life might have been like, if more years had been granted.

As a child, Martin had been an unquestioning believer, sitting at his mother's side in the church pews every Sunday. As a young man, he was a secret skeptic, whose doubts were tempered but not overcome by the summers he spent with his grandfather. The Reverend Coulter was the only man he knew who seemed to live according to his faith, which meant more to him than some story in a book. Everyone else seemed to use religion to rationalize their self interest. That's why Martin had taken some consolation from the belief that he was more honest than most folks, because he rejected God. After all, he stood to inherit his father's vast fortune, which was built on the backs of slaves. How could that be?

Martin had struggled with his conscience, but he couldn't get his mind around his grandfather's abolitionism. His travels with Harvey had only fanned the flames of cynicism, as his powerful father had hoped. Martin enjoyed drinking, gambling and having sex with prostitutes—and he expected to keep on enjoying himself for the foreseeable future. Now, he didn't know if he had a future. One particularly loud voice in Martin's head ridiculed him for imagining God might take an interest in his fate:

"If there is a God, why would he save you, when so many others have died? Surely you don't imagine you deserve to live, do you boy? If you beg God to save you now, wouldn't that be a dishonorable, cowardly thing to do, since you rejected Him when things were going well? Wouldn't God see through your falseness, if he exists at all?"

After allowing his cynical and hopeful selves to argue back and forth for a very long time, Martin decided to pray, humbly and sincerely, for the first time as a grown man.

"Lord," Martin began with a shake and a shiver. "You know I'm a sinner, and deserve to die. If You think I should go on living, I'm willing to try."

Martin stopped for a moment, suppressing pride and shame as he struggled to gather his thoughts.

"Jesus, I'm not asking for a miracle, to save myself. A true miracle would make something useful out of me, to serve some purpose, according to Your will. I'm thinking I should put myself in Your hands, but know I'm already there, whether I like it or not. I'm just saying I accept that now. Amen."

The long, lonely night finally ended when the sun rose in the east, illuminating a clear blue sky. Martin was still rising and falling on the ocean swells, but the wind softened quickly as he drifted between the distant arms of a stormy pinwheel. He woke with a thick crust of salt on his lips, which were beginning to crack. His head ached from dehydration and his body was numb with exposure, as the ocean was warm, after the long days of summer, but cooler than his body.

As his raft reached the peak of each swell, Martin scanned the horizon and searched for signs of life. Two hours later, his lagging attention was diverted by a school of dolphins swimming nearby. One of the larger dolphins drifted alongside. It seemed to fix Martin with a curious stare as its head rose above the water. Grateful for the company, his eyes continued to track the creature until it disappeared beneath the waves. Marveling at its beauty, he raised his head a little bit higher, hoping to catch another glimpse.

As he scanned the sea, Martin was thrilled to discover a lifeboat floating amongst the ocean swells, hanging like a pearl between the breasts of a giant mermaid. At first Martin assumed he must have been hallucinating, but the image remained after he rubbed his eyes and reached the top of the next wave. His heart jumped and fluttered as he considered the possibility that he might survive, after all.

Looking around, Martin could see his makeshift raft was settling lower in the water. How long would the contraption hold his weight? He knew it would be impossible to pull the debris all the way to the lifeboat: He would have to swim for it.

Martin was a strong swimmer, one of the best at Davidson College thanks to Harvey's training. When another student expressed admiration for his skills, following a competitive race, Martin shared a few stories about the family slave who could swim like an otter and rode horses like an Arab.

His stories were met with ridicule.

"Everybody knows niggers can't swim!" The young man from Wilmington, North Carolina had declared. "Their bones are too heavy, so they sink like stones. And my daddy would never let a nigger ride a horse. Makes 'em uppity and encourages the run-aways, he says. You must be one of those nigger-lovers, letting your chattel run wild, posing a danger to the rest of us white folks."

After that, Martin never talked about Harvey with the other students at his college.

The young man made good progress, at first, covering half the distance to the boat, but his muscles began to cramp. The pain was unbearable, forcing him to tread water with one arm and a leg while trying to massage a cramp out of the other leg. He swallowed a mouthful of seawater and retched before floating on his back, craning his neck to keep an eye on the lifeboat. He shouted for help, hoping someone might be alive, to no avail. He made one last attempt to swim, but the cramps were even worse than before, rendering both of his legs useless.

Just as Martin was about to give up hope, something brushed against his hand in the water. He panicked at first but calmed down immediately when he saw a dolphin floating casually alongside. He swore it was the same creature that had approached him on the raft. As a child, he heard stories about life-saving

101

dolphins, but never believed them. He was a believer, now.

In a smooth and effortless manner, the dolphin moved closer to Martin, using its body to support some of his weight. It made no effort to dive, so Martin rolled over and gripped the animal's dorsal fin. He was amazed by the feel of its skin and the power throbbing through his hands. The dolphin swam toward the lifeboat, maintaining a slow but steady pace. Several members of its tribe drifted by, inspecting the proceedings. One youngster was especially curious and nuzzled closer to the larger animal.

"My savior must be its mother!" Martin imagined, as he considered the possibilities: "Am I dreaming? Am I already dead?"

He had little time to ponder these essential questions as he soon found himself alongside the boat. Weak as a baby, he tried to haul himself over the side, but the boat rocked and tipped him back into the sea. Recovering his wits, Martin worked his way around to the stern, which offered more stability. With a final effort, he pulled himself up and and over, flopping into the bilge like an exhausted game fish. He summoned enough energy to look over the side, catching a final glimpse of the dolphins as they moved in gentle concert toward the west. He collapsed with a sigh, falling into a deep, dreamless slumber.

Martin awoke in the dark with an aching head and a parched throat. He rolled over and found himself gazing up into a clear, moonless sky. He recognized many of the constellations and began reciting their names: Ursa Major, the Great Bear; Cassiopeia, the Queen, and Andromeda, her daughter. The spectacle was awe-inspiring, moving Martin deeply, followed by an existential sense of dread.

"Were my prayers answered, or was it merely a coincidence? What will God expect from me, now? Why was the lifeboat empty? When so many died, why was I saved? Am I saved?"

The young man sat up abruptly. None of it mattered if he didn't survive. He needed to stop worrying about the future and focus on the present. First and foremost, he needed water. He had never gone without, but knew he wouldn't last long. During a quick inspection of the boat, his fears were confirmed: There was no fresh water on the boat, only a few inches of salty brine in the bilge. He found a pair of oars, two lengths of rope tied to the bow and stern and a little girl's doll tucked beneath a thwart. That was it. No food, no water, no shelter, no tools.

"What if it rains?" Martin wondered. "That might give me some fresh water, but I don't have anything to store it in!"

He slumped over, looked at the oars and laughed bitterly: "What good will they do?" He scoffed. "I can't row my way across the Atlantic!"

Taking stock, Martin tried to remember the little he had learned about navigation. He found the North Star quickly, which allowed him to sort east from west. The wind was coming from the south and west. That would blow him further away from the coast of the Carolinas. There was some hope he might be discovered by another ship, but he didn't know how far he had been blown off the main seaway running along the coast. He might be half way across the Atlantic, for all he knew.

Martin felt dizzy and disoriented. He decided to lay back and enjoy the night sky, while pondering his fate. It would be best to keep a lookout during the day, in hopes of spotting a passing ship. He would tie his shirt to an oar and use it as a signal flag—Yes, that's it! Comforted by the feeling that he had regained some control over his life, Martin relaxed. The boat rocked slowly and he soon fell asleep.

Martin's eyes were pried open by the sharp blades of a morning sun. His woolen clothes were still damp but the wrinkles had disappeared from his fingers and toes. His stomach cramped and he felt an urgent need to urinate. Steadying himself with one hand while opening his trousers with the other, Martin pissed over the side of the boat. He was shocked by the dark color of his urine and the painfulness of a stream that burned like liquid fire. The young man was no physician, but he knew he would die if he didn't find water. Gathering his resolve, he decided to keep a look out all day.

After a few hours, the glare from the sun was too much to bear, so Martin removed his jumper and used his shirt to fashion a makeshift turban, with slits for his eyes. At first the sun felt warm on his pale skin, but it didn't take long for the first signs of sunburn to appear, so he put his jumper back on. His sunburned skin crawled from the itchy wool, so he took it back off again.

After maintaining a long, lonely vigil, Martin sought refuge in the limited shade beneath the benches. The salt water in the bilge stung the skin on his back, but his eyes recovered from the glare. He decided to bale out the bilge, in case it rained, so the fresh water wouldn't be ruined immediately. He used his trousers as a makeshift bucket, tying the legs together and scooping water into the waist.

With time and patience, Martin began to see the results of his efforts. He enjoyed the sound of the bilge water slapping against the sea and he convinced himself it would rain before he died from thirst. His task was interrupted by an alarm in a primitive part of his brain, which processed sensory input faster than he could think. He stopped bailing, froze and looked around.

"What was that?" He wondered aloud, as he scanned the horizon, shielding his eyes with one hand. He began his search in the north, as the late afternoon sun was off to the west. He turned slowly in a clockwise direction, finding nothing in the east or south. He had to squint hard when his gaze turned back to the west, but he couldn't see anything in the glare. Instinctively, he cupped both hands to his ears and listened carefully. Nothing. Just as he was about to give up the search and resume bailing, Martin heard a faint shout. Donning his makeshift turban and squinting as hard as he could, he was able to make out a clump of debris floating in the distance. Was that an arm rising out of the water, waving in his direction, or just his imagination? He had to find out immediately.

Martin was weak, but determined to move the boat. He set the oars into a pair of locks and sat down on a thwart near the stern, which caused the bow to rise and didn't allow much progress. Recognizing the problem, Martin moved to a thwart further forward. He seemed to make better progress, hearing nothing but a steady clump and a splash as he focused on the task at hand. After two ocean swells passed under him, he shipped the oars and checked his position. Positioning himself in the bow of the boat, he shielded his eyes as best he could, still blinded by the sun as the glare moved lower on the horizon. Suddenly the shouts were much clearer, and he detected a sense of panic in the man's voice. Squinting harder and turning his head at an angle, Martin saw a man floating on a makeshift raft, with a cluster of barrels riding low in the water and dark shapes moving off to one side.

After rowing for another 15 minutes or so, Martin stopped again so he could hear the shouts more clearly. "Sharks!" The voice cried. "Sharks!" Leaning out from the bow, Martin looked into the glare and confirmed a castaway's worst fear: The wolves of the ocean, circling and waiting to rip the man to shreds. Tearing his eyes off the dark shadows in the water, Martin received another shock: The man on the raft was Harvey, and his only weapon was a piece of lumber.

Martin rushed back to his rowing position, cracking his shins on a thwart in the process, and pulled as hard as he could. One of the sharks shied away as he moved closer. The second shark became more aggressive, jostling one of the barrels in an effort to reach its prey. Martin continued to pull until every muscle in his body ached. When he felt he could row no longer, the bow of the boat collided with Harvey's contraption. Reaching over the side, Martin offered Harvey both of his hands, which the bigger man seized immediately. This motion caused the raft to separate from the boat, leaving Harvey scrambling with both legs hanging over the side of the boat. Harvey struggled to pull himself aboard, with Martin's help. The shark struck at that moment, seizing Harvey by the calf of his left leg.

Scared witless, Martin still managed to act when a voice burst inside his head. "Use an oar!"

Martin spun around, pulled one of the oars out of its lock and used it as a club, striking the shark repeatedly: Once, twice and a third time on the eye. The shark released its grip and Harvey fell into the boat, screaming with frustration. Martin inspected the crescent shaped wound, which oozed blood but did not spurt, and concluded no arteries had been damaged. He ripped an arm off his shirt and used that to fashion a bandage, which he wrapped around the wound.

"Quick!" Harvey shouted, between clinched teeth. "Get the barrel of water. It's tied to a line on the other side of the raft!"

In a panic, Martin realized he had dropped an oar over the side. The wind was light but still strong enough to push the boat, the oar and the raft further apart. Without pausing to think, Martin jumped over the side, swam to the oar, and struck out quickly toward the rear of the boat. He tossed the oar inside and ignored a curse as the handle struck a glancing blow on the side of Harvey's head. Using his legs to propel himself, Martin slipped back into the boat, just as the shark made another pass.

After regaining his breath, Martin rolled over and moved back to his rowing position, pulling slowly toward the raft and the life-saving barrel of water. It was surprisingly heavy, impossible to heave over the side, until Harvey gave him a hand, grimacing with pain. The barrel bounced off a bench before dropping into the bottom of the boat, rocking back and forth as its contents settled.

Harvey sat on the floorboards, with his long arms stretched out on bench. His eyes hid behind puffy slits and a trickle of blood ran down his ankle. The pale palms of his hands and the matching soles of his feet were withered and wrinkled. With his body half immersed in sea water since the ship went down, Harvey had suffered badly from exposure, but he hadn't lost his sense of humor:

"Don't suppose I've ever been happier to see you!" Harvey exclaimed, between clinched teeth.

Martin didn't respond immediately, because he was thinking the same thing.

"I'd be dead if you hadn't taught me how to swim." Martin responded with a shrug, "Besides, you saved my worthless self more than a few times over the years. Remember that she-wolf up in the mountains? She would have eaten me alive if you hadn't come along....and how 'about the time I climbed that live oak in Charleston and almost broke my neck? And then there's Lucy...."

Harvey answered with a deep chuckle that dissolved into a groan. Despite the distraction, he was struck by a change in Martin, which sparked his curiosity.

"That's right, Suh, you still owe me for Lucy, and don't you forget it!" The black man tried to relax as he rested the back of his head on the bench and closed his eyes.

"Now you listen to me, Harvey. Stop calling me Sir, when there's no other white folks around!" The latter comment elicited a chuckle and a groan from the former slave. "It's time you called me by my given name!" Martin exclaimed, as he adopted the tone of voice used by his father when posturing, not knowing the man was Harvey's father, too.

"All right, Martin. But don't you start calling me John, at least when there's other niggers around!" Harvey responded, adopting the same overbearing tone. "That would be too familiar!"

The tone men shook with laughter for a time, until both of their eyes settling on the injured leg.

"Sure wish I knew what to do about that bite, Harvey. Do you think we should use some of the water to wash the wound?" Martin learned over to take a closer look.

"Hell no!" Harvey responded as he sat up and stared down at his leg. "The bite might fester, that's for sure, but that water could make it worse. Do you remember Mammy Bester, down on your daddy's plantation? She's a healer, none better, and says there are only two ways to clean a wound: Fresh sea water, or fresh piss. We got plenty of one, if little of the other!"

"Fresh piss, that's disgusting!" Martin responded skeptically. "My last piss was the color of sulfur and burned like Greek fire!"

"I wouldn't have believed it, either, if I hadn't seen it for myself." Harvey admitted. "When old Mister Walsh, the overseer, whipped Big Pete for stealing some food, Mammy Bester had several of us men drink a pint of her special brew before we pissed on his back. I've never seen lash marks heal faster than the ones on Pete's back. Mammy said the body heals itself from the inside out, so fresh piss aimed by a healthy man was the next best thing to sea water, when it comes to healing a wound." Harvey squinted over at Martin to emphasize the truth of his story.

"Well, it's a good thing we've got plenty of sea water!" Martin responded, while sweeping his right hand around in an arc. "Because I'm not pissing on your leg! Besides, I haven't had any of Mammy Bester's brew, or anything else, since the ship sank!"

110

Harvey glanced over at the barrel of water, resting in the bottom of the boat, then back at Martin, without saying a word. Not wanting to put his needs before those of an injured man, Martin decided to take a closer look at Harvey's leg. He carefully unwound the bloody bandage and winched when he saw the oozing wounds. He counted six deep punctures, three on either side of the calf, and several shallower cuts.

"Here!" Martin instructed. "Prop your leg up on the gunnel, so I can wash it thoroughly, while keeping the blood out of the boat."

Harvey hoisted himself up onto the bench and lay back, allowing his injured left leg to extend over the opposite side. Martin dipped his jumper into the sea, held it over Harvey's leg and and twisted the wool fabric, repeating the process several times as he allowed fresh sea water to wash over the wounds.

"Stay right there!" He ordered, as he recovered the dirty bandage and rinsed it carefully, before shifting Harvey's leg back in the boat and retying the bandage.

"That should do it!" Martin exclaimed, while admiring his work. "I doubt Mammy Bester could 'a done any better! Suppose you should keep that leg up higher than your backside, so the blood won't pump out any quicker—although a slow, painful death is what you deserve!" Martin fell into the sharp-witted, insulting banter the two had shared in private during their adventures over the summer.

"Just in case we run out of sea water," Harvey quipped, "I suppose we better give you

111

something fit to drink, so you'll be able to piss when I need it. Here, set that barrel down next to me."

Martin complied by rolling the barrel under a bench until he could stand it up next to Harvey, with the bottom of the barrel resting on the floorboards.

"Go ahead, sit yourself down!" Harvey demanded, still hoping to conceal his hoard of gold. "I couldn't open the barrel on that flimsy raft—afraid I might ruin the water."

Reaching deep into a carefully buttoned pocket on his trousers, he retrieved a small gentleman's pocketknife, with ivory handles and two blades made of Damascus steel. He had taken the knife off a Creole gambler in New Orleans, who resented his losses and staged an ambush in a dark alley. Before Harvey was done, the man lost several teeth, and his will to fight.

Wrapping his right arm around the barrel, Harvey used his left hand to pry open the lid. Looking down, he saw a pint-sized tin cup and the gold ingot, resting safely in the bottom of the barrel. As he reached down to retrieve the cup, he glanced over at Martin with a possessive look on his face, which the younger man interpreted as concern for the limitations of their water supply. With a deliberate smile, Harvey filled the cup and passed it over to Martin, who drank the pint with relish. The water had a mild odor and tasted woody, but that didn't spoil his enjoyment.

"That was finer than the best beer in Charleston!" He exclaimed, while passing the cup

112

back to Harvey. "I suppose we better make it last!"

"That's all we're likely to see for some time." Harvey agreed. "The sailors told me it's often dry after a cyclone, so we're probably not gonna see any rain."

He filled his own cup to the brim and savored it slowly. His stomach responded with a gurgle and a groan. After dropping the cup back into the barrel, he re-secured the lid, tapping the edges with the palm of his hand until it popped back into place.

The two men sat silently as the sun set, somewhere over the Carolinas. Along the western horizon, the clouds glowed red, like crimson curtains in a marble hall, with paler shades of pink and red illuminating a ceiling of alabaster and bone. The boat rocked gently on rising swells as the wind drove them further to the east, toward the distant shores of North Africa.

CHAPTER 8:
THE PACKET TRADE

The schooner Birkenhead was a British packet-ship carrying mail, cargo and passengers on a regularly scheduled run from Barbados to Liverpool, with a stop in Bermuda. Once Britain's richest colony in the West Indies, Barbados produced most of the sugar consumed in Great Britain, sustaining the gentile lifestyles of the great island planters and yielding generous profits for British commerce.

Profits had fallen after the British Empire abolished slavery in 1837, but the freedmen of Barbados still worked the plantations. They had no other choice. The planters received financial compensation for every slave they lost, but the freed men and women were forced to work the fields for miserly wages, if they wanted to keep their ramshackle huts and vegetable plots. During the first six

115

years of "freedom," they were forced to serve as un-paid apprentices, to soften the blow for British men of property.

By 1857, much had changed in Bridgetown, Barbados—and much remained the same. The city was still one of the most important ports in the Empire, the center of British commerce in the West Indies. The same wealthy families controlled the island, and their prosperity still depended on the sugar trade.

One of the real changes was represented by Samuel Prescond, the first black member of the Barbadian House of Assembly. On that day in 1857, he stood in the bow of the schooner, looking out to sea as he considered the work that lay ahead. He had accepted an invitation from the British and Foreign Anti-Slavery Society, which was working to outlaw slavery everywhere, to extend the emancipation established by the British Empire. Prescond was accompanied by the Reverend Robert Nichols, a Quaker from Liverpool, as they discussed the many obstacles in their path.

"We have very little influence in Liverpool or Manchester." Reverend Nichols admitted. "The prosperity of both cities depends on the cotton trade. Every man takes a share of the profits, from the bankers to the factors, the warehousers to the carters, the shippers, spinners, weavers and exporters. All MP's in the region are bitterly opposed to the goals of our Society."

Prescond listened carefully and nodded his head thoughtfully before responding.

"There must be some leverage," he suggested, "if we are clever enough to find it. For example, the planters of Barbados supported the ban on the slave trade in 1807, because they wanted to prevent the other islands of the West Indies from establishing sugar plantations. The ban on the slave trade created an artificial shortage of labor, advancing their agenda. I suggest we identify those members of Parliament who wish to frustrate the interests of their rivals and competitors in Liverpool and Manchester. The bankers of London and Bristol, for example, or those who contemplate the development of cotton plantations elsewhere. I've understand new plantations are being established in Egypt and India. Surely we can find allies who are motivated by self-interest, if not their religious convictions?"

Not for the first or the last time, Rev. Nichols was impressed by Prescond's insight. He was just the sort of man his Society needed to find the political allies they required. The Barbadian was impressive in his person, well-spoken; clearly a man to be reckoned with, despite the color of his skin.

"You grasp our situation precisely," the Reverend responded. "As you know, we Quakers are dissenters, ineligible to vote. Only Anglican men of property enjoy that privilege. Of course, the only votes that truly count are wielded by great men of commerce. That's why our trip only begins in Liverpool: We'll be moving on to London at the first opportunity."

117

Leaning against the ship's railing, Samuel Prescond thought of his wife and children, waiting back home in Bridgetown. He wouldn't see then again until spring. Gathering his resolve, he tried to ignore the pangs of loneliness. After staring grimly at his shoes for a moment, Prescond blinked and lifted his eyes to the horizon. His gaze was distracted by a flash, an odd reflection off to the north.

"What might that be?" The Barbadian asked Reverend Nichols, who responded by squinting helplessly through his spectacles.

"I can't see a thing," the Reverend responded, "but that's not unusual!"

"O'Byrne—come take a look, what can you see?" The Reverend addressed a young sailor from Liverpool with whom he had established a cordial relationship during the voyage from Bridgetown. O'Byrne was tall and thin as a willow, with sandy blond hair and sharp green eyes.

The sailor dropped the line he was coiling and moved over to the rail, shielding his eyes with one hand. "Aye, Reverend, there's a small boat sitting on the horizon!"

In a flash, O'Byrne climbed the ratlines to gain a better view, a motion that was not lost on Captain Johnston. He moved forward to investigate.

"What is it, Timothy?" He shouted in a thundering voice that could rise above any storm.

"A lifeboat, Captain, with two men aboard."

"Now that was unexpected," thought the captain. "A boat cast adrift, along the packet route to Bermuda. Their ship must have been lost in the cyclone, poor devils."

"Helmsman!" He shouted over his shoulder, "Bring her about, five points to larboard!"

"Albert!" The Captain shouted to his first mate, "Rally the rest of the crew, prepare to drop sail!"

A gentle breeze woke Martin from his fatigue-induced torpor. He rubbed his eyes and glanced over at Harvey, whose mind was addled by fever. Martin had done his best to clean the wound with salt water, but the deepest puncture was inflamed. After several days in the boat, with nothing to eat and little to drink, both men had found it difficult to maintain a consistent watch on the horizon. A brief rain shower had darkened the sky earlier that morning, teasing the dehydrated men from a distance, but none of the precious moisture had fallen into their boat.

It was time for a drink. Until that morning, Harvey had doled out their rations, but his condition had worsened overnight. Not wishing to disturb his companion, Martin moved quietly from bench to thwart, reaching for the water barrel. He removed the lid carefully, squinting as the sun reflected off the water. Reaching down, Martin used his left hand to lift Harvey's head, while raising a cup to the older man's lips. Harvey groaned incoherently, but his lips recognized the cup and accepted the drink.

He closed his eyes immediately, mumbling quietly as he shifted to one side.

Martin turned to place the cup back in the barrel, pausing for a moment to examine their dwindling supply. He was confused at first, as the surface of the water seemed to glow. Shielding his eyes from the sun, Martin looked again and was greeted by a golden reflection floating in the bottom of the barrel. Addled by hunger and exposure, Martin sat dumbly as the feeble connections between brain and body were restored. Finally, a voice commanded him to reach into the water. He responded slowly, reluctant to spoil the last of their precious water. When his fingers reached the bottom, he felt something smooth, hard and heavy—that didn't belong. His curiosity ignited, Martin reached into the barrel with both hands and emerged with a breathtakingly beautiful ingot of gold. Instinctively, he held the ingot over his head, allowing a few droplets of water to fall in his mouth.

Martin lowered the ingot down to his lap and sat in stunned silence. His mind was impaired, but the implications were clear enough.

"Harvey, wake up!" Martin demanded as his hands began to shake, whether from nervousness or exhaustion he knew not. Impulsively, he slammed the ingot down on the nearest bench, cracking the wood. Harvey didn't respond, even when Martin kicked his foot.

At that precise moment, Martin's attention was diverted by the sound of a ship's bell, carried across the waves by the wind. When he turned, he saw a ship bearing down, less than half a mile away. Instantly, Martin recalled the feelings of fear and panic he experienced when his father caught him playing with a chest of gold coins at their house in Charleston, when he was only six years old. Hiding behind a door, he had watched his father counting the gold, and made note of its hiding place. The subsequent beating was ferocious, never to be forgotten.

The rush of emotion cleared the fog and Martin grasped the situation immediately. The gold was stolen, undoubtedly by Harvey. That would explain why he was so protective when they first retrieved the little barrel of water. If they were caught with the gold, Harvey would be hung—and he might be accused, himself. There was nothing else to do: Martin lifted the ingot with both hands and dropped it over the side, using his body to screen his movements from the approaching ship. When the deed was done, he turned and climbed into the bow of the boat, waving enthusiastically.

The schooner's crew was well-practiced. In a smooth, easy ballet they lowered the ship's sails and brought her alongside the small boat. A heavy net was draped over the side, enabling two members of the crew to scramble into the boat, where they quickly secured a pair of lines to bow and stern. The sea was relatively calm, so Martin was able to climb up the net, with assistance from Nichols. The sailor could easily get by with one arm for himself and a second for the castaway. Three sailors rigged a sling for

Harvey. They hauled the wounded man aboard carefully, with respect to his condition.

Martin's head spun precariously when he attempted to stand upright. He slumped into a hump, not exactly falling but landing with a bit of a bump. He shielded his sun-burned eyes with both hands and tried to focus his attention on the somber but sympathetic faces surrounding him.

Reverend Nichols spoke first.

"Young man, tell us your name," he asked with a kindly voice.

"Martin, Martin McCrary—from South Carolina..." Martin swallowed hard and croaked, unable to recognize the sound of his own voice.

"I know this man, or at least his family!" A stout gentleman from Charleston spoke up. "His father is Hank McCrary, one of the richest men in South Carolina. My firm does business with his plantations. He has but one son and heir. No doubt he'll be grateful we found the boy!"

Theodore Sharpwell was a cotton factor, on his way to Liverpool to consult with the Exchange. He and Reverend Nichols despised one another, the one a man who profited from slavery, the other an unforgiving abolitionist. The Quaker stepped back, with a look of regret on his face.

His place was taken by Captain Johnston, who booked no quarrel with any of the wealthy families his livelihood depended on, be they British or American.

"Mr. McCrary, I see your boat bears the name of the *S.S. Central America*. Pray tell us, what happened to your ship?"

Martin tried to stand, but stumbled immediately.

"She sank in a great storm," Martin whispered.

A murmur moved through the passengers and crew as the news spread from lip to ear. The world seemed to spin when Martin looked up at the Captain's face.

"One last question, Mister McCrary, and we'll allow you to rest. Who is this black man and how did he come by his wound?"

"His name is John Harvey, my companion and servant. He saved my life, by taking the bite of a shark that wished to take me."

Martin didn't know why he lied. Harvey had saved his life, in the past, but he had returned the favor. And there was the issue of the stolen gold to consider. For reasons he couldn't explain, even to himself, Martin felt a bond with the freedman and wanted him to live.

"All right, young man. We're fortunate to have a pair of skilled physicians onboard. They'll treat the both of you." The Captain turned to issue a command:

"Albert, take some men and carry Mister McCrary down below. Have Nichols round up some fresh clothing. You'll find Dr. Snow in my cabin, send him up."

"Aye, Sir."

Albert Oates, the first mate, was the son and grandson of seamen; both men were lost when he was a boy. After many years at sea, he was still moved by the plight of castaways.

"All right, the rest of you, raise sail and get us back on course!" The Captain moved towards the helmsman's position, to supervise the proceedings. His presence was expected by not required, as the crew was well practiced. The ship was soon underway.

Dr. John Snow was a famous physician who had traced the source of an infamous outbreak of cholera to a public water pump in Soho, contaminated by an abandoned cesspool. He was also a pioneer in the use of surgical anesthetics and had administered chloroform to Queen Victoria when her last child was born in April of 1857. He had traveled to Barbados over the summer, to study cholera in tropical conditions, with the assistance of his assistant, Dr. Michael Satterwhite.

During their visit in Bridgetown, Dr. Snow became friendly with the Barbadian assemblyman, Samuel Prescond. For his part, Prescond was surprised to learn the famous physician was a self-made man, the son of a laborer working the coal yards of Northumbria. Building on their friendship, Prescond persuaded Snow to advocate better sanitation conditions for freed slaves, by making perfectly rational arguments that appealed to the financial interests of the planters themselves. Harvey was incredibly fortunate to be treated by such an accomplished physician.

No longer a young man, Dr. Snow was still vigorous and placed hands on every patient he met. He emerged from the Captain's cabin wearing a wool waistcoat, with his shirt sleeves rolled up, as he had been working on a manuscript and wished to avoid getting ink on his shirt. He knelt beside Harvey and carefully removed Martin's makeshift bandage.

"The infection hasn't spread, Michael. Boil some water and prepare some clean bandages—we'll lay him out under the skylight in the Captain's cabin."

"Captain!" Dr. Snow shouted, "With your permission, I would treat this man in your cabin down below, as the light is ideal for our purposes!"

"Yes, of course, Doctor." The captain responded, "I'll have the crew bring him down shortly, as soon as the sails are set."

"That won't be necessary," Prescond spoke up, "the Reverend and I will do it."

"Of course, of course." Reverend Nichols responded, as he helped Prescond and Dr. Satterwhite carry Harvey down a ladder behind the mizzen mast. Seaman O'Byrne steeped in when the Reverend stumbled a bit at the bottom of the stairs.

The injured man moaned as his body was laid out on the deck, temporarily. The physicians scrambled to remove paper and pen from a large table dominating the Captain's cabin. Harvey tried to examine his surroundings, as he was lifted up on the table, but his fever burned and he couldn't think clearly. The ceiling was low and heavily beamed; tall men like Dr. Satterwhite had to duck to avoid cracking their skulls.

Harvey squinted when his body was positioned under the skylight. He didn't notice Martin standing in the doorway, with a concerned look on his face.

"Why don't you tell us what happened, while we get to work?" Dr. Snow glanced up at Martin as he washed his hands thoroughly in a large basin.

Martin nodded and paused before speaking, wondering if he could avoid telling a more elaborate lie to support the first.

"It's simple, really. Harvey jumped into the water to rescue me and was bitten by a shark as he climbed back aboard the boat." Neither physician looked up as they carefully cleaned Harvey's wound with alcohol and boiled water, probing each puncture with small instruments.

"Can you remember how many days ago that might have been?" Dr. Snow asked kindly.

"No Sir, I cannot." Martin answered, truthfully, as he sank to the deck to take the weight off his feet. "At least three days, maybe more."

"Here, I found it!' Dr. Snow exclaimed, as he pulled a shark's tooth from the largest wound. Stepping back, he held the object up to the skylight, admiring the fine serrations on either edge.

"We'll save this souvenir for your friend— he may wish to have it, when he's recovered." The tooth clinked loudly as it dropped into a basin. Snow continued: "He's fortunate, as the infection is concentrated here, in the wound where the tooth lay hidden." The physician held the wound open and pointed with a probe, as if he were lecturing to a medical student. "We'll flush everything carefully, stitch up the worst of it and bind his leg with gauze. The bandages will need to be changed frequently. A fine specimen like him should heal quickly. I don't suppose he's the sickly sort?"

"No, not at all. In fact, I can't recall Harvey having ever been sick, and I've known him all my life. I'm far more susceptible to illness, myself," Martin offered honestly.

"Is this man a slave?" Reverend Nichols asked in a somber tone, as he helped Martin to his feet and moved him to a seat in a corner of the cabin.

"No. He was born a slave, but my father freed him three years ago."

Martin gratefully accepted a glass of water offered by the Quaker.

"Well, I'm pleased to hear that, as you have been rescued by a British ship, bound for a British port, and slavery is outlawed throughout the British Empire." The Reverend tried to take each man as he found them, but he didn't expect much from the son of a wealthy South Carolinian.

"Yes, of course." Martin nodded as he took another sip of water. "No doubt my father thought of that when he selected Harvey to accompany me on my first journey abroad. We were bound for Liverpool ourselves, by way of New York, had our ship made it that far."

During his journey to San Francisco and back, Martin had acquired some experience in

127

dealing with abolitionists. He wasn't the type to mount an open defense of the South's "peculiar institution" unless pressed. If it came to that, his father had educated him on the conditions of the working poor in the great cities of the North, and in England, where children labored in factories from dawn 'till dusk.

"We'll have the crew move your man to a space in the bow of the ship. The forepeak is well ventilated during fine weather, when the hatches are open. That should speed his recovery. Dr. Satterwhite will attend regularly. With any luck, he'll be back on his feet again before we reach port."

"I'm truly grateful, Dr. Snow."

Martin sank deeper into the chair, relieved for Harvey but exhausted by his own ordeal.

"All right then, Mister McCrary, you need to rest. When you wake, we'll put some food in you. Nothing heavy, mind, just enough to restore your strength."

Four sturdy sailors entered the cabin and lifted Harvey off the table, carrying him forward to a hold near the bow of the ship. The physicians helped Martin to his feet and guided him to a narrow bunk on one side of the Captain's cabin, closing the dark curtain behind them. Martin could hear the men talking in low voices as they put their equipment away and rearranged their writing materials on the table. They spoke of the importance of sanitation and the need to maintain a proper distance between sources of drinking water and the latrines that served the plantation workers and their families. Martin drifted into a deep, dreamless sleep as the ship swayed gently, driven by a fair breeze in a milky blue sky.

Harvey woke up in a hammock, some 18 hours later. His head was free of delirium, but the pain in his leg was persistent. He didn't know how long he had slept, and certainly didn't know his slumber had been facilitated by milk of the poppy, administered by a famous physician who had attended the Queen of England. Opening his eyes, Harvey was surprised to find a white man he didn't recognize, gently wrapping his leg with surgical gauze that had been boiled earlier that morning.

"My name is Michael," Dr. Satterwhite began. "I see you're feeling better, but the question remains, what should I call you?"

There was something striking in the young physician's expression, which was illuminated by a skylight and an open hatch. He seemed genuinely interested in his patient's condition, and his person, with no trace of the posturing the former slave had come to expect from white men.

"The name's Harvey," he responded softly. "Where am I?"

"You're on a British packet ship, bound for Liverpool. We'll be making a brief stop in Bermuda. That's British territory, of course. Free territory."

Harvey raised his torso a few inches, resting his weight on his elbows.

"Yes Suh, I know. Been there before."

"Your companion, Mr. McCrary, he says you're a free man. Is that a fact?"

Harvey nodded affirmatively, but didn't speak.

"If not, I should tell you the truth: You are a guest on a British ship, and we will soon reach a British port. You needn't go back to America, if you'd rather not."

"Well, it's true, I'm a free man." Martin finally responded, "But my mother and sister are slaves, working a plantation in South Carolina."

"I see." The British physician continued. "Then you aren't free at all, are you?"

Harvey smiled grimly, as he lay back in the hammock, with his hands behind his head.

"Some day I'll buy their freedom!" Harvey asserted, as the doctor finished his work, gently placing the wounded leg back in the hammock.

At that moment, the wheels in Harvey's mind engaged and he remembered the stolen gold.

"Oh my God!" He thought to himself. "If they find the ingot, I'm a dead man!" Since he was being treated with respect, he assumed they hadn't.

But what about the double eagles?

Lifting his blanket, Harvey realized he wasn't wearing his trousers. The gold coins were hidden in the secret pocket sewn into the waistband of his trousers. He tried to hoist himself out of the hammock, as he scanned the room with a panicked look on his face.

"Don't worry," Dr. Satterwhite spoke calmly, "your secret is safe with me. The trousers and their contents are hanging up to dry, over there in the corner. I would recognize the handiwork of the Scotsman's seamstress anywhere. In fact, I have a pair just like them."

Harvey's initial reaction was cautious, as he had never spoken to anyone about his patron, the man who had given his life a purpose. He wanted to trust this man, Michael, but how could he? As his life was already in the physician's hands, he decided to test him.

"If you wish to speak of the Scotsman," Harvey intoned, "tell me his name."

"Ah, you're a careful man, that's good, very good!' Dr. Satterwhite responded enthusiastically. "A mention of clan McDonald should suffice, don't you think?"

The physician paused long enough to examine Harvey's face as he spoke.

"Yes, more than enough." Harvey turned away, to give himself time to ponder his predicament. He was tempted to let down his guard, but too many questions raced through his mind.

In the end, he decided to take a risk:

"I expect to see him in Liverpool, but he may not welcome me, as the items I collected in Cuba were lost with the ship."

"I'm sure he will be pleased to see you alive," the doctor retorted, "as there is always more work to be done. When I see the Scotsman myself," he continued, "I will be sure to relay my esteem for your resourcefulness, in surviving the cyclone and saving the only son of your former master, whose activities and influence in

America are undoubtedly of greater interest than Cuba."

The last remark raised obvious questions in Harvey's mind.

"The truth is," Harvey admitted, "the young man saved me, not the other way around. I was lost on a raft, with the sharks circling, when he found me."

"So, it seems you enjoy his trust, and he is willing to lie to help you? That's interesting, as I understand he will inherit all of his father's property, and his connections, as his only son."

Dr. Satterwhite was surprised and offended by Harvey's reaction, a laugh that began deep in his belly, ending in a groan when the shaking disturbed his wound.

"Is there something I need to know?" The British spy asked between tight lips.

"Pardon me, Doc, couldn't help myself!"

Harvey locked eyes with Satterwhite as he shared another secret:

"I'm Hank McCrary's oldest son, his bastard son, and I'll inherit nothing!"

Having developed a deeper appreciation for his patient, the Englishman was curious:

"Does Martin know?"

"No, Sir, he does not! Mr. McCrary threatened to keep my mother and sister in bondage for all their days, if I disobey him and reveal the secret of our brotherhood."

Their conversation was interrupted by footsteps and voices. Moments later, Captain Johnston entered the forepeak, followed by Martin, eager to check on Harvey's progress.

132

Martin, looking clean and well fed, was wearing a set of clothes borrowed from the first mate, Albert Oates.

"Aha, it's good to see your man is feeling better!" The Captain began, speaking to Martin as if Harvey wasn't in the room. "Once you've had a chance to meet with the American Consul in Hamilton, I hope you'll join us on the rest of our voyage to Liverpool!"

"Thank you Captain, that's my intention!"

Looking pleased with himself, Martin stepped closer and spoke directly to Harvey:

"You look famished—Lord knows I was! Here, we've brought some food, Dr. Snow's orders!"

Martin removed a cloth to reveal a bowl of beef broth and a heel of bread. Harvey tucked in immediately, relishing the first hot meal he had enjoyed since the cyclone struck.

Dr. Satterwhite and the Captain left the two Americans alone. They laughed and joked for hours until, exhausted, they collapsed in a pair of hammocks, still weak but growing stronger. They were awakened in the morning upon their arrival in Hamilton, the capital of British Bermuda.

CHAPTER 9:
ISLAND INTRIGUE

In 1815, The British authorities moved the capital of Bermuda to Hamilton, as the harbor was larger and more easily defended. St. George's town, the former capitol, was the oldest continuously inhabited English-speaking settlement in the New World and still served as the center of commerce. By 1857, Hamilton boasted a Parliament building, the Government House, the Admiralty House, a British Army garrison and a few thousand residents enjoying a fine climate and a comfortable life.

After most of its famous cedars were harvested by the shipwrights, and the colony lost control of the lucrative salt trade to the Bahamas, Bermuda was primarily a military outpost, protecting British trade in the Atlantic. Most of that trade was focused on the American South, where the ports were peppered with immigrants from the colony. On both sides of the Atlantic, vast fortunes were being made off the backs of American slaves, as King Cotton fueled English textile mills and the profits were used to purchase goods from British merchants, craftsmen and manufacturers. Much of the trade was financed by British banks, extending the tentacles of self-interest deep into the upper levels of British society.

The Birkenhead was met by a pilot boat, as the entrance to Hamilton harbor was difficult to navigate without local expertise. Only one man aboard the Birkenhead recognized the true significance of their arrival, as the news of the lost gold had not yet reached the colony, or the capitols of Europe.

Theodore Sharpwell, the cotton factor from Charleston, grasped the implications immediately, as he was an experienced businessman with connections in Liverpool and London. The first men to receive the news would enjoy a tremendous advantage, before the shock hit the financial markets and the bankers were exposed to the loss. As a representative of Fraser, Trenholm and Company, Sharpwell knew he had an obligation to relay the news immediately. An ambitious man, he was also motivated by the knowledge that quick and decisive action could improve his position in the company.

Keen to exploit the situation, Sharpwell hitched a ride back to the harbor aboard the pilot boat, which docked well before the Birkenhead. Sharpwell hired a carriage at dockside and rushed to the company office, which was located behind Government House. Much to his surprise, he found Charles Prileau, the influential head of Fraser's Liverpool office, engaging in quiet conversation with their local representative, Stephen Phelps. Prileau didn't hide his irritation when Sharpwell burst into the room:

"Give us a moment, will you Theodore—Stephen and I have important business to discuss." Prileau was a senior partner and never hesitated to remind his inferiors.

"I regret I can't do that, Mr. Prileau, as my news will surely convince."

Sharpwell smiled respectfully and waited for an invitation to be seated.

"Well, all right then, please join us—it better be good!" Prileau warned.

The implied threat wasn't lost on Sharpwell, who gathered his thoughts, removed his hat and sat down next to Phelps, facing their superior.

"The news is tragic, but the opportunity is great. The steamship *Central America* was lost in the cyclone—you must have felt the effects of the storm here in Bermuda?"

Sharpwell waited for Prileau to nod affirmatively before continuing.

"Officially, she was carrying three tons of gold from California, and who knows how much additional gold was being carried by the passengers? When the news reaches New York and London, chaos will ensue. It's too late to stay ahead of the markets in America, as some survivors have undoubtedly reached port. We could be the first to act in Europe, if we move quickly."

Sharpwell paused again, waiting for the news to settle.

"Oh, there's one more thing," Sharpwell continued, "Hank McCrary's son was on the ship, he was rescued by the Birkenhead. I thought you'd like to know."

In an instant, the chain of logic worked its way through Prileau's mind. Fraser and Company held a large volume of stock in British, French and American banks, and many of those banks were overextended. With the loss of all that gold, a financial panic would ensue. Fraser and Company could limit their exposure if they were the first to act. The news about the McCrary boy could be useful, too.

"You've done well, Theodore, in bringing this to me. We'll relay the news immediately, by the fastest possible means."

"My thoughts exactly, Charles. I've already prepared several letters."

Sharpwell reached into his breast pocket and retrieved three envelopes addressed to Fraser and Trenholm representatives in Liverpool, London and Paris. Prileau's name was on one of the packets, which Sharpwell proudly presented.

Prileau calculated and made a decision.

"You've shown admirable initiative, Theodore, which I will bring to the attention of our partners at the first opportunity. Here's what we're going to do: I will carry the news to Liverpool, as I'm responsible for that office, by

138

taking your berth on the Birkenhead. You'll travel to London aboard our company ship, the Herald, and send word on to Paris. The Herald is in St. Georges, ready to sail. Stephen here will charter the fastest boat in Hamilton to run you over, with orders for the captain, but no mention of the lost gold. You will arrive in London first, as the Herald is a fast steamer and the Birkenhead won't leave for Liverpool until late tomorrow. That is your reward."

The three businessmen set to work immediately, making all reasonable preparations. Forty minutes later, Theodore Sharpwell was enjoying a cool drink on a fast cutter, basking in his good fortune and day-dreaming about his glorious arrival in London, where he would conceal the secret of the *Central America*'s loss until after his company had improved its position in the markets.

Sharpwell wouldn't have been quite so pleased if he had known the truth: George Trenholm, the senior partner and President of their company, was visiting Hamilton at that moment, and Prileau was already on his way to share the news, taking full credit for himself.

Henry Brown, the American Consul in Hamilton, was nervous. George Alfred Trenholm was the most distinguished guest he had hosted during his tenure in Hamilton. He was very familiar with Trenholm's business interests, as he was a beneficiary of his largesse. Brown was a North Carolinian, from Wilmington, and he owed his position to Trenholm's influence in Congress.

"Mr. Trenholm, you'll be pleased to know I have reached agreement with the British authorities, to decrease the harbor fees for your ships. Your local representative did much to facilitate the matter, by securing provisioning contracts with the Governor's associates. The authorities are also pleased with your proposal to build new hotels in Hamilton and St. Georges. Your donation to the parish fund was a nice touch, as the vicar was recently married to the Governor's niece."

Brown smiled broadly, while lowering his eyes in a respectful manner. The deference came naturally, as George Trenholm was an imposing figure, a handsome, impeccably dressed man of vigorous middle age with the bearing and manners of a European nobleman.

"You've done well, Henry." Trenholm conceded. "As well as could be expected. Should I assume the prospective builders of our new hotels are also close associates of the Governor?"

"Indeed they are, Mr. Trenholm, but I'll spare you the details."

Early in their relationship, Brown had observed Trenholm's disdain for local entanglements, as long as his interests were well served.

"Good, good." Trenholm continued. "How is the Governor, by the way? Are we expected at the reception this evening?"

"Yes, indeed, Sir. Colonel Murray is well disposed. I have learned he is a leading member of a faction which believes it would be in the best interests of the United Kingdom if the Southern states were to peacefully secede from the Union, at some point in the future. During our most private conversations, he mentioned your father, whom he described as a highly regarded Loyalist during the Revolutionary War. He is also aware of my family's connections in that regard."

"That's a valuable piece of intelligence, Mr. Brown, but we shan't speak of it again, until you hear otherwise from my local representative." Trenholm stared deliberately at Brown, to stress the seriousness of his command.

"You may rely on my discretion, Sir, but there is more you need to know...."

The sharing of confidences between one of the most powerful men in America and his loyal public servant was interrupted by a brisk knock on the door.

"Yes, come in!" Brown stood and faced the door, with the air of authority he adopted when dealing with subordinates at the Consulate.

"Sorry to interrupt you, Sir, but two men have arrived, demanding an immediate audience. The first is Mr. Trenholm's associate, Mr. Prileau. The second is a runner from the harbor, carrying news of a shipwreck and two American survivors rescued by the packet from Barbados."

The clerk was a young man from Wilmington, one of Brown's distant relations. The Consul glanced over at Trenholm, who responded with a nod.

"Please escort Mr. Prileau up to my office, where he can converse with Mr. Trenholm in comfort. Bring the runner's message when you return."

141

The two men waited quietly, listening to the footfalls as the clerk skipped down the stairs and returned a few minutes later, with a steadier rhythm on the uphill climb. The clerk opened the door, allowing Prileau to enter, and handed a sealed envelope to the Consul before departing.

"Sorry to interrupt, George, but the news is urgent." Prileau acknowledged Brown's presence as the Consul reached for his letter opener.

"Well, out with it, Charles." Trenholm knew Prileau wasn't a man to waste his time, so he assumed the news must be urgent.

"The *Central America* sank a few days ago, off the Carolina coast. Several tons of gold were lost. The financial implications are grave." Prileau knew better than to condescend to Trenholm, by offering a detailed explanation.

The distinguished gentleman stood up, his mind racing but his bearing undisturbed.

"Yes, we must act at once. I'm familiar with the ship's cargo—we have interests in California."

Trenholm turned and stared out the large window hanging behind the Consul's desk, raising one finger to his lips as he considered the news. The value of the cotton crop gave the South huge advantages in the increasingly bitter competition with the industrial and commercial North, which was vulnerable to financial upheavals. In recent months he had received intelligence that many Northern banks were starved for cash, hence the importance of the expected shipment of gold from California. A financial panic in the North would greatly enhance the political position of the cotton states, just as the debate over slavery was heating up. The consequences would highlight the superiority of Southern society. Perfect!

Interupting Trenholm's revere, Prileau seized his opportunity:

"I've already dispatched one of our representatives to St. Georges, with orders for the captain of the Herald to proceed immediately to London. That should give our associates time to act before the news reaches the rest of the market. With your consent, I will return immediately to Liverpool aboard the same British packet that brought the news, to pursue our interests there."

"Yes, yes, of course—you're a reliable man, Charles—I won't forget it." Trenholm was as generous with his most capable colleagues as he was unforgiving with the incompetent.

"There is no rush in relaying the news to America, as the wreck occurred near the coast of South Carolina and a number of passengers were rescued. They will have reached port several days ago." Consul Brown would prepare the usual messages for the State Department in Washington, but his primary concern at the moment was serving the interests of his powerful patron.

"There's more to this story, George," Prileau offered. "Hank McCrary's son was on the ship. He was rescued by the Birkenhead and is on his way to the Consulate."

143

"Why, that's remarkable!" Trenholm responded enthusiastically, as Hank McCrary was one of the wealthiest men in South Carolina, second only to himself, and a close associate on many levels.

"Brown, I shall provide whatever funds the young man requires, to speed his recovery. Charles, do you remember the boy's name?" Trenholm turned to face Prileau.

"Yes, of course, his name is Martin, after his maternal grandfather. McCrary has but one son, so he'll be grateful for any assistance you can provide." Speaking for himself, Prileau was more than pleased to ingratiate himself with another powerful South Carolinian.

"I'll put McCrary up in the Consulate, in the guest room across from yours, if you have no objection." Solicitous as ever, Brown practically groveled as he spoke.

"Good. That will do nicely, an excellent opportunity to take the young man's measure." Trenholm glanced at Brown, wondering if the letter contained any other useful information.

Brown noticed his interest and summarized the contents:

"Captain Johnston informs us that McCrary is well and would be welcome to continue his journey to Liverpool as a passenger on his vessel. He notes the young man lost all of his possessions and will need re-provisioning. There is a passing reference to his servant, a freed nigger who survived the wreck. He was bitten by a shark while rescuing his master."

"Fascinating. Perhaps we can find suitable clothes for McCrary, so he can join us at the reception this evening? I imagine the Governor would like to hear his story, first hand."

Trenholm turned to face Prileau and continued:

"Charles, I would be grateful if you could arrange for Phelps and the other men at our local office to look after McCrary's re-provisioning. I have other business to attend to and must be on my way as soon as I've had a chance to greet McCrary's heir."

Before Prileau could respond, their conversation was interrupted by a firm rap at the door.

"Sir!" The clerk began, his head inserted through the doorway. "A carriage has arrived!"

All three men followed the clerk down the broad staircase to the front lobby. The double door was open, embracing a fresh breeze and offering a clear view of an open carriage pulled by a pair of sturdy horses. A young man in oversized clothes stepping gingerly to the pavement. A vigorous-looking black man sat next to the driver, and a tall white man with observant eyes sat behind them.

The Consul was the first to great Martin.

"Welcome, Mr. McCrary, we just received the news. I'm Henry Brown, the American Consul here in Hamilton. You'll be my guest until you're ready to continue your journey."

Martin accepted Brown's hand with a smile and looked over his shoulder to find a man he recognized immediately.

"Mr. Trenholm!" Martin exclaimed, "It's good to see you again, Sir! It's been a few years, but you were often a guest at my father's townhouse in Charleston, before I went off to college!"

"Of course, of course!" Trenholm responded graciously. I remember you playing with my boys in the garden at Ashley Hall, but you were only a lad at the time. We're all very glad you survived the storm. I'm staying across the hall from you here at the Consulate and we shall have an opportunity to get acquainted before we continue on our way. I've asked my local representatives to see to your provisioning and hope you will join me at the Governor's reception this evening."

George Trenholm was famous for his hospitality and treated the families of his most important business associates generously.

"I would be honored, Sir!" Martin didn't know what else to say. He was nervous about appearing before the Governor, so he offered no embellishment.

"All right then, young man. I'm off on other business, but I shall see you again this evening, for the ride up to the Governor's mansion." Trenholm whispered quickly into the consul's ear before taking Prileau by the arm and walking towards their waiting carriage.

"Mr. McCrary, what shall we do with your servant, before we show you to your room?"

Consul Brown spoke as if Harvey didn't exist, which had its advantages, as far as the ignored party was concerned.

"Harvey was treated by Dr. Snow, a physician from London. His associate, Dr. Satterwhite here, will see to his bandages."

Martin pointed to the tall Englishman as he stepped down from the carriage.

"My apologies, Dr. Satterwhite! I should have introduced you to Mr. Trenholm and his colleague."

Brown knew a properly trained physician would be in great demand during his stay in Hamilton. Trenholm himself had complained of a minor ailment during a previous conversation.

"My pleasure, Mr. Brown. Perhaps you would be kind enough to introduce us later?"

Satterwhite knew the Scotsman was intensely interested in the powerful Mr. Trenholm. He would need to take full advantage of the opportunity during their stay in Hamilton.

Martin interrupted, to steer the conversation back to Harvey:

"The good doctor says my man is healing quickly, but he needs to stay off his feet. Do you have a place he can rest?"

A nigger treated by a pair of British physicians? Brown had never heard of such a thing, but he was willing to oblige the son of a rich and powerful man like McCrary.

"In light of his service to you, we can make room for him above the carriage house around back. My servants will see to his needs."

147

Brown was never one to become familiar with black men, even the house niggers back home in Wilmington. He resented the fact that he was unable to bring any of his well-trained slaves to his diplomatic post in Bermuda, given the British prohibition.

The Consul's clerk and butler settled Martin in a comfortable room upstairs and made arrangements for him to visit the best men's provisioner in Hamilton. Harvey and Dr. Satterwhite were escorted around back to the carriage house. Harvey was offered help climbing the stairs up to the loft, but he refused. Once his patient was settled on a straw mattress below an open window, the doctor dismissed Brown's stable hand and attended Harvey's bandages.

"You won't believe our good fortune, Harvey, and I'm not talking about your trivial wound."

Dr. Satterwhite spoke in low tones as he unwrapped the bandage, pleased to see the inflammation had fully abated. He continued:

"During my last meeting with the Scotsman, he mentioned his interest in the American businessman, George Trenholm, who by chance or providence is staying in a room across the hall from Martin."

"You've got my attention, Doc, but why?" Harvey was keenly interested in doing something of value for the Scotsman, before he reached Liverpool.

"As I mentioned aboard the Birkenhead, McDonald has bigger fish to fry than the Spanish mackerel in Havana. There is a growing faction

148

in Britain that wishes to facilitate the demise of the United States, as your nation is seen by some as a threat to British hegemony. These men are primarily members of the aristocracy, supported by a handful of senior officers, some of whom still resent your Revolution, among them Governor Murray. Their allies in commerce wish the Southern states to secede from the Union, to preserve the cotton trade. Mr. Trenholm is a key player in that game."

Harvey seized on the issues that mattered most to him: Some powerful Englishmen wished to perpetuate slavery in America because it profited them. If the Southern states seceded from the Union, his mother, sister and all the blacks in South Carolina might remain slaves forever.

"What can I do?"

Harvey looked down at his leg as the doctor finished wrapping his wound.

"No doubt Dr. Snow and I will be invited to attend the Governor's reception this evening, as the doctor is well connected with the Royal Family. That should give me a chance to gain some insights, but you have the greater opportunity: Everyone of importance will be away from the Consulate this evening. Mr. Trenholm has just returned from England, and we must assume documents related to his affairs are present in his room. If you can, you must find those documents and prepare a list of his associates in England, which we can pass to McDonald when we arrive in Liverpool."

Dr. Satterwhite knew he was putting Harvey at risk, but the potential reward was great.

"I can manage that." Harvey responded, without hesitation. "When Martin returns from the provisioner, I'll show up in his room, to organize his belongings and help him dress for the reception. When the gentlemen leave, I'll make my way into Trenholm's room."

"You're a good man, Harvey."

Dr. Satterwhite opened a leather case, to replace his medical supplies, and retrieved a small wooden pencil, square in shape, and a stiff sheet of paper.

"It's important that we identify as many of Mr. Trenholm's British contacts as possible, so the Scotsman will know where to focus his investigation on the other end. As you know, McDonald is a leader of the opposing faction in Britain, which wishes to end slavery everywhere and sees America as a valuable ally against the aspirations of other European powers."

"I understand, Doc—consider it done!"

Satterwhite shook hands with Harvey and bid adieu. He scrambled back down the stairs, as the coachman was still waiting out front.

As he lay quietly in the loft, Harvey's heart filled with resolve. He was grateful for the sense of purpose his life had gained after he agreed to spy for Sir Ian McDonald. He closed his eyes and considered the implications of everything he had learned. He mind drifted off into a chaotic dream filled with images from his boyhood, growing up on one of his father's plantation, where his mother was hidden away by her white lover. He remembered the moment he first understood her relationship with Hank McCrary, which he discovered when he was only five years old. His face still stung from the white man's slap. After that, he never opened the door to his mother's cabin without knocking.

Two hours later, the stable boy clopped up the stairs to inform Harvey that his "master" had returned. An undersized lad of mixed race, he shifted from foot to foot before speaking:

"Mr. McCrary is back from town, but Mr. Brown won't like it if you go inside the big house!" The boy declared, while trying to determine if Harvey was friend or foe.

"Don't you worry 'bout a thing, Isaac!" Harvey retorted with a confident smile. "Mr. Brown won't expect a man like McCrary to organize his own belongings, much less dress himself!"

"He'll beat me if I show you the way!"

He wasn't exaggerating. Harvey turned toward the boy, with his hands on his hips.

"You're free like me, Isaac—why work for the man if he beats you?"

"Cause my Momma is his cook...and more, I guess."

Isaac's pride was stung by Harvey's question, and it showed in his response:

"Why are you working for that white boy, he's younger than you?"

"Well, I'm pleased to see you've got some spunk, Isaac!" Harvey responded with a laugh and a compliment. "We all got our reasons, don't

151

we? Now, if the Man beats you, there's always a way to get even, without getting caught. I could teach you, if you like?"

Harvey had used this approach to recruit any number of allies over the years.

Isaac liked the sound of that. "I was told to fetch you some food. I could take you down to the kitchen, in the basement. There's a service staircase running upstairs from there."

Harvey followed Isaac through the courtyard to a small brick staircase leading down to the kitchen, which was illuminated by several windows mounted just above ground level.

"Mamma, this is John Harvey, the man who got himself bit by a shark!"

Isaac's Mamma was a nice looking mulatto woman, about 28 years of age, short of stature, wearing a simple cotton dress. She had remarkable bronze-colored eyes, which liked what they saw.

"A shark, you say? That sounds more like good luck than bad, Mr. Harvey, seeing as how you're still walking! Isaac calls me Momma, but everybody else calls me Sue—that'll do for you, too!"

As a child at her mother's knee, Sue learned to love the sound of words and had been playing with them ever since. She had a remarkable memory and could tell colorful stories for hours.

"Pleased to meet you, Sue!" Harvey responded, truthfully. "I don't know about that shark, but I would feel lucky if you treated me to some of your fine cooking!"

Sue was easy to look at, so Harvey smiled broadly as he openly admired her.

"Run along now, Isaac, before Mr. Brown sees you!"

Sue did her best to protect her son, by keeping him out of sight, as the boy reminded Brown he wasn't the first man to take his liberties.

"I've got fresh cornbread in the oven and soup on the stove, but they won't be ready for a while. You're welcome to visit, in the meantime!"

Sue rarely met a man she could rely on; something about this man seemed trustworthy.

"I'd be lucky, indeed, if I could stay for a while, but I best get upstairs to Mister McCrary's room, to sort out his things. If I come back later, maybe you'll take mercy on my appetite!"

Sue was a bright woman and she knew what Harvey meant.

"Mmm, I'll be sure to keep something hot for you!"

Sue's eyes flashed brightly as she stirred her pots on a new iron stove. After sharing a smile and a laugh, Harvey opened the door leading to a narrow service staircase. He admired the craftsmanship reflected in the fine woodwork as he climbed up to the second floor, two levels above the kitchen. The staircase was illuminated and well-ventilated by a pair of small windows, so he had no trouble finding his way, despite the pain in his leg. He listened carefully before cracking the door and peaked before stepping into the hallway. He felt exposed, largely because he was poorly dressed, wearing a

153

sailor's hand-me-downs and a pair of worn out shoes in a finely decorated hall. Hearing some noises behind the door to his left, Harvey stepped softly before tapping lightly on the door.

"Yes, who is it?" Martin asked as he opened the door. "Oh, it's you Harvey—come in, come in!"

"I figured you could use a hand with your things!" Harvey suggested, as he scanned the young man's spacious accommodations, which included a sitting area in front of a window, a large bed and the usual wash basin, mirror and chamber pot.

"Speaking of which," Martin responded proudly, "I procured a new set of clothes for you, in deference to your vanity!"

"My vanity?" Harvey asked, in mock offense, touched by the young man's consideration. "You're the young dandy, parading around like a peacock!"

"If I'm a peacock, you're a damned rooster, Harvey, and a thieving rooster at that!"

Martin had avoiding raising the topic before, when the big black man was recovering from his wound, but the gold ingot troubled him deeply, so he decided to clear the air.

"Why, you know full well I'd never steal anything from you or your family!"

Harvey maintained a tone of mock offense, hoping to avoid a confrontation.

"Well, that's true enough, Harvey, but your gambling and reckless thieving has to stop! We could have been killed by those men back in Havana, and just imagine what the British authorities would have done if they'd found that gold!"

Martin looked directly in Harvey's eyes as he spoke, having grown up a bit after the shipwreck. It was hard to put his finger on it, but Martin felt he deserved more respect from Harvey, as a fellow man—not the degrading relationship of "master" and "servant." Theirs was no longer a relationship in which a young, incompetent man depended on the older, competent one; they needed each other. Somehow, if that fact could be acknowledged, Martin felt the empty posturing and petty resentments that shamed his conscience would fade away.

Harvey's response was heartfelt:

"If you found that gold, why didn't you turn me in and leave me for the hangman's noose? Why did you lie about shark, when it was you that saved me?"

"I'm not sure if I understand that, myself," Martin responded sincerely. "I suppose I was damn glad to see your black ass, all alone in the middle of the ocean like that. Besides, you've done more for me over the years, that's for sure. So I guess we're even, and you can stop treating me like that little boy you used to lead around the plantation like a puppy."

"All right," Harvey responded with a smile. "We're even, and then some. I am curious, though: What did you do with that gold?"

Martin rolled his eyes and walked across the room before answering.

"A man's got to keep his secrets, Harvey, so you'll just have to use your imagination!"

Harvey decided he could live with that. Might as well change the topic.

"Now what have we here?" Harvey asked, looking over at two suits of clothes arrayed on the bed.

"You won't believe our luck!" Martin replied. "The local provisioner had some of those newfangled suits made of cotton khaki. The tailor is a Hindu man from British India; he spent most of the last 20 years whipping up suits to fit their climate, which sounds a lot like South Carolina in summer, only it lasts all year. It seems the men here in Bermuda have taken a fancy to the style, and I've been assured my suit will do well enough for the event with the Governor this evening."

Glancing over at the pair of suits on the bed, Harvey couldn't help but notice the sizes were considerably different. One suit was finely made and featured narrow shoulders, accompanied by matching trousers and a colorful waistcoat; the second suit was much larger, if simply cut, with a sturdy pair of suspenders on the side. In a flash, Harvey understood: The second suit was meant for him.

Reaching over, Martin handed Harvey a few coins, breaking the silence.

"In the morning, have that boy Isaac hire you a carriage to run down to the provisioners. They're expecting you first thing in the morning. Run around back and they'll let you in. Bring the suit with you and they'll finish things up to your

156

liking. It may be a little large, until we fatten you up!"

"I don't know what to say," Harvey responded honestly.

"A simple thanks will do!" Martin continued. "They'll also fit you for a hat and a pair of ready-made shoes; that'll have to do until we can get you a new pair of boots in Liverpool. Everything has been paid in advance, so don't let that clever old man swindle you!"

"Well thanks, then!" Harvey teased, "I wouldn't want to shame you when we arrive in England!"

"Speaking of that," Martin interrupted. "The khaki won't do in Liverpool; the Hindu promised to stay up late tonight to finish my wool morning coat and trousers. I'll have to wait to procure a frock coat and all the usual trappings when we get to England. Be sure to pick that up in the morning, too!"

Harvey ruminated for a while before asking: "Are you sure you want to go on to Liverpool, right now? We could catch the next packet to Charleston and be home in a few days."

He couldn't have been more pleased with Martin's answer:

"The last thing I want to do is go home to my parents." Martin glanced over at Harvey and was rewarded with a grin. "Mother would dote over me and try to forbid me from traveling, and Father would watch in silence and wonder if I'm too weak to follow in his footsteps. They'd fight over my future, with Mother arguing for the seminary again, and that's not the path for me.

We've got business to attend, so it's off to England we go! I'll send them a short letter and be done with it."

With little else to say, Harvey spent the next hour organizing Martin's new trunk, with plenty of room for all the belongings needed by a young man of means. Among other things, Martin had picked up a new copy of the King James Bible, along with a frayed edition of a novel by Charles Dickens, Harvey's favorite. When Martin left to join Trenholm and Consul Brown in the foyer, Harvey took his leisure in a chair by the window, reading "The Adventures of Oliver Twist." He identified with the band of thieves, as he prepared to enter Trenholm's room, uninvited.

CHAPTER 10:
A GREAT MAN'S SECRET

Harvey was familiar with "Oliver Twist," having found the book in Hank McCrary's library when he was only 12 years old, but the pleasure was fresh as he thumbed the pages, scanning his favorite passages:

"Such is the influence which the condition of our own thoughts, exercises, even over the appearance of external objects. Men who look on nature, and their fellow-men, and cry that all is dark and gloomy, are in the right; but the somber colors are reflections from their own jaundiced eyes and hearts. The real hues are delicate, and need a clearer vision."

The words rang true, based on the lessons Harvey had learned from his mother. She was a slave woman who embraced the simple joys of life and never allowed herself to wallow in gloom or despair. As his mind turned to the task at

159

hand, he flipped the pages until he found the inspiration he needed: "... (He) listened to everything without seeming to, which showed he understood his business."

Harvey was a good listener, to be sure. Turning his senses outward, he noticed two things: First, the second floor had been silent, since the white men departed in their carriage; and second, the aroma drifting up the staircase from the kitchen was more than he could bear, for long.

First things first. Harvey set the book down on the table, stood up and walked quietly to the door. He pressed his ear against the cool mahogany and listened carefully before turning the knob slowly. The hinges were well oiled and the door opened silently. Steeping softly in his borrowed woolen socks, Harvey slipped across the hall to Trenholm's door. Much to his relief, he found the door unlocked. He hesitated briefly, before stepping into the room and shutting the door quietly behind him. The suite was larger than Martin's, with open windows facing north toward a line of distant thunderstorms glowing brightly above the treetops. It took a moment for Harvey's eyes to adjust to the light, as fine linen curtains and specks of dust drifted slowly on the breeze. He moved one foot toward the desk on the far side of the room, but froze when the old floor creaked in response. Stepping to one side, he found a path that followed the edge of a thick Persian carpet, which absorbed the sound of his footsteps.

When Harvey reached the desk, a door slam downstairs and his heart skipped a beat. Listening carefully for footsteps on the staircase, and hearing none, he began his search in earnest. The Scotsman had prepared him well: Harvey paused and made a mental note of the arrangement of Trenholm's papers before disturbing them, to avoid leaving any trace of his passing presence. He knew the most important documents wouldn't be left out in the open; more likely they would be secured in some fashion. Glancing at the papers on the desk, he could see most of the letters were commercial in nature, complicated business transactions documented by Trenholm's subordinates. Harvey stopped for a moment and tried to put himself in the great man's shoes: Where would he place his most important documents? The answer revealed itself when he conducted a more thorough search and found a finely-made leather folder, with a monogram and a pair of brass clasps, tucked away on the floor beneath the desk.

"That's a good place to start!" Harvey concluded as he pressed the buttons on both of the clasps. He found a collection of letters, all with similar texts. He read the first letter twice:

"Regarding the matter of mutual interest we discussed at my club in London, I wish to assure you my principle is favorably disposed in regards to your proposal. He wishes to offer his assurances that his friends in Parliament would seek to recognize a newly independent Republic formed by the Southern States, should you and your associates choose to proceed down that path. You may relay said assurances to your most trusted confidants, along with our expression of support for decisive action, which is surely the only way to avoid the imposition of Emancipation by the Northern states, which resent the superiority of Southern society. You are well aware of the financial ruin wrought on many of our finest families when misguided men destroyed the foundation of our wealth in the colonies, with their reckless Prohibitions. The cotton trade stands at the foundation of our mutual prosperity; we believe the formation of a deep partnership with you and your associates is the only path capable of preserving it."

The letter was signed by a certain George Betram. Harvey copied the names at the bottom of each letter, 22 names in all. None of the men appeared to be Members of Parliament, themselves, but all made reference to support from unnamed Members. Surely the information would be invaluable to the Scotsman? Harvey was tempted to take one of the letters, to prove the story they told, but he knew McDonald would disapprove:

"I am rarely interested in secrets the owner knows he has lost." The Scotsman had tutored him, during one of his training sessions in Liverpool. "The value of a secret is multiplied many times over when the owner believes it has been kept. If you come upon any intelligence which satisfies the tasks I have given you, do your best to conceal the knowledge. You have an excellent memory, Harvey, and read as well as any man I know. I trust you to bring me what I need, ever delicately."

Satisfied he had found exactly the kind of intelligence the Scotsman and Dr. Satterwhite required, Harvey double-checked the names on each letter, secured the paper and pencil in his pocket and placed every item exactly where he had found them. Hearing nothing when he approached the door, Harvey stepped out in the hall and closed the door gently, just as Sue emerged from the servant's staircase.

"There you are, Harvey! You never came down to the kitchen, so I brought something up!"

Sue was a bright woman and she understood discretion. Still carrying her tray, she stepped over to the confront Harvey in the middle of the hallway and whispered harshly:

"What do you think you're doing, sneaking into Mr. Trenholm's room? Brown would have you hanged for less! If anything is missing, they might blame me or my son—did you think about that?"

The words stung.

"Don't you worry, Miss Sue!" Harvey whispered in response, as he gently escorted her into Martin's room. "Go ahead and check my pockets—you won't find anything of value!"

Harvey took the tray from Sue's hands and set it on a side table before stepping closer and placing her hands on his pockets, before raising his arms above his shoulders.

"Go ahead, now—search me, I'm innocent!" Harvey grinned as he turned slowly.

163

Unable to resist Harvey's charm, Sue suppressed a laugh and conducted a thorough search. Reaching into a back pocket, she pulled out a folded sheet of paper and a pencil. She held it up to the light, ashamed to admit she was illiterate.

"What's this?" Sue asked, as she unfolded the sheet and held it up to a window.

"Nothing but a list of things Mr. McCrary needs me to pick up at the provisioners tomorrow morning, before our ship sails for Liverpool. I couldn't find anything to write with, so I borrowed a sheet of paper and a pencil from Mr. Trenholm's room."

Harvey had a gift for concocting credible cover stories at the drop of a hat.

"So you're an educated man, then?" Sue asked coyly. "Next time, you better ask if you need anything, otherwise Mr. Brown might catch you—and that wouldn't do!"

"Now, Sue, I can't believe you're worried about Mr. Brown catching me doing anything at all. Otherwise you wouldn't be alone in this room with me, would you?"

Harvey lowered his arms and placed his massive hands on Sue's slim shoulders. She wasn't a shy woman, and longed to feel the embrace of a real man, a man she chose for herself. Placing her hands on Harvey's hips, she slid her fingers down to his front pockets.

"I best search you again..." Sue suggested, as she found what she was looking for and smiled at Harvey's response. "What's this?" She asked, "A billy club or a black jack?" She asked with

164

mock concern and genuine interest, as she conducted a thorough investigation.

"You disarm me," Harvey whispered.

Sue stepped back and pulled the straps off her shoulders, allowing her dress to drop to the floor. Turning around, she allowed Harvey to unbutton her undergarment, while reaching behind to stroke the front of his trousers again. Both man and woman were famished: They sated each other's appetites as quietly as they could, with Sue leaning over a sofa as Harvey stood behind her, his hands roaming at will. When they were done, Harvey washed Sue gently and silently, using the towel and basin on a stand by the window, and helped her with her clothes. He knew a woman's heart would be touched by simple acts of kindness, when her man's desires had already been sated. A simple "thank you" was exchanged, as Sue smiled and waved goodbye at the door, stepping carefully as she moved down the servant's staircase to her refuge in the kitchen. She sang softly over her pots and pans, grateful to be alive, on that day.

Harvey shared Sue's sense of gratitude, as he donned his clothes and secured the list of names in the pocket of his waistband, next to his gold coins.

"No matter what happens," he thought to himself. "I have to get that list to McDonald!"

Harvey's reverie was interrupted by a growling sound, as his stomach demanded attention. Resting by the window, he relished Sue's simple meal, which tasted as fine as any banquet in New Orleans, washed down with a beaker of cold tea laced with rum.

As Harvey mopped up the last of his soup with a heel of fresh bread, Martin was enjoying a carriage ride up Cedar Avenue toward the Governor's residence on Langton Hill. It was a fine September evening and the shadows were lengthening rapidly as the sun dipped closer to the horizon. As the youngest of the four men in the carriage, he was content to remain silent, barely listening to the conversation dominated by George Trenholm. A refreshing breeze rose up from the harbor as the carriage moved towards the north shore. To his right, Martin admired the outlines of a new Anglican Cathedral, which was only half-completed after 14 years of labor. The structure was built in the Early English style, his personal favorite, and tall lancet windows of imported stone were rising under a latticework of timber.

When they reached the crest of Langton Hill, a fine view awaited them. The sky above was deep blue and clear, with the ocean spread out below. On the horizon, a wall of thunderstorms glowed brightly with the last hour of sunlight. Pillars of ebony rain supported vaults of pure white, as bolts of silent lightning revealed more subtle colors where the sea and the sky embraced.

The grounds of Government House, known locally as Mount Langton, encompassed 30 acres of gardens. The drive leading up to the house was lined with Bermuda cedars, planted by a former governor who lamented the loss of so many native trees to the shipwrights and ambitions of Empire. The trees had a magical quality, with their twisted trunks clothed in serrated bark, and dark evergreen boughs that seemed to match the coats worn by the Scottish riflemen guarding the gate.

Martin's apprehensions grew louder as they approached the main house, knowing he was a very young man among so many men of power; his fears lessoned when he realized none of the men could be as fearsome as his own father, or the storm he had survived.

Several riflemen stood at attention on either side of the main entrance to the grounds, wearing a uniform that looked strange to an American eye. The soldiers wore shorts of khaki cloth, matching pith helmets, stiff-looking brown leather shoes and knee high socks turned down at the top. The shorts looked odd, topped with formal-looking jackets of dark green. The men carried long rifled muskets, with brass handled bayonets strapped to their belts. The house they protected had a distinctive colonial appearance, with steep-pitched tin roofs covering massive verandas, offering unobstructed views of the ocean.

"Any success procuring one of those rifles?" Trenholm asked, as the carriage approach the house.

Not wishing to spoil the surprise he had orchestrated so carefully, Consul Brown replied coyly:

"I did mention your interest to the Governor, and he is a most gracious host."

An elaborately dressed doorman opened the carriage door, deftly kicking a fresh horse apple under the front wheels, to avoid embarrassing the Governor's guests. A young British officer approached, dressed in a white tropical uniform embellished with elaborate decorations.

"Welcome to Mount Langton, Mr. Trenholm, Consul Brown." The officer exclaimed. "Please allow me to escort you to the reception room."

Martin trailed behind the older men as they entered the house, which boasted high ceilings and rows of tall windows embracing a fresh breeze rising up from the sea. With no tropical sun to bake them in the evening, the Americans were reasonably comfortable in what passed for formal attire in the tropics. Small groups of men and women nodded politely as the Americans passed, some acknowledging Consul Brown by name. Off to the left, they entered a large reception room, with a line of guests waiting to greet the Governor. Almost immediately, an aide standing behind Colonel Murray whispered in his ear. The Governor looked across the room and politely disengaged, leavening his wife to handle the formalities. Accompanied by his aide, the Governor strode across the room, extending his hand to Consul Brown.

"This must be the esteemed gentleman from the great state of South Carolina!" The Colonel remarked warmly. "I've been looking forward to this meeting."

"Please allow me to introduce Mr. George Trenholm, of Charleston." The Consul replied rather formally, in a tone that seemed to acknowledge his own lesser status. The two great men shared a firm handshake as the Governor scanned the faces in Trenholm's party.

"Welcome, welcome to you and your colleagues, Mr. Trenholm. Please, follow me out to the veranda: I've set aside an area where we might engage in uninterrupted conversation. I'm eager to hear more about the fate of the *Central America*—a tragedy unknown to us until yesterday."

The Governor's aide led the group through a double door to a corner of the spacious veranda, which was populated by comfortable chairs and sofas surrounding low tables covered with local delicacies. Two servants stood to one side, ready to serve iced wine, punch and other refreshments.

"Please, gentlemen, make yourselves comfortable!" The governor's aide suggested.

As soon as the group settled and each man had a drink in hand, a tall British officer wearing a tropical white uniform approached. The man had a full head of dark hair, a square jaw and deep-set blue eyes that seemed to assess the Americans in a casual but predatory manner.

"Gentlemen, this is Lieutenant Walter Tisdale, Royal Navy. I've asked him to attend our informal gathering, so he can prepare a report for the Admiralty."

The Governor wasn't asking anyone's permission, but he didn't wish to offend of his guests, either. The lieutenant nodded politely to the Americans and stood a few steps behind the Governor's chair, an elaborately cushioned teak affair imported from India.

"Before we begin, I'd like to make a presentation." The Governor continued, as he nodded to an aide. With a clap of his hands, a servant wearing white shorts and a colorful tunic carried a long wooden box out to the veranda and placed it on a table in front of George Trenholm. The crate was crafted from polished wood, with brass fittings and leather handles.

"Mr. Trenholm, I understand you share my appreciation for fine armaments. Please accept this gift, as a token of my respect: A pair of rifle-muskets, made by the best British craftsmen at Enfield."

At a nod from the Governor, an aide opened the crate and invited Mr. Trenholm to admire his gift. The British were notoriously protective of their rifled muskets, which had given them such an advantage in warfare, dating back to the Napoleonic era. These Enfield's were the latest model, Pattern 1853. After much lobbying, The Governor had succeeded in re-equipping his garrison with the weapons. The gift was deliberate, given his desire to see the United States divided into its more natural and less dangerous components. His motivations were both personal and professional, as his mother was an American loyalist whose family had fled the Revolution and his father was gravely wounded when the Americans invaded

Canada in 1812. Murray was only 10 years old at the time and he had worshiped his father.

Trenholm smiled broadly as he admired the rifles. He was well informed, regarding the Governor's Loyalist sympathies and future intentions, and appreciated the gift and its symbolism. If the South seceded from the Union, as they both desired, Trenholm hoped to import tens of thousands of the rifles, to give Southern troops an advantage on the battlefield, if war was necessary. The fact that both he and the Governor stood to profit greatly from the transaction seemed perfectly natural to him.

"Governor Murray, please allow me to express my deepest appreciation for your generous gift, as a Southern gentleman who appreciates the superiority of British weaponry!"

His enthusiasm ignited, the Governor rose and reached inside the case to retrieve a powder cartridge and one of the new Minie balls used with the rifled muskets.

"As you can see, the balls are cone-shaped, with groves circling the base. Their accuracy is most impressive, better than the famous Baker rifles used by our light infantry when the British army defeated Napoleon. If you please, we can arrange a demonstration before your departure."

Martin shared the older men's' enthusiasm for fine guns and a boyish corner of his young heart couldn't resist interrupting the great men with an impudent question:

"Governor, is that the cartridge the sepoys of India rebelled against, earlier this year?"

Martin had heard about the Indian Rebellion during his trip to San Francisco over the summer. Following rumors of mass murder and rape perpetrated against their colonial masters, the rebellion was brutally crushed by the British, with overwhelming force. The story was repeated and embellished by Southern newspapers and politicians, who feared a similar rebellion by their African slaves.

The Governor glowered at first, both at the interruption and the reminder of what could easily have been a historic disaster for the British Empire. He repressed a frown by recalling the identity of the young American, and his connections with the gentry of South Carolina.

"That's true, young man." The Governor replied. "The sepoys, both Muhammadans and Hindus alike, feared the cartridges were greased with beef tallow or pork fat. Their fears were fanned by brigands who spread rumors of a conspiracy to humiliate their religion. Many rose against us, but the rebels were repressed with the very weapons they refused to employ."

"Is it true, Governor," Trenholm asked, "The British government may divest the Honorable East India Company of its responsibilities for managing the colony?"

"You are well informed, Mr. Trenholm." Governor Murray responded respectfully. "Within a year, I suspect India will become a Crown Colony, the direct responsibility of Her Majesty's Government, but fear not for our men of commerce: They will be free to pursue the

172

interests of Trade, without the burden of Government or the financing of private armies."

Trenholm already knew the answer to his question, having divested himself of his company's shares in the East India Company before any real damage could be done. The Indian Rebellion had been one of the motives behind his recent trip to England, not so much to protect his existing interests but to take advantage of the opportunities presented when some British businessmen were forced to sell plum investments to cover the losses arising from the expected demise of the East India Company.

After discussing the Indian rebellion with Trenholm in some detail, the Governor turned the conversation to the sinking of the *Central America.*

"I understand you've brought the honorable Henry McCrary's son with you this evening. He seems no worse for the wear, having survived the disaster!"

The Governor turned to smile at Martin, with a grandfatherly glint in his eye.

"He seems fit enough to me," Trenholm admitted. "Martin, could you share your story?"

Martin's mind had drifted during the conversation about India, his imagination ignited by images of exotic lands on the far side of the world. He shifted in his seat and moved to clear his throat, but was interrupted by the Governor.

"Before you began, I should confess I know your father, Mister McCrary. We met when last he journeyed to England, as he stopped off in

Hamilton along the way. During a long and pleasant conversation, we discovered our families share a connection, as my brother's wife was born in Charleston. She was a Calloway—does that name sound familiar?"

"Yes, of course!" Martin responded with youthful enthusiasm. My father once told me we have relations in Nova Scotia, a cousin who was born in Charleston. Could that be her?" Like all men of his station raised in the South, Martin was trained from a young age to recall the details of family histories and connections, which counted for so much in Southern Society.

"That would be my younger brother's wife, Elizabeth Calloway. Her father was a prominent loyalist who settled his family in Nova Scotia a few years before I was born. My brother Howard is a Captain in the Royal Navy, responsible for the port. If you find yourself in Halifax during your travels, you must look them up, as you will be warmly received!"

"Why thank you, Sir, for the recommendation. Hopefully the cyclone season will have passed, by the time we make our way home. I hear the voyage from Liverpool to Halifax is a shorter and safer route than we might otherwise employ."

"Speaking of cyclones, Mr. McCrary, please share your story with the rest of us."

The Governor smiled encouragingly and listened carefully as Martin recited his tale. The young American made no mention of the stolen gold or Harvey, or his rescue by a dolphin, less they think him a criminal or a mad man, but

174

focused on the storm and the sinking itself, the subject of primary interest to the group. Martin responded as best he could to questions offered by Lt. Tisdale, which focused on the source of the first leak (the shaft driving the paddle wheel), the location of the coal bunker (deep in the hold) and problems maintaining headway (Martin recounted every detail he could remember). The Lieutenant also asked about the ships boats (how many lost, how many functional) and the fate of the passengers and crew. The group was relieved to hear most of the women and children were saved by a passing ship. The older men were impressed with Martin's ability to offer a clear and concise accounting, while confessing gaps in his knowledge and observations, as appropriate. The conversation continued for over an hour, as most of the men smoked cigars and sipped their drinks in silent respect.

Meanwhile, Dr. Satterwhite was strolling in the moonlit gardens with a secret ally and confidant, Edward Benton of Baltimore. Benton was a merchant and a spy working for the Scotsman's network in North America. In all his dealings with Governor Murray and his associates over the past two years, Benton had portrayed himself as an ardent supporter of slavery, a ship-owner whose wealth depending on the cotton trade. In so doing, he had gained the Governor's confidence and was on the brink of a major discovery. He had urgent news to share with Satterwhite, who would relay everything to Sir McDonald when he reached Liverpool.

175

"Tell me more about the Governor's proposal, Edward." Dr. Satterwhite asked.

"It's simple, really." Benton replied. "It seems the soon-to-be-dismantled British East India Company procured a very large quantity of the latest Enfield rifles, some of which never made their way to the subcontinent before the mutiny. One of Governor Murray's associates procured 5,000 of those rifles, and Mr. Trenholm has offered to purchase them for the South Carolina Militia."

"That hardly seems credible," Satterwhite remarked. "Given the history of the Militia and its role in defeating British forces during the Revolution."

"It's true the men who founded the South Carolina Militia were American Patriots engaged in a long and dirty war against Loyalists, but the political geography has changed. Wealthy Southerners like Trenholm, who now fund the Militia, see the British as an essential ally against the North. Besides, credible or not, I know this arrangement is true, as Governor Murray's man has asked me to handle the shipment to Charleston, when the rifles arrive."

"Who is is the Governor's man, Edward, and when will the guns arrive?" As a trained physician, the process of asking detailed questions came naturally to Satterwhite.

"Why, that would be Lieutenant Tisdale himself. I would imagine he's upstairs with the Governor right now. A nasty piece of work, that one. Polished enough on the outside, but viscous in a fight. He was lurking around the docks one

176

night last year, spying on one of my ships—checking me out for the Governor, I suspect. He was attacked by a trio of dock rats—sailors no captain would hire, it seems. He killed all three of them with a dagger, pretty as you please, and threw their bodies in the water. Saw the whole thing myself, and I'm damn glad he didn't see me!"

Clearly Lt. Tisdale deserved a closer examination. The doctor decided to save that for later.

"All right then, when will the guns arrive in Hamilton?" Satterwhite asked.

"Not Hamilton, the old port up in St. George's. Should be sometime in November or December. I'm supposed to work out the details with Lt. Tisdale next week." Benton waited patently while Dr. Satterwhite pondered the information.

"Is there more I should know?" Satterwhite asked.

"Believe so, Doc. The lieutenant promised this would be the first of many shipments over the next several years, if I do a good job for the Governor. Tisdale told me business would be even better if the South decides to go its own way."

"Incredible!" Dr. Satterwhite thought to himself. He had uncovered a plot to supply South Carolina with the best rifled muskets in the world, in the expectation they might be needed if the South seceded from the Union. The Scotsman would be furious, and he would need every ally and every skill at his disposal to frustrate the ambitions of men like Murray and Trenholm.

"You've done well, Edward." Satterwhite offered. "McDonald will be ever grateful for your service. I suspect we will need to deploy a man here in Bermuda, to monitor this development. I'm thinking of volunteering myself, knowing men of quality like you are working on his behalf."

"That would be a pleasure, Doc! As you know, I spend half my time here in Bermuda and the other half in Baltimore. I wouldn't feel half so lonely if I had someone to share the burden."

Satterwhite shook hands with Edward Benton and thanked him warmly for his service. Neither man realized they were being observed at that moment by Lt. Tisdale, who was leaning against the railing of the veranda above the garden path and had recognized the ship captain, making a mental note to identify his companion. By the time Satterwhite made his way back to the reception, the Governor had finished his interview with Martin and was engaged in a conversation with Dr. Snow, accompanied by Lt. Tisdale.

"Ah, Dr. Satterwhite!" Dr. Snow exclaimed, when he noticed his colleague's approach. "You must join us! Governor Murray, please allow me to introduce my associate, Dr. Satterwhite. His advice and assistance was much appreciated during my trip to Barbados."

"Governor," Satterwhite responded, with a respectful tip of his head, as Dr. Snow continued.

178

"It seems last year's yellow fever outbreak in Bermuda was worse than we imagined. The garrison lost more than a score of its prime soldiers and many families lost a child." Snow provided a concise, professional assessment of the situation. "The Governor has found it extremely difficult to secure a qualified physician, to develop preventative measures and treat the victims properly, should another outbreak occur. I have just explained to the Governor I'm unavailable, given my commitments in London. I can think of no one better than yourself, if you're willing to accept the task."

Sometimes the solution to a problem presents itself before the problem has been digested, Satterwhite thought to himself, as he formed a response.

"Of course, I would be honored! As a bachelor, my life is rather simple, but I do have some affairs to arrange back home. With the Governor's permission, I would accompany you on the Birkenhead back to Liverpool and return by ship from London before the year is out."

"That would do nicely, Dr. Satterwhite, nicely indeed! Lieutenant Tisdale will speak with Colonel Hemphill, the commander of the garrison, so he can make the necessary arrangements with Whitehall. It will do the Colony good to have a real physician on hand. Now, if you will pardon me gentlemen, I must attend the rest of my guests, having abandoned my wife for too long!"

Dr. Snow patted Satterwhite fondly on the shoulder and muttered, "Good man!" Before moving off toward a group of familiar faces on the far side of the room. Surprisingly, Lt. Tisdale had not turned to follow the Governor, but remained to face Satterwhite, instead.

"I suppose you're from Norfolk, like Dr. Snow?" The naval officer asked, beginning the process of elicitation. Satterwhite knew what the man was about, having played this game all his life: Based on his accent and mannerism, the Lt. hailed from good family. As such, he could not rest until he had established his relative status and position with a new acquaintance.

"A good guess, I suppose, but no—my family hails from Lancashire. My grandfather was a cooper, clever enough to move his business to Liverpool, before I was born. Like Dr. Snow, I'm the first physician in my family." Satterwhite felt no sense of shame in his humble family origins and often found advantage when loftier men underestimated him.

"Tradesmen, then, I see." The Lieutenant responded with satisfaction. I suppose doctoring is also a trade, although perhaps more prestigious than coopering."

The put-down was the expected climax of such conversations, in Satterwhite's experience, so he simply smiled and nodded pleasantly when Lt. Tisdale turned and walked away.

The taste of revenge will be all the sweeter, Satterwhite thought to himself, as he considered his good fortune: A unique opportunity to be of service to the Scotsman. Like

180

McDonald, Satterwhite opposed the reckless adventurism of those Englishmen who resented American independence and still hoped to derail their experiment in self-government. He had even less respect for their allies in Commerce, men who couldn't see beyond next year's profits. Clearly Bermuda was the place he needed to be.

CHAPTER 11:
AN UNEXPECTED OFFER

With no time to waste, John Harvey was up and away soon after sunrise, with a belly full of biscuits and a smile on his face. He had enjoyed a few minutes in the kitchen with Sue, who bore no grudges and expressed no regrets in the wake of their previous liaison.

"You come and see me, John Harvey, if you find yourself back in Bermuda!" Was her only request.

Sue made arrangements for Harvey to ride back to town in the produce wagon that stopped by the Consulate every morning. A breeze was blowing off the harbor as the wagon worked its way to the Gentleman's Emporium on Burnaby Street, where Martin's new clothes were waiting for the voyage to Liverpool. Climbing down from the wagon, Harvey tipped his hat at the driver and paused to admire the morning before continuing on his way. Intimately familiar with the unspoken rules of the world he inhabited, the black man approached the servant's entrance cheerfully, as the indignity he used to feel on such occasions had been lessened by the sense of purpose he found in a secret life.

Moments before he could rap on the back door, three white men stepped around the corner and approached him. Two of the men were British sailors, senior petty officers wearing blue jackets and white trousers, with heavy pistols on their belts. The third man was dressed in the unmistakable uniform of a British naval officer, a tall gentleman with dark hair and penetrating blue eyes. He approached Harvey with both hands open, in a friendly but authoritative manner.

"Mr. Harvey, may I have a word with you?" Although his words were politely phrased, his demeanor implied more of a demand than a question.

"And who might you be, Sir?" Harvey asked, as the sailors moved closer, cutting off any possible avenue of escape.

"An officer of Her Majesty's Navy, and a potential friend, if you'll hear me out, in private."

The lieutenant stood directly in front of Harvey and gestured with his right hand toward the end of the alley, where an enclosed carriage was waiting.

"A man like me could always use a friend!" Harvey replied submissively, as he followed the officer and was followed in turn by the sailors, who relaxed in the face of his compliance.

The British officer joined Harvey inside the carriage, with the curtains closed. One of the sailors took the reigns and the other sat on the bench beside him. Moments later, the rig moved out smartly.

"Mister Harvey, may I call you John?" The officer asked politely, with a predatory smile.

"Yes Sir, that's my name." Harvey replied timidly, assuming the habitually humble persona that allowed white men to underestimate him, although they rarely needed much encouragement.

"Good man! This is your lucky day, John, as I have a proposal that will undoubtedly be of great interest you. How would you like to make some real money?"

Lieutenant Tisdale had recruited several American negroes over the years. Based on his experience, there was no need to waste time with a subtle approach.

"Well, Sir, I already has a job, of sorts."

The wheels were turning in Harvey's mind, as the Scotsman had warned him he might be a tempting target for recruitment by rival intelligence operatives, British or otherwise, given his access to prominent personalities in South Carolina. Sir McDonald had encouraged Harvey to accept such an approach, within set parameters, as a double agent could be a precious asset.

"How much does your Master pay?" The Lieutenant asked solicitously.

"Well, he feeds me and buys my clothes and puts a roof over my head most days, plus I gets two dollars a month, if I does what I'm told."

"Two dollar a month?" Tisdale asked, with mock incredulity:

"Listen up, John: I'll give you 20 dollars, right now, plus another 20 dollars when you get to Liverpool, if you'll work for me, on the side, with no one the wiser."

"How could I work for you, Sir?" Harvey asked the obvious question, "Our ship is leaving today!"

"That's exactly where you're needed, John—on that ship. What I require is a pair of eyes and ears on the Birkenhead. If you accept my proposal, I would only ask that you listen quietly to what certain people have to say and report to my associate when you reach Liverpool. He'll give you the other 20 dollars and, assuming you do well, we could make a long term arrangement that could set you up for life. Think on this, John Harvey: If you provide good service over a number of years, I could make arrangements for you to settle right here in Bermuda, where slavery is forbidden and all men are free."

"What if I gets caught?" Harvey asked, feigning caution in an effort to conceal his true intentions. "I could lose my job and my place...worse yet, they might hang me or sell me back into slavery when we gets back to South Carolina."

"I can see you're a man who thinks clearly, John. You have that reputation. That's

186

why my proposal is a perfect opportunity for you. The Birkenhead is headed to Liverpool, where British law reigns. All you have to so is to give my proposal a try. If you come up empty-handed when you arrive in Liverpool, you can keep the first 20 dollars and we'll go our separate ways. If you do well, you'll have double the money right away, and the opportunity to earn more in the future. All you have to do is to listen, which I imagine comes natural to a man of your station, and meet my associate when you get to Liverpool."

"Well," Harvey continued: "I fear I might disappoint, but you seems like a fair man who would understand if I changes my mind. What exactly do you want me to do?" Harvey hoped to more elicit information that might be of value to Dr. Satterwhite and the Scotsman.

"It's simple, John. There's a man traveling on the Birkenhead you already know, a Dr. Satterwhite. He's been asked to to return to Bermuda in a couple of months, to serve as the official physician for the colony. In that position, he'll have regular contact with all of our senior officers and government officials, so I need to check him out carefully, to make sure he deserves that level of trust. I want you to find out if he drinks too much, or if he abuses his own medications, as some physicians do. Does he gamble? Is he in debt? Who are his friends, who are his enemies? What are his political opinions? Does he have friends or connections in the United States? You don't have to go out of your way, John. It's well known you have a friendly relationship with the Doctor. In fact, you'll be doing him a favor, in secret, by helping him secure such an important position here in the Colony."

Harvey nodded his understanding before the officer continued.

"Then there's Samuel Prescond, the Barbadian, and his friend, Reverend Nichols. I want you to pay close attention to both men, especially their relationship with Dr. Satterwhite. Do they meet privately on the ship? What do they talk about when you observe them together? Very simple, really."

Not for the first or the last time, Harvey savored the feeling of power derived from secret knowledge. The joy and the irony of being a co-conspirator with Dr. Satterwhite and the Scotsman, and the ability to be of service to men who shared his goals, both personal and political.

Harvey responded carefully, hoping to learn more about the officer's identity.

"I could use the money, Sir, as I've got family back home in South Carolina to worry about, but I don't even know your name or how to find your man when I gets to Liverpool."

"You can call me Mister Walter. The rest is easy."

Lieutenant Tisdale went on to brief Harvey in a professional manner. He provided a simple contact plan to be implemented on his arrival in Liverpool, which required him to approach a certain door at the local Admiralty office and ask for an officer by the name of Wallace. He gave Harvey a $20 Double Eagle, as promised, and dropped Harvey off on a quiet side street around the corner from the Gentlemen's Emporium, a mere 30 minutes after their initial encounter.

Harvey experienced a strange sense of detachment when he approached the rear entrance to the Emporium, as he forced the memory of his encounter with the Lieutenant into a compartment in his mind and resumed the role of a man-servant. A sharp rap on the door was answered by shuffling feet and mumbling voices, followed immediately by the rasping sound of a sliding bolt. The door was opened by a tiny mulatto woman with a pinched face, her short grey hair covered by a cotton scarf. The skin on the hand that held the edge of the door was wrinkled, but her fingers looked lean and powerful.

"And who might you be?" The old woman asked as she peered up at Harvey.

"Good morning, Cleopatra! I'm John Harvey, Mr. McCrary's servant—here to retrieve his furnishings." Harvey wore his brightest smile and bowed dramatically, as if he were Mark Antony presenting himself to the Queen of Egypt.

"Uh, huh—and a scoundrel too, trying to flatter an old woman like me. As you can surely see, I'm long past flattering, John Harvey, so best keep your charm to yourself!"

Chuckling, she turned and gestured for Harvey to enter.

"They call me Cleo—I suppose Sue told you that. Now that's a woman worth flattering!"

189

Reading Harvey's face like a book, Cleo laughed out loud before continuing:

"I can see you're well acquainted—she does like handsome men, when she can find 'em!"

Harvey couldn't restrain a smile of his own before responding:

"I'm sure I don't know what you're talking about, although I was asked to relay Sue's regards, and an invitation to share a pew with her on Sunday."

"Don't know why that woman is so worried about my soul—she knows I don't care for that nosy old pastor. You tell her to mind her own business!"

Cleo began to bustle about the room, placing a last few items into a large steamer trunk before stepping through a curtained doorway towards the front of the shop. Harvey took the opportunity to survey the old woman's lair, a tidy affair featuring a pair of sewing tables surrounded by cupboards. Moments later, a portly white man with a balding head and spectacles emerged, followed by Cleo.

"You must be McCrary's man." The shopkeeper began, without bothering to introduce himself. "Is everything in order?" He asked, without turning to face Cleo.

"Yes Suh, just like you said—everything on the list, including that old mended suit for Mr. Harvey here. Should I have him try it on before he leaves?"

"No, don't bother—it's loose enough to do the job, with a pair of leather suspenders. I hope it serves him better than the previous owner, who died last month and was buried in a new frock coat, at the insistence of his foolish relations. Waste of fine clothes, if you ask me."

The sour look on the shopkeeper's face made it clear he was referring to both the recently interred new suit and the old mended one for Harvey. As Harvey shuddered at the thought of wearing an ill-fitting suit that most recently belonged to an anonymous dead man, the shopkeeper kept talking:

"Mr. McCrary can pay for the adjustments when they get to Liverpool, if he wants. Roust up a wagon and make sure the trunk is loaded safely for the trip down to the harbor."

The shopkeeper turned dismissively and exited the storeroom, leaving Cleo and Harvey to roll their eyes and shrug their shoulders in mutual understanding.

"Let me guess." Harvey asked rhetorically, "You do the work and he keeps the money?"

"Sure enough, but old Mr. Bueller ain't so bad—I'm the best paid seamstress in the Colony and has my own little cottage with a garden and some chickens. I run a little business out of there, me and my daughters making clothes for colored folk."

"Well, Mamma Cleo, I hope to do as well, myself, someday. Sue told me you was a wonder, with more spring in your step than many a young girl!" Harvey missed his own mother and saw more than a little of her resourcefulness in Cleo.

191

"There you go, flattering an old woman again. You best be glad my husband ain't around no more! Go on now, be own your way before I forgets my manners!"

Moving with surprising quickness for a woman of her age, Cleo popped out the back door and whistled energetically for a little colored boy sitting on the corner.

"Felix! Fetch a wagon—and be quick about it!" Her voice rang with authority.

Harvey grabbed the steamer trunk by its handles and followed Cleo up to the corner. He watched with amusement as the boy's feet kicked up the dust as he ran down the street. Harvey barely had time to set the heavy trunk down on the ground before the boy returned, riding in the back of an open wagon drawn by an old mule. The driver, a rough looking character wearing a straw hat and an impudent grin, stepped down to help Harvey load the trunk, which was protected by metal fittings on every corner. Harvey was surprised when Cleo stepped forward and gave the driver a couple of small coins.

"The fee for this wagon was included in the bill paid by Mr. Trenholm." She explained. "So don't let this rascal take advantage of you when you gets down to your ship!"

One glance from Cleo was enough to set the rascal straight, as he knew he might lose his regular trade with the Gentleman's Emporium if he steeped out of line.

"She's a tough old hen!" The driver observed when they were out of earshot. "Boston's my name!" He offered confidentially, while snapping the reigns and clucking at the mule.

"Boston? What kind of name is that?" Harvey asked, without offering his own.

Boston smiled in response, pleased to meet a black man with some spunk.

"My daddy was a sailor from Boston. That's all my mamma knows, so that's my name. I've got three brothers, all named after their daddies. There's Will, don't ever call him Wilmington! And Baltimore, he's the youngest. Then there's Galveston—everyone knows where his daddy came from, but nobody knows where the hell he is now."

Seeing the driver meant no harm, Harvey offered his name and a handshake. The driver responded with a mock tone of surprise:

"John Harvey? You're a lucky man, havin' two first names, like one of those fancy white men from Virginia! How'd you come by that?" Boston was a curious man, by nature, and not at all stupid. His job offered little stimulation, other than conversation with strangers in the little port city he called home.

"You get right to the heart of it, don't you Boston? Well, here's the truth: My mother is a slave. Her father was called John and his father was called Harvey, so there you are!"

"So, if you has a son of your own someday," Boston asked lightheartedly, "Will you call him John Harvey something or another? Three first names, that would be grand! You could call him JHW or JHP and dress him up in fine clothes, with the letters sewn in front for everyone to see!"

Boston was a talker and could riff for hours.

"So you're a reading man?" Harvey asked politely, enjoying the driver's good cheer.

"Well enough!" Boston replied. "Even the poorest children in this town go to school when they's young, learning to read the Bible in the missionary school. I never did care for old King James, too stuffy for me, but you can't beat the Bible for a good story!"

"No you can't!" Agreed Harvey. "What's your favorite?"

"Why, Moses, of course!" Boston narrated the familiar story with passion, as the wagon worked its way down Front Street. A number of tall ships were anchored out in the harbor, but a packet ship like the Birkenhead was small and important enough to dock at a pier, simplifying the loading process. Boston continued to talk as the two men unloaded Martin's trunk. He finished the story with a flourish:

"Bermuda is my promised land, wouldn't live anywheres else. What about you, Harvey? You're a free man—why would you ever go back to South Carolina?"

"I better think on that, Boston!" Harvey conceded, as they bid farewell.

John Harvey considered the question carefully during the voyage to Liverpool, both when resting quietly down below or when staring out over the North Atlantic in silent reverie. Part of him wanted to run, far away, and never return. He had some gold in his pocket and could make a living most anywhere. He listened to that cowardly, selfish voice but never wavered in his commitment to his mother and sister. If he abandoned them, who would set them free? No, his path was set, no way to change that.

There was more: An idea that grew in his imagination, a conviction that he had some larger role to play. He wondered if his secret life could help bring an end to slavery in America, not just for his family, but for everyone. He also had a darker side, a rage-filled heart that longed to kill the men who kept other human beings as chattel. His rage was clean and pure, fanned by flames of righteous indignation and the sure knowledge that slavery was evil incarnate. Harvey began to see himself as an avenging angel, bringing justice to men who deserved no mercy. Part of him laughed at the grandiosity of this notion, but his true self knew he would strike without hesitation, when the time came.

CHAPTER 12:
LIVERPOOL GAOL

A pleasant fortnight passed during the voyage from Bermuda to Liverpool, with the prevailing westerly winds aided by warm Gulfstream currents. Harvey spent his time listening, but not in the way Lt. Tisdale had intended. He kept a close eye on Charles Prileau, Trenholm's representative in Liverpool, and learned a few things about the financial and political implications of the lost gold from the *Central America*. He also spent as much time as he could with Dr. Satterwhite, soaking up advice on how best to handle Tisdale's approach as they prepared for their long-awaited conversations with the Scotsman. Both men grew closer and developed a keen appreciation or one another, forming a partnership that would serve them well in the future. By the time the Birkenhead reached England, Harvey's leg was completely healed, with a few jagged scars to show for his misadventure.

During the voyage, Martin noticed some changes in Harvey's behavior, but said nothing. His former slave treated him with genuine respect now, as his own man and not as the boy he had once known. They spoke of it only once, up on deck when the Birkenhead skirted close to the southern coast of Ireland before turning north to reach Liverpool. Harvey's remarks were brief but heartfelt:

"I want you to know," Harvey began, "I appreciate what you did."

Martin nodded and responded with equal simplicity: "You would have done the same for me."

"Well," Harvey admitted, with a contrarian's sense of humor, "I might have saved you from that shark, but I never would have dropped a fortune into the sea!"

"If you'd been smart enough to steal something smaller, I might have kept it myself!" Martin retorted, "Where did you think you were going to hide a brick of that size? In your trousers?"

Harvey laughed heartily in response, in part because he had successfully concealed a handful of gold coins in his waist-band, without Martin's knowledge, but also because he appreciated the self-confidence his unwitting half-brother had gained since the shipwreck.

"Guess you'll have to pay for the drinks and the women, when we get to Liverpool—

there's nobody to blame but yourself!" Harvey replied pointedly.

"It makes no difference to me!" Martin responded: "You would have lost that gold in a game of cards, anyway!"

"Hum, maybe so, maybe so..." Harvey was more of a gambler than Martin knew.

"Speaking of the city, tell me about Liverpool." Martin requested.

"Alright." Harvey agreed, gathering his thoughts. "It's the greatest city you'll ever see, until we get to London." Harvey described the bustling port, with its acres of docks and miles of quays, unlike anything Martin had ever seen in the New World. He also painted a frank but fair picture of a city bursting with energy and enterprise, driven by the blind ambition of cut-throat merchants who shared much in common with the pirates and privateers of old.

The Irish Sea was slate grey and peaceful as they approached Liverpool on a damp Monday in early October 1857, a little more than a month after the sinking of the *Central America*. A gentle northwesterly breeze pushed the Birkenhead softly into the mouth of the River Mersey, where they were met by a pilot in a sturdy-looking paddle-wheeled tugboat. Both banks of the estuary were forested with the masts of tall ships, still the most reliable means of transporting goods over long distances. Coastal steamers and sturdy little tugboats moved briskly across the harbor, ferrying passengers and running all of the innumerable errands needed to facilitate the trade that sustained the largest commercial empire the world had ever known. The colors and sounds of the harbor were muted by the damp air, which would turn to fog by morning. The Birkenhead seemed to float in a bowl of thick grey soup, backlit by a sun that couldn't quite break through the clouds.

Despite several attempts to lay a cable on the ocean floor, there was no functioning trans-Atlantic telegraph in the Fall of 1857. Nevertheless, the news of the sinking of the *Central America* had already reached Liverpool before the Birkenhead, as the American cotton factor Theodore Sharpwell, had arrived in London aboard Trenholm's private steamer the week before. Lacking any form of communication aboard the Birkenhead and unable to know if Sharpwell had carried out the instructions he received in Bermuda, Charles Prileau, the head of Trenholm's Liverpool office, was the first to disembark, rushing to his office on Rumsford Place. Martin and Harvey took their time, as they wanted to thank the captain and crew for rescuing them after the hurricane. The moment they set foot on English soil, they were approached by a boy carrying a stack of newspapers. The headline of the Liverpool Mercury demanded their immediate attention:

"Lost Gold Invites Panic in America and Europe."

Martin reached into his pocket and offered a few pennies to the boy. He scanned the article, which referred to the loss of the *Central America*'s gold and detailed a financial crisis that began well before the sinking. One passage, a

200

quote from President James Buchanan, caught his eye.

He read the passage out loud, for Harvey's benefit:

"It is apparent that our existing misfortunes have proceeded solely from our extravagant and vicious system of paper currency and bank credits, exciting the people to wild speculations and gambling in stocks. These revulsions must continue to recur at successive intervals so long as the amount of the paper currency and bank loans and discounts of the country shall be left to the discretion of 1,400 irresponsible banking institutions, which from the very law of their nature will consult the interest of their stockholders rather than the public welfare."

The article went on to praise the virtues of England's Bank Charter Act of 1844, which established a gold standard and gave exclusive power to the Bank of England to print notes. The author expressed reservations regarding Prime Minister Palmerston's plans to suspend the Act temporarily, to help the British Government deal with the expanding crisis.

"I have little experience in finance," Martin admitted, while turning to face Harvey, "but surely Father's interests are at risk. We best make our way to the Exchange."

Harvey remained silent as he flagged a carriage. His mind raced, distracted by the bustling harbor and the need to make contact with Dr. Satterwhite, without attracting attention from Martin.

He would have to bide his time, as always.

"Exchange Flags!" Harvey ordered, while loading Martin's trunk. Most of the family's business in England was based at the cotton exchange, an open air market located behind Liverpool's Town Hall.

"Tain't open today!" The coachman responded, "Everyone's gone to the hanging!"

"What hanging?" Martin asked, his curiosity peaked.

"There's four of them, Sir—two men, a woman and a boy, going to meet their maker, they is, over at Walton Prison. If we hurry, we could still make it!" The coachman wanted to see hanging as much as anyone, so much the better if he got paid for it.

"Drive us there, straightaway. You can take us to the Angel Hotel afterwards." Part of Martin's youthful soul was shamed by his desire to witness a public execution, which his deeply religious mother and grandfather opposed outspokenly, but his curiosity got the better of him. Besides, he had drunk and womanized his way to San Francisco and back: What harm would a little execution do?

The streets of Liverpool where unusually empty until their carriage turned left on Southport Road. The driver stopped the carriage to admire the spectacle. Tens of thousands of people were converging on the prison, from every direction and from every class. The road a half mile ahead was jammed with wagons and carriages of every description. Some the younger observers attempted to circumvent the crush by running across an empty field. The coachman offered a solution:

"The best we can do, Sir, is to make our way to that hill over there," the driver suggested, as he pointed with the handle of his whip. "I know the keeper in the cemetery yonder. He'll open his gates if we give him a few pence. The hill is set back a bit from the gaol, but we'll enjoy a clear view of the proceedings. We won't get any closer, at this late hour."

Martin nodded his assent and the driver cracked his whip. Ten minutes later, they approached the graveyard, which seemed like a suitable location to view a hanging. The keeper of the cemetery recognized the driver, as the carriage approached, and he opened his gate without hesitation. The coachman dropped a few pennies in his hand and asked:

"Georgie, why don't you join us up on the hill?"

"No need," the crusty old man responded, spitting tobacco juice over his shoulder. "I'll see 'em up close, soon enough, unless the surgeons claim their bodies, first. Besides, there's money to be made," he exclaimed, pointing to an approaching carriage filled with jolly matrons and laughing young ladies. It seemed likely the women hoped to follow their example by finding a vantage point inside the cemetery.

The coachman followed a series of winding gravel driveways, moving past headstones and markers that grew progressively older as they moved further north, towards the prison. One of the narrow paths wound up a steep slope to reach a small crest pegged with crooked memorials, like the teeth of a beached whale washed up by some long forgotten storm. The stones were etched with letters that had faded with the passage of time, reminding Harvey of his mortality. Scattered graves and stubby trees spread out on the slope below, ending at a stone wall topped by an iron fence, with sharpened points like the spears of a Greek Phalanx, to discourage grave robbers. The field between the fence and the prison was packed with bystanders of every variety, the shorter ones bobbing and ducking in an effort to improve their view. Small children clung precariously on the shoulders of their fathers, uncles and older brothers. The crowd was hushed, as they strained to hear the words of the uniformed official standing on a large wooden platform topped by a pair of sturdy posts. Four ropes hung from a heavy cross-beam.

Although they were located a good distance from the crowd, the coachman spoke in a rasping whisper. He stood uncomfortably close to Martin and the stench of his unwashed body and soggy woolen clothes smelled like death itself, causing the young man's eyes to water. He resisted the urge to step away, as he wanted to hear what the coachman had to say.

"Both of those men are murderers, half-crazed Fenians from Ireland. The papers say they stabbed a constable to death. Liverpool is infested with the bastards! More of them arrive every day, looking for work and food, as they have none at home."

The coachman nodded absentmindedly, agreeing with himself.

"What about the woman and the child?" Martin asked, having never heard of a child being hanged back home in South Carolina.

"Don't worry yourself!" The coachman chuckled, "They both deserve it! The woman's a prostitute—she slit a man's throat with a razor. The boy's a real devil: He poked out the eyes of a chaplain at his workhouse, while the man slept! The pastor survived, but he'll never read the Good Book again."

The men stopped talking when the crowd issued a collective sigh as the trap doors were tested, one last time. Martin recalled what he had learned about the "long drop method" of hanging, which was the standard at home and in England. This method was considered more humane because it relied on the weight of the human body to snap the victim's neck when it reached the end of a long rope, rather than leaving the victim dangling at the end of a shorter one.

Martin's revere was interrupted when two additional carriages reached the top of the hill. A dozen or more women climbed down, rushing to gain a better view of the proceedings. The wives and daughters of prosperous shopkeepers kept a safe distance from the male strangers. One of the young ladies cast an admiring gaze at Martin, her eyelids fluttering like the wings of a hummingbird. Her attention was rewarded with a thin smile, which disappeared when shouts began to rise above the crowd.

Martin watched with fascination as the prisoners where lead to the scaffold, their hands bound before them. All four of the condemned wore long white gowns over their street clothes, to mark their status and to conceal the distasteful release of bodily fluids from the crowd. It was hard to tell from that distance, but the boy seemed to meet his fate with more courage than the adults. He stood defiantly when the hood was placed over his head and the noose was secured around his neck. The hangman was tall and patriarchal, with long flowing hair. He did his duty efficiently, not pausing for effect but pulling the lever without hesitation. The trap doors fell and the four condemned followed, with the crowd crying out in unison, like a single living creature in the throws of orgasm.

The Fenians died immediately, their necks and lives broken in a painless instant. The woman took a bit longer, her feet kicking wildly and her back arching terribly before her corpse dangled quietly at the end of a rope, like a fly in a spider's web. The boy's death was more difficult, as his neck was strong and he weighed very little. He wiggled and jumped and twirled until the hangman's assistant walked under the gallows and added his weight to that of the boy, pulling on his feet from below. The assistant knew his business and it was over in less than a minute. The crowd began to move, clustering in small group, to recount what they had seen and to compare the scene with other executions they had witnessed in the past. Some shook their heads in disapproval over the boy's painful

206

death, many of them with children tugging at their apron strings. Other parents took the opportunity to school their boys on the obvious consequences, should they stray from the path of righteous obedience. Worst of all where the street urchins, some of whom had known the boy before he was taken into an orphanage. One of the boy's acquaintances was badly beaten by a swirling mob of miscreants when he suggested his friend had been molested by the workhouse chaplain the night before the incident.

Martin ordered his coachman to wait until the women and girls had cleared the cemetery before departing. The streets and lanes of Liverpool were packed with horses, carriages and pedestrians of every variety, all enjoying a festive carnival atmosphere. Street peddlers took advantage of the special occasion by offering an amazing variety of finger-foods, beverages and trinkets. One enterprising young man made a tidy sum selling hang-man's toys: Small sticks with tiny dolls dangling from a noose, each made to resemble one of the condemned. The little boy was popular, second only to the Fenians, as they both hung from the same stick. Martin watched with fascination as a well-dressed child riding in a fine carriage manipulated the rope on his toy, making the legs of the boyish effigy dance merrily.

The scene was surreal and exhausting, as was the slow journey back to the Angel Hotel, near Liverpool's Town Hall. Harvey followed Martin into the lobby, carrying two leather valet cases, with Martin's steamer trunk left in the care of the doorman. The clerk behind the desk was polite and efficient. After examining Martin's new passport, issued at the Consulate in Hamilton, he stood at attention:

"Of course, Mr. McCrary, we have suitable accommodations. Your father has been a regular visitor over the years and your family's credit is good with us. Please let us know if you require any assistance, or perhaps separate accommodations for your manservant."

Curiously irritated by the courtesy and privilege derived from his father's name and connections, Martin's response was less than polite:

"It's been a long and trying day. Please send up a simple evening meal within an hour. I'll also have breakfast in my room at precisely 8 am, coffee not tea." Martin turned to leave.

"Yes, of course, Sir, but there's one other thing: A Dr. Satterwhite stopped by this afternoon and left a note requiring your attention." The clerk extended his right hand formally, with palm up.

"Thank you, Mr. ah..." Martin mumbled, regretting his boorish manners.

"Green, Sir, Mr. Green at your service."

"Well thank you Mr. Green," Martin offered, while turning to read the note:

"Dear Martin: I recall you planned to seek accommodations at the Angel, so I took advantage of the opportunity to pay a brief call. As you have not yet arrived, I find it necessary to relay my request in this note, rather than personally. For this I beg your pardon. I would be sincerely grateful if I might borrow your man Harvey for one day this week, to assist me in moving some medical supplies to a local hospital. I'm staying at the George, a hostel on the far side of the Exchange, until Saturday, when I must be off to London. I hope you find Liverpool to be as hospitable as Hamilton; if you continue your journey to the capital, I would be honored to receive you. Sincerely, Michael."

Martin was grateful for Dr. Satterwhite's competent treatment of Harvey, and his friendship aboard the Birkenhead.

"Of course, of course." Martin uttered aloud. "It seems Dr. Satterwhite requires your assistance one day this week. You can find him at the George Hostel, once we've taken care of urgent business at the Exchange tomorrow. I'll entertain myself on Wednesday."

"We do owe him a debt of gratitude!" Harvey agreed, relieved to know when and where he would be able to make contact with the Doctor, and presumably the Scotsman.

Both men were exhausted and settled in for the night, with a light meal followed by a hot bath. Harvey carefully brushed the shoes and clothing acquired during their brief stay in Bermuda, as Martin wanted to make a good first impression when meeting his father's associates the following morning. The two men spoke very little before drifting off to sleep, sharing the same stormy visions filled with breaking waves and drowning men. A particularly vivid dream disturbed Harvey's sleep, leaving him tossing and turning until he could stand it no more.

Draping a blanket over his broad shoulders, he stood by the window and gazed out over an endless sea of jagged rooftops, with countless chimneys breathing smoky trails in a moonlit sky. "Let tomorrow come," he thought, "no matter what the day might bring."

CHAPTER 13:
A CHANCE ENCOUNTER

The morning after the hangings, the fog had
lifted and the skies were clear, so Martin and
Harvey decided to walk over to the Exchange.
The streets of Liverpool were humming with life,
like the veins of a great beast pumping blood into
the heart of the city. The sounds of the wagons
and carts and the horses that drew them rose to
a crescendo as they approached Town Hall. The
building was an elaborate structure, with two
lofty stories rising above a rusticated ground
level. The stones were stained by a hundred
years of rain-washed soot and the bronze fittings
glowed with a soft, green patina. A large portico
lined with Corinthian pillars projected from the
front of the building. On the summit, smaller
pillars supported a voluptuous dome topped by
an imposing figure of Britannia. After admiring
the fierce-looking Amazon, the Americans paused

to study an elaborate monument to Nelson, which was erected in 1813. Harvey provided a narrative, as he was familiar with the Admiral's story.

"The Hero is up there!" Harvey began, pointing with his left hand, "He was killed in battle, so an angel is watching over him, see? Now, can you make out those fine-looking sailors? Well, they ain't so fine on the streets of the city, especially at night, so watch your back! Now, do you see that man in chains down below? He's one of the French prisoners held right here in Liverpool during Nelson's war with Napoleon. Pay close attention, 'cause you'll rarely see a white man in chains!"

Harvey leaned back with his hands on his hips and admired the monument with a theatrical flourish. The statue was too ornate for Martin's taste and he was in no mood to encourage Harvey's antics, so he feigned disinterest with a shrug of his shoulders.

When Harvey realized he wasn't going to get a rise out of Martin, he turned to lead his "master" through the crowds at the Exchange. The big black man was uncomfortable in his ill-fitting suit, which only served to highlight his status as a servant, as if the color of his skin wasn't enough. Martin was properly dressed, in a new frock coat and trousers with all the accoutrements. He walked gingerly, as there was no opportunity to break in a new pair of shoes during the voyage from Bermuda.

The scene at the Exchange was chaotic. Groups of men stood in tight circles, holding fistfuls of paper over their heads as they shouted at elevated figures offering various goods for sale. The organized chaos reminded Harvey of a bee hive, with frantic workers surrounding the all-important Queen. The largest crowds surrounded the cotton brokers. To a man, they wore serious-looking faces and projected a fungible air of authority, as cotton was the fuel that sustained Great Britain during the first decades of the industrial age. The demand for cotton was insatiable, as the white stuff supported the legions of men and women who grew it, sold it, bought it, moved it and turned it into clothing and other textiles. By 1857, hundreds of thousands of Britons depending on cotton to support their families, at a time when charity was limited, the debtors' prisons were packed and the destitute littered the streets.

Great men on both sides of the Atlantic made vast fortunes financing King Cotton, from the slaves in the fields to the finest shops of London. The loss of the *Central America*'s gold fanned the flames of the first global financial crisis, which began with a series of bank failures in New York City, caused by inadequate regulation and reckless business practices. During the crisis, the rich and powerful sought refuge in commodities—and the demand for cotton grew stronger. The crisis boosted the morale of the Southern states and deepened the conviction that their way of life was superior to the North. They found natural allies on the far side of the Atlantic, where many prominent Englishmen felt threatened by the industrializing, commercialized and sea-faring Northern states.

This sense of relative strength increased the odds that Southerners would be willing to fight to preserve the status quo, and some bolder men advocated aggressive expansionism. In Bleeding Kansas, thousands of pro-slavery men threw themselves into an undeclared war, in an effort to expand the borders of their profitable institution. In states where slavery was long-established, many believed their prosperity was based on a superior culture, as ordained by God. His blessings rang from the pulpit, with harmonious melodies arising from courthouse and statehouse. The minds of weaker men were lost in the myth, but hard-headed businessmen like George Trenholm knew the truth: Their world was built on the backs of slaves, and everything would come crashing down if those weary backs were taken away.

Watching the cotton brokers from a distance, Harvey tutored Martin on the basics, helping him make sense of the chaos. After observing the proceedings for an hour or so, Harvey escorted Martin across the square to a row of brick buildings on the far side of the Exchange. One building sported a large white sign, with black lettering, which read: "Small and Sons, Cotton Brokers." Harvey stood to one side as he gestured and dipped his head, signaling Martin to enter the establishment before him. A bell rang at the top of the door as the two Americans entered, interrupting a conversation by three remarkably similar men

214

huddling around a wooden desk on the far side of the room. The space was illuminated by a row of large windows overlooking the exchange, casting shadows in the back of the room. The ceiling was 12' high, decorated with tin panels hammered into intricate patterns depicting every aspect of the cotton trade. The wall behind the men was dominated by a chalkboard, with rows of abbreviated figures arranged in neat columns. A telegraph operator sat at a small desk in the back, tapping out a stack of messages prepared by his superiors. The oldest of the three men looked irritated, at first—but his frown morphed into a grin when he recognized Harvey, as he stepped out from behind Martin, with his hat in hand.

"Look, boys, it's Harvey—Hank McCrary's man! And that must be McCrary's son, Martin!"

The younger men stood and turned to face the door. Their father, Paul Small, was a shrewd businessman, but they all knew their family's success depended on his personal connections with Hank McCrary, the powerful South Carolinian.

"Come in, come in!" The older man continued, as he walked toward the door. "Your father must have told you about me: I'm Paul Small, his broker, and these are my sons, Paul Jr. and David."

Both of the younger men donned their frock coats, which were hanging from the backs of their chairs, before approaching and shaking Martin's hand. Paul Jr. ignored Harvey; David nodded politely, having been accompanied by Harvey on an excursion in the past.

"We were expecting you a fortnight ago!" Paul Sr. began, while shaking Martin's hand. "When we first heard the news about the *Central America*, we feared the worst, but soon afterwards the good people at Fraser and Trenholm send over a runner with a message from their man in London, explaining that you had survived and planned to continue on to Liverpool. Remarkable!"

All three of the Smalls wanted to make a good impression on Martin, as they knew Hank McCrary wouldn't live forever and they hoped to maintain fruitful relations with his son. Paul Jr. was already married, with two children of his own, so the task of building a bridge for the next generation was assigned to David, as he was closest in age to Martin. The youngest of the Small men was bright and eager to rise above the shadow cast by his domineering older brother.

"Is it true?" David Small asked, "Like they say in the papers, that you saved your man Harvey from the sharks?"

Little did Martin know, a garbled version of their survival story had been picked up by the British press, after Theodore Sharpwell reached London. Seeking to ingratiate himself with the McCrary family, Sharpwell had portrayed Martin as a hero during an interview with a British newspaper. The subsequent article was popular with the British public, which had long embraced Rudyard Kipling's notion of the "White

216

Man's Burden" and assumed the hero in every story should look like Martin.

"Quite the opposite!' Martin replied, sticking to his original fable. "Harvey saved me from the sharks, and got himself bit in the process! Plus, he taught me how to swim when I was a boy. I would have drowned, if not for him, that's for sure!"

After some good-natured ribbing from the youngest Englishman, Harvey rolled up his trousers and showed off his scars, which formed a semi-circle around a muscular calf. The display aroused suitable exclamations from all three of the Small men, but the father and oldest son backed away, discomfited by their proximity to an African American and a former slave. With the introductions completed, it was time for business, and Harvey was no longer welcome, as the Smalls moved toward a private room in the back of the establishment. Martin turned to engage Harvey in a private conversation and handed his manservant several coins, part of the generous sum provided by George Trenholm back in Bermuda.

"Why don't you find yourself some better clothes," Martin whispered, "so you can make a good impression on the ladies? I'll see you back at the hotel this evening."

Harvey nodded and smiled in return, pleased to save his own money for more important purposes. He was also eager to have a few hours to himself, as Dr. Satterwhite wasn't expecting him until the following day. As Harvey shut the door behind himself and stepped down to the street, he took a deep breath of pungent city air and paused to think for a moment. He realized his appetite for women, drink and gambling was muted by a desire to do something useful. There would be plenty of time for distractions, he decided, but few opportunities to move about the city on his own.

His first stop: A simple tailor's shop near the harbor, popular with prosperous members of the working class, successful craftsmen and the like. With the measurements made and specifications agreed, Harvey moved on to a second establishment that sold cutlery. After carefully examining the inventory, he used some of his own money to purchase a fine Solingen hunting knife with a bone handle and leather sheath, knowing it was unsafe to move about the city unarmed. He selected the knife both for the quality of the workmanship and the knowledge, gained from experience, that he could conceal the weapon on his person without difficulty. He regretted the loss of his Italian stiletto, almost as much as the Spanish documents that were lost at sea, and vowed to find a similar blade in the future. Harvey could almost feel the touch of the stiletto's ebony handle as he slipped it between the Spaniard's ribs back in Havana. A voice in Harvey's head suggested he should feel ashamed, but he felt only satisfaction. He reckoned there would be time to take stock of his morals tomorrow, or the next day.

After eating a simple lunch in a familiar sailors' tavern, and resisting the tastier dishes offered on the second floor of the establishment,

Harvey walked over to the Fraser and Trenholm office on Rumsford Place, to see what Charles Prileau and company where up to. He hoped his initiative would impress Dr. Satterwhite and the Scotsman, when they met the following day. Harvey was familiar with the local office, having escorted Hank McCrary to meetings with Mr. Prileau during previous trips to Liverpool. He wasn't worried about being recognized, as he had never been allowed inside the building. Besides, the employees were raised in the American South and would pay him no more attention than any anonymous nigger back home, as long as he stayed quiet and looked like he knew his place. In any event, Liverpool hosted a sizable black population, so it would be easy to blend in on a street so close to the quays. After studying the area carefully, Harvey identified a favorable location to maintain his watch by moving a few steps up a small brick staircase, with a clear view of his objective on the opposite side of the street, further down the block. A pair of evergreen shrubs offering good screening from passersby, making it less likely anyone would notice a man sitting casually on the steps. Over the next hour or two, several carriages approached and a number of well-dressed men entered and exited the building, which featured a small pedestrian entrance and a large archway leading to an inner courtyard.

Harvey wasn't sure what he expected to see, but he felt the need to keep watch, anyway. No one seemed to note his presence and his patience was rewarded at about 4 pm, when

Charles Prileau emerged from the doorway, vigorously shaking the hand of a younger man. "Now that was curious!" Harvey thought to himself: Who was important enough to cause the head of Trenholm's local office to emerge from his lair, to offer a lavish show of respect for his visitor? Fortunately, Rumsford Place was relatively quiet at the moment, so Harvey was able to catch some of their conversation:

"It was a pleasure to meet you, Mr. Bullock!" Prileau's remarks were easy to follow, as he spoke with authority and was facing in Harvey's general direction. "I wish you and the Cromwell Steamship Company success in your venture, and I'm certain we'll need your services in the future." Harvey couldn't follow Bullock's response, as the younger man's back was turned towards him.

His curiosity piqued, Harvey decided to learn what he could. The stranger was well-dressed, but not showy enough to be an Englishman, Harvey decided. His height and build were average, with dark brown hair, a full mustache and muttonchops whiskers. He appeared to be about 35 years old and dressed in civilian clothes, although he projected a military bearing. He carried a cane, which the stranger moved about in a subdued fashion, more like an American than an English dandy. Harvey followed a half block back, sometimes staying on the opposite side of the street. Once or twice he lost contact, when larger carriages blocked his view, but he always managed to reacquire his subject. After ten blocks or so, skirting north along a path parallel to the harbor, Harvey's efforts were rewarded: The mysterious stranger entered a door below a large sign marked, "John Laird and Sons, Shipbuilders."

Alright then, Harvey thought to himself. The man's name is Bullock. That's easy to remember. He works for Cromwell Steamship Company. I've heard of 'em, they run most of the coastal steamers from Charleston up to Philadelphia and New York. He's visiting a shipbuilding company. So, I suppose Cromwell wants to buy some steamships. Well, that's something I didn't know this morning!

Before Harvey could decide his next move, Bullock emerged from the Laird company building in a rush and continued walking east on a side street that should take him over to Old Hall. Rather than running to catch up, which might attract unwanted attention, Harvey decided to take a short cut along a parallel road, where he hoped to require his target. Sure enough, Harvey reached the next block in time to observe Bullock moving north up a quiet street lined with empty wagons. Harvey held back for a moment, trying to decide if he should follow, when four men emerged from the shadows and surrounded Bullock. The stranger immediately pulled a long, narrow blade from the staff of his cane and adopted the stance of a man who knew how to fight with a sword, with his left hand behind his back and the blade held up in the classic style. He checked the balance of the blade by slicing the air twice, making a swooshing sound that was audible down the street.

The four assailants kept their distance but didn't back off, circling Bullock as they swung their clubs and gathered their courage for a coordinated attack. In a rush, they were on him: No matter which way Bullock turned, at least one man danced behind him, ready to land a quick blow. Bullock managed to run his blade through one man's thigh, but he lost his grip on the handle when he was clubbed on the back the head, and dropped to the ground when he was struck on the back of his left knee. Dazed but determined, Bullock rolled in an attempt to evade his attackers.

Without giving it a thought, Harvey ran directly at Bullock's assailants, shouting at the top of his lungs. One of the men turned and ran, but the remaining assailants faced Harvey, spreading out in their customary fashion. Harvey faked a move toward the smaller of the two men, a wiry looking ferret wearing a merchant sailor's clothes, before ducking under a killing blow from the larger man, who sported a full beard hanging over a thick torso. Spinning on the balls of his feet, Harvey drove the tip of his German knife into the back of the bearded man's head, killing him instantly. Before he could remove the knife and turn around, the ferret managed to land a blow on Harvey's shoulder, leaving his right arm stunned and temporarily useless. Harvey left his knife in the dead man's skull and used his left arm to block a second blow from his attacker, whose drooling grin emitted a piggish squeal as Bullock pushed his cane-blade all the way through the sailor's torso and out the other side.

The squealing continued until Bullock withdrew his blade and drove the point into the pig's throat, silencing him.

Bullock dropped to his knees, his head still spinning from the first blow to his head. The attacker with the leg wound tried to scramble away and called for help from his cowardly accomplice. Harvey followed the man calmly, shaking the pain out of his right shoulder, before reaching down to strike him on the back of the head with the butt of his dagger. He watched for a moment, trying to decide if he should cut the man's throat or bandage his leg. In the end, Harvey decided to let him bleed.

Still wondering why he had bothered to save the man called Bullock, Harvey turned to survey the scene. As far as he could tell, no one had witnessed the incident, and he didn't want to hang around until someone else showed up.

"We'd best move on, Suh, before anyone sees us." Harvey insisted with a soft Carolina accent, as he helped Bullock to his feet.

"Never thought I'd be so happy to see a nigger in Liverpool!" Bullock responded with a sharper accent, using the only honorific he gave any black man. Dusting himself off and reaching around to collect his hat and his cane-sheath, he continued:

"The names Bulloch, with an "H." James Bulloch, from Georgia."

Harvey knew better than to offer his hand, but he didn't want to offend a man he'd just saved, as the Scotsman had tutored him on the need to cultivate good relations with subjects of potential interest.

"The name's Harvey, John Harvey, from Charleston. I's a free man now, but my master was Hank McCrary. I work for his son, Martin, now."

"Well I'll be damned!" Bulloch responded. "I know Hank McCrary, he's a fine man, none better! Never met his son, though, but...wait a minute," he continued, as they worked their way down the street and around a corner. "I heard Martin McCrary's name just the other day, at the train station. You must be the house nigger he saved from the sharks, after the *Central America* Sank! I'll be damned, read all about that in the papers, everyone's talking about it!"

"Yes Suh, that's me." Harvey knew he would learn more if he shut up and listened.

"Why, that's the biggest story in the world right now, the loss of the *Central America*. I'm a former naval officer myself and would like to hear your master's story, first hand. Where's young McCrary staying? I need to meet him, so I can thank him properly for your service."

Although he was widely respected as a thoughtful, intelligent man, it never occurred to Bulloch that Harvey could tell the *Central America*'s story himself, or that he should thank a black man for saving him from a beating and a robbery, or worse. Blacks served whites and that was that, as God intended.

Harvey understood all that. Once again, he would bide his time and make his presence felt when the opportunity arose. Putting on his best, "aw shucks" manner, Harvey responded exactly the way Bulloch expected from a well-trained servant, freeman or not.

"He's staying at the Angel Hotel, over by the Town Hall." Harvey didn't make eye contact, but lowered his head a bit and shuffled his feet in mock respect.

"All right then!" Bulloch responded, feeling comfortable. "Run tell your master what happened here and tell him I'd like to pay him a call this evening. Here's my card."

"Yes Suh, right away Suh!" Every little humiliation and indignity added fuel to the fire raging in Harvey's heart. He knew one man couldn't tear down the South, all by himself, but he might achieve that lofty goal, with help from powerful allies.

Harvey raised a knuckle to his forehead, as he had seen many sailors do when showing respect to their officers, and turned to walk back to Martin's hotel. Not wanting to reveal his ability to read, Harvey waited until he turned a corner before examining the card:

"James Dunwoody Bulloch, Lt. USN (retired), Cromwell Steamship Company, New York."

CHAPTER 14:
ST. GEORGE'S HALL

While Harvey was making his way back to the
Hotel, Martin was finishing up business with the
Small men, who had invited him to attend a
cultural event at St. George's Hall later that
evening. A group of local charitable organizations
had organized a recital and reception by the
daughters of some prominent families, to raise
monies for gutter children and helpless waifs
before Christmas. Martin accepted the invitation
immediately, although he had planned to pursue
other entertainments with Harvey that evening.
Over lunch, David Small had promised to send
over a proper tailcoat and accessories, as he and
Martin shared the same height and slight build.

By the time Martin returned to the Angel
Hotel, a package containing his evening attire
was waiting for him at the front desk. The black
wool tailcoat sported matching silk buttons and

facings. The dark wool trousers Martin wore with his everyday frock coat would have to do, until he could order a complete evening ensemble of his own during their stay in Liverpool. Martin looked forward to the outing, as he had never met an Englishwoman younger than his mother. He wondered if they might be different from the Southern girls he tried to avoid back home, with their artificial manners and empty conversation. When Harvey returned, Martin was already dressing for the evening. Harvey made a show of dusting off Martin's shoulders and admiring his borrowed tailcoat before recounting the incident with Mr. Bulloch, which he described as a chance encounter.

"I'm surprised you didn't slit the wounded man's throat!" Martin exclaimed, "He deserved nothing better, and I doubt you would have been so charitable back home!"

"A moment of weakness." Harvey responded, shrugging his shoulders. "I figured two dead men was enough for one day. The two who survived won't be talking, 'cause theirs was a hanging offense!"

"I hope your streak of good luck continues, Harvey, but you'd better stay away from the harbor for the rest of our stay—someone might recognize you."

Martin was genuinely worried about Harvey's safety—and he knew he would need the big man's help during the rest of their journey.

"I suppose it will be more difficult to find a suitable whorehouse, now, as they are usually clustered near the harbor" Martin wondered aloud, trying not to sound peevish.

"Plenty of fine establishments lay on the east side of town, near Lime Street station, if you can find the time!" Harvey needed a drink and a woman himself but preferred not to use his own money.

"I'll leave a note with the front desk," Martin said, "inviting Mr. Bulloch to meet me for for lunch tomorrow. You'll be busy helping Dr. Satterwhite, so I might as well make Bulloch's acquaintance. After our obligations are fulfilled, let's visit the train station tomorrow evening!"

With the original basis of their friendship reaffirmed, Martin trotted off downstairs and found David Small in the lobby, with a small carriage waiting outside. The journey up Victoria Street was pleasant, with gas lights illuminating a broad avenue leading to Queen's Square. David Small instructed the coachman to drop them around the corner, to avoid waiting in a long line of carriages. Martin's view was blocked by a line of trees, until they crossed the street and reached an open plaza. Martin gasped audibly, as David took him by the arm and hurried toward their objective.

St. George's Hall was majestic, one of the finest neoclassical buildings in the world. The glorious structure was only three years old but seemed rooted in the ground, as if it had stood at that location for ages. David led Martin up the broad stone steps towards a set of massive bronze doors, marked in Roman style with the letters "SPQL," which David explained stood for

"The Senate and People of Liverpool." The main entrance overlooked the square, known locally as St. George's Plateau. The two young men paused for a moment, enjoying the view. Lime Street station was located across the way, with its curved iron roof and innumerable glass panels. The scene was remarkable.

"Will you be taking the train to London?" David asked. "It's a splendid journey!"

"I won't know until I hear from Father," Martin responded wistfully, "I'm hoping he'll release the necessary funds, although I imagine Mother will insist I return before Christmas."

Catching the discontented tone in Martin's voice, David asked:

"Do you ever wish you could be your own man, free to make your own decisions, without waiting for permission from your father? If so, we're rowing the same boat!"

Instinctively, David understood he could cultivate a friendship with Martin by identifying shared concerns. In this case, his question was sincere and the frustration was heartfelt.

"Hum," Martin began, recognizing a kindred spirit: "You understand my situation precisely. I suppose the two of us are indentured servants, really, pledged to our familial patriarchs!"

"Ah, but your prospects are brighter, as you don't have an older brother!" David responded with a grimace. Neither David nor Martin knew Harvey was Hank McCrary's oldest son, but that wouldn't have made any difference in either society.

"True enough," Martin admitted, "but Old Hank is tough as nails, likely to live forever!"

Both men shared a laugh and nods of mutual understanding. With the connection established, David changed the subject:

"Let's forget about work, tonight! Nothing in London can match St. George's Hall, and nothing should be allowed to spoil such a fine evening!" David was rightly proud of his city's finest attraction.

When the crowd at the main entrance slackened a bit, David led Martin inside, across the lobby and on to the man concert hall. Martin's heart skipped a beat as he admired the spectacle: The tunneled vault was 82' high, supported by polished red granite columns. The ceiling was decorated with paneled plasterwork depicting allegorical figures of the virtues, sciences and the arts. Looking down, Martin discovered he was standing on an impossibly elaborate tile floor. Distracted by the mosaics, the American was barely able to follow David's words as he explained how the tiles were normally protected by a portable wooden floor, which was removed on special occasions such as this. Razing his eyes, Martin found himself looking at a pair of lovely young ladies, gazing with amusement at the bumpkin who had obviously never seen the hall before. David recognized one of the women immediately.

"Come on, let me introduce you!" He insisted, leading Martin by the elbow.

"Good evening, ladies, Miss Ryder. Please allow me to introduce my American friend,

231

Martin McCrary. His family is very prominent in South Carolina."

"A pleasure, I'm sure." Miss Rebecca Ryder was a pretty young lady, the daughter of a successful tobacco importer who attended the same Anglican church as the Smalls. She wore her strawberry blond hair tied up behind her head and covered, highlighting her delicate features. She acknowledged David and smiled at Martin before continuing:

"Allow me to introduce my friend, Jane Jevons. She comes from a literary family." Miss Ryder stood to one side as she gestured toward her friend, who nodded confidently in Martin's direction before turning to David, who dipped his head politely as they exchanged pleasantries.

The American was speechless. He was already feeling rather small, having just entered St. George's Hall. How could a single Englishwoman overshadow such magnificence? Martin's cheeks flushed as he admired Jane surreptitiously, as she chatted cheerfully with Rebecca and David. She had the largest eyes he had ever seen, warm and wise and mysterious. She was no man's idea of a traditional beauty, but the hard angles of her face were softened by luminescent skin that seemed to glow with vitality. An infinite variety of auburn highlights added interest to that portion of her luxurious brown hair revealed by a delicate covering of ivory fabric. Martin struggled to avoid staring at the perfection of her neck and shoulders, which hinted at an unusual athleticism, reminding him of a statue of the goddess Diana. Her poise and posture projected quiet self-confidence, with no trace of pretense.

Martin noticed a spark of mischief in Jane's eyes, as she glanced in his direction before speaking:

"Gentlemen, did you know the great Charles Dickens is here this evening? If we hurry, we should be able to catch the last moments of a public reading, in the small concert hall. He's a wonderful philanthropist and always makes an effort to attend charitable events such as ours."

David struggled to hide his discomfort, as his father loathed Dickens, whom he condemned as a dangerous radical. And there was the matter of his abolitionist views, which might offend Martin.

Before David could think of a suitable objection, Rebecca spoke up.

"That's a brilliant idea, Jane. Come, gentlemen, we must hurry!"

With their youthful enthusiasm tempered by a sense of propriety, the two ladies lead David and Martin down a long corridor to a more intimate concert hall, elliptical in shape. The room was crowded, but the four young people managed to find a place to the right of the stage, with a reasonably good view of an energetic middle-aged man sporting a long mustache and matching goatee.

"There he is!" Rebecca whispered as they gathered together. The crowd was hushed, anticipating the famous author's next words.

233

A young lady standing near their group provided some helpful orientation, in a soft voice:

"He's reading from Little Dorrit!"

Rebecca reached out appreciatively to touch the girl's arm in thanks.

Dickens' voice was clear and precise:

"A person who can't pay gets another person who can't pay, to guarantee that he can pay. Like a person with two wooden legs getting another person with two wooden legs, to guarantee that he has got two natural legs. It don't make either of them able to do a walking match."

The crowd laughed appreciatively, although some with a hint of nervousness in their voices, as the financial crisis was on everyone's minds.

Dickens continued reading in a voice that carried well, like an actor, with his volume enhanced by the room's superb acoustics:

"I am the only child of parents who weighed, measured, and priced everything; for whom what could not be weighed, measured, and priced, had no existence. Strict people as the phrase is, professors of a stern religion, their very religion was a gloomy sacrifice of tastes and sympathies that were never their own, offered up as a part of a bargain for the security of their possessions. Austere faces, inexorable discipline, penance in this world and terror in the next—nothing graceful or gentle anywhere, and the void in my cowed heart everywhere—this was my childhood."

The crowd murmured appreciatively, but only a few scions of the upper class laughed, as Dicken's words awakened feelings of superiority directed at Liverpool's grasping merchants.

Ending on a hopeful note, Dickens concluded with the following passage:

"And thus ever, by day and night, under the sun and under the stars, climbing the dusty hills and toiling along the weary plains, journeying by land and journeying by sea, coming and going so strangely, to meet and to act and react on one another, move all we restless travelers through the pilgrimage of life."

The crowd responded with enthusiastic applause and polite nods of approval. Dickens smiled and bowed in response, before returning to the center of the stage and gesturing for quiet. A beautiful young lady stepped to his side and spoke in a clear, ringing voice.

"Mr. Dickens would be pleased to take a request from the crowd, for one final reading."

"That's Miss Ellen Ternan, the actress from London! I'm afraid you missed her performance, a scene from a play, "The Frozen Deep." Isn't she lovely?" The helpful young lady whispered.

Martin recalled some of his favorite works, but could never bring himself to speak up in such circumstances. Secretly, he wished Harvey was at hand, as he was by far the greater authority on Dickens. "What an odd thought, but true!" Martin admitted to himself.

Other members of the audience weren't so shy, and several made requests, but Dickens

235

seemed to be waiting for a passage that moved him. Much to Martin's surprise, Jane offered a suggestion of her own:

"Please, Sir, read something from your American Notes, as there is at least one Southern gentleman in the room and he would surely treasure your wisdom!"

Dicken's eyes lit up in response to Jane's request, not the least because it was offered by a woman almost as beautiful as his companion, Miss Ternan.

"Yes, of course—my American Notes. With pleasure!" Dickens nodded as he turned to retrieve one of the heavy volumes resting on a bookcase at back of the stage. After flipping through the pages, Dickens cleared his voice and took a sip of water from a glass offered by Miss Ternan. His posture became more erect and his tone more serious as he repeated the words he wrote in 1842:

"The upholders of slavery in America—of the atrocities of which system, I shall not write one word for which I have not had ample proof and warrant—may be divided into three great classes."

"The first, are those more moderate and rational owners of human cattle, who have come into the possession of them as so many coins in their trading capital, but who admit the frightful nature of the Institution in the abstract, and perceive the dangers to society with which it is fraught: dangers which however distant they may be, or howsoever tardy in their coming on, are as certain to fall upon its guilty head, as is the Day of Judgment."

"The second, consists of all those owners, breeders, users, buyers and sellers of slaves, who will, until the bloody chapter has a bloody end, own, breed, use, buy, and sell them at all hazards: who doggedly deny the horrors of the system in the teeth of such a mass of evidence as never was brought to bear on any other subject, and to which the experience of every day contributes its immense amount; who would at this or any other moment, gladly involve America in a war, civil or foreign, provided that it had for its sole end and object the assertion of their right to perpetuate slavery, and to whip and work and torture slaves, unquestioned by any human authority, and unassailed by any human power; who, when they speak of Freedom, mean the Freedom to oppress their kind, and to be savage, merciless, and cruel; and of whom every man on his own ground, in republican America, is a more exacting, and a sterner, and a less responsible despot than the Caliph Haroun Al-Raschid in his angry robe of scarlet."

"The third, and not the least numerous or influential, is composed of all that delicate gentility which cannot bear a superior, and cannot brook an equal; of that class whose Republicanism means, 'I will not tolerate a man above me: and of those below, none must approach too near;' whose pride, in a land where voluntary servitude is shunned as a disgrace, must be ministered to by slaves; and whose inalienable rights can only have their growth in negro wrongs."

The reaction from the crowd was mixed. Any critique of the upstart Americans was bound to stir the heart of an Englishman, but the merchants of Liverpool knew their prosperity depending on cotton and cotton depended on the institution of slavery. The room was divided between those who accepted this reality and those who hated slavery with a passion. In Liverpool, at least, many of the most fervent abolitionists were hard-headed apples falling from the Presbyterian branch of the Reformation tree.

Jane Jevons was a member of the latter group, which applauded vigorously. David Small was not.

"Miss Jevons!" David said, with an accusing tone. "How could you? Mr. McCrary is a friend of my family and has done you no harm!"

"Please, Mr. Small, I'm sure Mr. McCrary can defend himself, if he chooses. I recognize his surname—isn't his father one of the largest slave owners in America?"

Martin was hurt, far more than he could show, not because he was stung by Dickens, but because he was so badly taken with Jane Jevons.

"Don't worry, David, I'm not in the least offended by his words, which sound exactly like the sentiments of my Grandfather, an abolitionist pastor and the best man I know. Think nothing of it."

Jane was surprised and a bit ashamed of herself, although she didn't show it. Rebecca was more certain in her assessment, as she admired David Small and didn't wish to offend his family.

"You have a generous heart, Mr. McCrary, unlike my friend Jane. When it comes to political opinion, she's a bit of a radical, like her Grandfather, William Roscoe."

With those words, the two ladies bid farewell and moved back toward the main hall. Rebecca's posture suggested she was still chastising her friend, who continued to hold her head high.

"Of course!" David exclaimed, "Now I can place her: Jane Jevons is the granddaughter of William Roscoe, a leading figure in Liverpool before he died, and a rare abolitionist of the most radical variety." David hoped the encounter didn't spoil the evening or sour his budding friendship with Martin.

"I thought she was delightful and refreshingly outspoken." Martin was only beginning to understand his appreciation for strong women, as his own mother was loving but weak and inclined to nervousness, dominated as she was by a controlling husband.

"Ah, I suspected as much: You're under her spell! Jane is striking it's true, but far too independent for my tastes. Her friend Rebecca is superior in every way!" David asserted.

"Surely both ladies are exceptional? I would be heart-broken indeed if the ladies back home compared so poorly to English girls, in every example!" Martin's compliment was heartfelt and his mind began to consider how he might arrange to meet Jane again.

Before the two young men could turn and follow the crowd back to the majestic main hall, they were approached by an older man:

"Well if it isn't Master Small! How is your father?" The man spoke with a New England accent. He appeared to be about 50 years old, with a vigorous bearing.

"Mr. Hawthorne—I'm surprised to see you, as I believed you had left Liverpool behind!"

David shook the American's hand vigorously, pleased to be recognized by one of his father's more important acquaintances, Nathaniel Hawthorne. For several years, the great writer had served as Consul in Liverpool, the second most prestigious post for American diplomats, after the Ambassador in London.

"That's true enough. My term ended when President Pierce left office in March of this year, but I couldn't miss a reading by Dickens himself! My family and I have been touring your beautiful island since April, and we're off to France and Italy next week. But enough about me: Is this the Southern gentleman the young lady spoke of, when she made her request?" The older man turned to face Martin.

"Of course, pardon me. Allow me to introduce Martin McCrary. I'm sure you know his father, Hank McCrary of South Carolina. Martin, this is Nathaniel Hawthorne, a writer no less gifted than our Mr. Dickens—and the American Consul in Liverpool until this Spring."

Martin reached over and shook hands with the second famous man he had seen in one day.

240

"Yes, of course—The Scarlet Letter! My father spoke very highly of you," Martin continued politely, "as he shared your enthusiasm for President Pierce."

"At times it seems I wear the Scarlet Letter, myself, as that book seems to be the first thing that comes to everyone's mind upon first acquaintance!" Hawthorne displayed a self-effacing sense of humor and used it to good effect in putting the younger men at ease.

"Your and I father met several times over the years, most recently during his last trip to Liverpool. Our backgrounds are diverse, as I hail from New Hampshire, but we share many of the same concerns." Hawthorne was well spoken, with only the hint of a politician in his voice.

"It seems radicals are thriving on both sides of the Atlantic!" David Small suggested.

"Indeed!" Hawthorne agreed. "The abolitionists are a small but vocal minority here in Liverpool. The leading men of the city are more pragmatic, as they understand the commercial ties that sustain our mutual prosperity. The truth be told, however, it's not just the abolitionists who pose a threat to the Union, in their headlong rush to destroy the delicate balance that holds our country together. A growing minority of opinion among prominent Englishmen suggests the British Empire would be better off if our United States divided themselves into two or perhaps three sovereign nations. The more precarious the political situation back home, the more popular this opinion becomes."

"I've heard such talk, myself!" David interjected, "but Father says it's all rubbish."

"The opinion is real enough, and I've spent much of the last six months trying to tamp down this foolish notion, making the case that there is far more binding the United States together than dividing us. President Pierce devoted himself entirely to preserving the Union through prudence and moderation. I fear his contribution has been greatly underestimated by his own people," Hawthorne concluded, with genuine sadness for his dear friend.

Responding to some hidden contrarian instinct, Martin offered a challenge:

"My father was a supporter of President Pierce, but he feels the Kansas-Nebraska Act was a disaster. Allowing the settlers to decide the issue of slavery has ignited a war, with thousands of men pouring over the border in an effort to swing the elections to one side or the other. Father feels the President was weak, enabling the abolitionists to gain a foothold and a battle cry in Kansas."

"I see you're an educated young man, and well informed. How inspiring!" Hawthorne enjoyed a vigorous debate and would have made a fine professor. He took to his rostrum:

"Speaking for myself, I believe the murderous abolitionists committing atrocities in Kansas are a great threat to the Republic. Your father and I agree on that issue. Regarding President Pierce's decision to support local sovereignty on the issue of slavery in the new territories, do you imagine the results would have been better if the decision had been left to Congress? Do you recall what happened last year, when Congressman Brooks nearly killed Senator Sumner over his abolitionist views, on the floor of the Senate itself? No, we need prudent, practical men like President Pierce to navigate our differences. There are more than enough radicals on both sides of this debate!"

"Your argument is persuasive!" Martin conceded. "I've met Congressman Brooks, he hails from my home state and I wouldn't trust him to settle an argument peacefully, even when sober!"

In an effort to steer the conversation away from politics, David Small offered a question of his own:

"What can you tell us about the young lady, Jane Jevons?" He asked Hawthrone. "I fear my friend is smitten!"

"Was I that obvious?" Martin asked cheerfully, ignoring any sense of embarrassment he may have felt, as he was eager to learn more about Jane.

"Ah, Ms. Jevons! Yes, she makes quite an impression." Hawthorne placed two fingers on his chin as he accessed his extraordinary memory for character and personality. "Let's see, her mother was a famous beauty, Mary Anne Roscoe, the daughter of the late great William Roscoe. Doubtless you won't be surprised to learn Mr. Roscoe was a prominent abolitionist; much to his credit, he was also an early supporter of independence for the American colonies, with his friends Thomas Coke and Charles Fox. Roscoe's favorite daughter, Mary Anne, married Thomas Jevons, a successful iron merchant. Somehow she found the time to write a collection of the most delicate poetry. Sadly, the stress of giving birth to 11 children ruined Mrs. Jevon's health and she died some years ago, leaving Jane and her siblings without a mother. All of the children received an excellent education. I hold Miss Jevons' brother William in high regard; they say he is one of the most promising mathematicians England has ever produced."

As Martin listened, his esteem for Jane Jevons was reinforced. His own family entertained no intellectual pretensions, although he had enjoyed the benefits of a decent education at Davidson College. He felt a sense of shame when he remembered how he had always concealed his passion for poetry, as his father who had no patience for such pursuits. He was struck by the revelation that Jane's mother had written poetry admired by Hawthorne himself. He wondered if Jane shared her mother's inclination, and found himself burning with desire to read something, anything she had written. Martin imagined he shared much in common with the beautiful young Englishwoman, as both of their families were Presbyterian and his mother's father was no less an abolitionist than her famous grandfather.

"You have a most prodigious memory, Mr. Hawthrone!" David exclaimed. "I'm afraid to ask what insights you might offer on Ms. Ryder!"

Nathaniel Hawthorne took David by the arm and walked with him toward the main concert hall, followed by Martin.

"Your question causes me to reflect on the most delightful thing about my years in Liverpool." Hawthorne continued energetically, "I've assembled the most delightful cast of characters to support my writing—all protected, of course, by the anonymity of colorful pseudonyms!"

Hawthorne's enthusiasm was infectious. Both of the young men were reluctant to part ways when the writer's attention was distracted by other acquaintances. Coming after all of his experiences since the sinking of the *Central America*, the evening had a remarkable effect on Martin, shaking his assumptions about the future. He was forced to consider the possibility that he had more choices than he ever imagined. He dared wonder if could pursue a fate beyond that ordained by his father, if he could rise above the soul-killing world of profit, if he could learn to write poetry worth reading, if he could avoid an arranged marriage and find true love, if he could choose a life for himself.

Dazed, confused and a bit overwhelmed, Martin was happy to be alive, for one night in Liverpool. His heart was on fire, his imagination soared and his spirit was set free.

It would be hard to go home after that.

CHAPTER 15:
THE SPYMASTER

When Harvey emerged from the Angel Hotel on Wednesday morning, he was intercepted by a tall figure emerging from the shadows as soon as he rounded the first corner down the street.

"It's good to see you again, Harvey."

Dr. Satterwhite was dressed for the outdoors, wearing sturdy boots and a wool cloak. His face was partially concealed by a long scarf and a low-brimmed hat.

"Pardon the surprise. Given everything at stake, I thought it best if we avoid advertising our connection. Liverpool is not friendly to our cause." The physician gripped Harvey's hand as he spoke.

"I understand, Michael." Harvey acknowledged, pleased to see his friend and accomplice. "Are we off to see the Scotsman this morning?"

"Indeed we are, but not in the city! Too many prying eyes and loose tongues! Here, try these."

The Englishman offered Harvey a sturdy bowler hat and a dark cloak of his own, which were warmly received, given the chill in the air.

In a moment, Harvey was ready and Dr. Satterwhite led the way, with long-legged strides and a deceptively fast pace that warmed both men quickly. The companions walked north and east, turning left and right and left again until they reached a broad boulevard, where they hailed an open carriage. Michael positioned himself on the bench directly behind the coachman, with a view to the rear, to see if anyone was following. After continuing along the boulevard for 20 minutes or so, Michael instructed the coachman to stop at a location just around a sharp curve in the road, where they would be invisible to anyone moving more than two blocks behind them. At that point along the boulevard, there were no options for a carriage or wagon to reverse course, as the narrow park running down the middle of the road was lined with shrubs and a low fence. Michael gave the coachman a generous tip and led Harvey directly across the street, jumping the fence and crossing the narrow park to reach the far side of the boulevard. Michael paid close attention to a pair of horsemen moving along a bridal path, but decided they posed no threat when they turned their horses and moved in a different direction.

From the far side of the boulevard, Michael guided Harvey through a maze of narrow streets and lanes, cutting through a series of poorly tended gardens and abandoned yards. Harvey had to suppress a laugh when Michael dealt with a pair of barking dogs by tossing them a few scraps of dried meat he kept in his pocket, for that express purpose. After a series of turns and maneuvers, they approached a stable located behind an ancient inn on Brunswick Road. The stable boy waited at the entrance, with two sturdy-looking horses, saddled and ready for the road.

"Can we expect you back before nightfall?" The stable boy asked. "The innkeeper will double his fee if you brings 'em back after dark, all wet and hobbly!"

"As promised!" Michael answered cheerfully, placing a few pennies in the boy's hands. "Your horses as in good hands—we'll bring them back well before sunset, fresh as ponies!

Harvey's heart soared as he mounted the mare, a chestnut with ivory socks and and a splash of white paint on it's face. The animal seemed to sense his energy and enthusiasm and danced in place for a moment. The two men started out slowly, allowing the horses to warm up before pressing the pace, giving free reign along empty stretches of roadway and slowing to a walk when they approached a farmer's cart or a tradesman's wagon. They spoke very little, embracing the simple pleasures of a ride in the country, enhanced by the inimitable view from the back of a horse. A soft shower passed quickly, leaving little droplets of water glistening on the

249

chestnut's ears and eyelashes. The companions paused long enough for the horses to take a drink from a clear running stream.

"We're almost there!" Dr. Satterwhite remarked, as they continued up the winding road to the crest of a treeless hill. When they reached the top, both men stopped to admire the view. A fine brick mansion sat in a deep green valley, surrounded by manicured gardens, immaculate groves and well-maintained fields. The sunlight reflected off the surface of a small lake, brightening an otherwise grey day.

"Croxteth Hall." Michael said simply. "The Earl is a friend of the Scotsman. He's waiting for us in the warden's cottage.

Both men were eager to see Sir Ian McDonald again, to share the results of their collaboration and to seek his guidance. Nevertheless, they didn't rush down the hill but allowed their horses to walk at a natural pace along a series of lanes until they reached a tidy cottage, screened from the north winds by a stand of dense evergreens. As they dismounted, their reigns were taken by a fierce looking man of early middle age wearing a leather hunting jacket and a soldier's bearing.

"It's good to see you again, Dr. Satterwhite. He's expecting you."

"Thank you, Tom. Harvey, this is Sargent Tom Bowler, Sir Ian's man. You can trust him with your life, as Sir Ian has done for many a year."

Sgt. Bowler didn't hesitate when Harvey extended his hand. Both characters were satisfied with the exchange, a firm greeting between powerful men. Tom took Harvey's measure with an appreciative smile and turned to walk the horses around back to a small stable, where they were gently brushed down and allowed to rest. Harvey's chestnut snorted a greeting to a pair of fine horses already housed in the stable, the mounts used by Sir Ian and Sgt. Bowler when they rode down from the mansion.

Michael opened the front door of the cottage and found Sir Ian sitting by the fire. He looked older and frailer than last they met, but his eyes blazed with intelligence as he rose to greet them.

"Aha, Michael and Harvey together! I've never seen a more unlikely pair of conspirators!"

Sir Ian McDonald was a wealthy man, the owner of several estates and well respected by his peers. Still, he was restless, single-minded in pursuit of his work and filled with a desire to accomplish more with his life, before he grew too old and sick to be effective.

"I was afraid you didn't receive my letters, until your messenger turned up at my hostel yesterday!" Dr. Satterwhite took both of Sir Ian's hands in his own, smiling broadly.

"Received them I did, with great enthusiasm! I had to decode and read both letters twice, to believe my eyes. Somehow you found Harvey on the open ocean, after he survived a cyclone and a shipwreck, only to discover your mutual connections and establish a partnership—marvelous!"

251

Sir Ian turned to face Harvey, whose heart was filled with concern as he imagined the old man must be ill, having aged so much since their last encounter, a little more than a year ago. The concern showed plainly on Harvey's face.

"Don't worry about me!" Sir Ian demanded, as he embraced Harvey firmly, in a show of genuine affection. "God willing, I have some years left to serve, before my days are done!"

Harvey's eyes welled up, as he embraced an Englishman who had treated him like a son, when his own sire wrapped his fatherhood in secret shame and kept his mother and sister in bondage.

"Now then!" Sir Ian continued, stepping back to admire Harvey and Dr. Satterwhite. "It does my heart good to see the two of you together, but there'll be no business until we've taken refreshment!"

Gesturing across the room, Sir Ian invited his friends to take a seat at a table under a south-facing window, which offered natural lighting for their meal. Sgt. Bowler appeared and filled their pewter bowls with venison stew and their cups with ale, returning moments later with a platter of sliced bread and butter. The three men tucked into their meal with relish. When finished, Harvey described the sinking of the *Central America*, his encounter with Martin and their rescue by the Birkenhead, leaving nothing out. Sir Ian laughed when Harvey described the theft and subsequent loss of the massive gold ingot, tossed overboard by Martin when the Birkenhead approached. Dr. Satterwhite was shocked.

"I can only imagine what might have happened, if the Captain had found that ingot when the two of you were recovered!" Dr. Satterwhite exclaimed, with a pained tone in his voice. He was troubled more by the omission in his previous conversations with Harvey than he was by the theft itself, as he had found several gold coins sewn into the waistband of the black man's trousers when treating his wounds.

"Harvey has always shown remarkable initiative!" Sir Ian offered with a laugh, "but so has young Martin McCrary! Imagine the presence of mind, recognizing the need to throw the offending object overboard, least it be discovered and his servant hanged!"

Harvey was embarrassed, but relieved to find his confession had not lowered his value in Sir Ian's eyes. The Scotsman continued to laugh, as he winked at Harvey and elbowed Michael in the ribs, until both men joined him in a round of uncontrolled laughter.

"I'd like to learn more about Martin," Sir Ian admitted, after taking a long drink from his pewter cup. "Why do you suppose he felt the need to protect you? Has he discovered your father's secret?"

Sir Ian looked thoughtfully at Harvey, with icy blue eyes and an unflinchingly honest expression framed by a full head of grey hair and a dense white beard. He wore a wool hunting jacket with leather trim over a pair of jodhpurs and riding boots, which slid on the floor as he leaned forward.

Harvey answered without hesitation:

"No, Sir—he's clueless. I'm not sure how he would react, if he learned the son of a slave woman is his older brother. We grew up together, and I always served him well, but some distance grew between us when he went off to college and I was freed by our father. He seemed to resent my change of status, but didn't reject my service when Mr. McCrary sent us off to San Francisco."

Harvey cleaned his bowl with a heal of bread, waiting for the inevitable questions.

"Tell me," Sir Ian asked: "What effect has his Grandfather had on his upbringing? I remember you said he spent several summers with Reverend Coulter, up in the mountains of North Carolina."

"That's true, and the old gentleman continues to move every slave I bring him along the road to freedom, with help from his friends up North. One thing's for sure: I'm confident Martin admires his Grandfather, who's so unlike his father, but he's never been one to talk about the source of his family's wealth or his status as the only heir to a great fortune."

"It's only a matter of time before the institution of slavery collapses, Harvey. The question is when and how violent the upheaval will be. That means the basis of the wealth Martin stands to inherit is unsound, like quicksand. I wonder if he understands that."

Sir Ian was a visionary, a man able to perceive patterns in the muddy ebb and flow of

254

history. He was also born with the gift of empathy, the ability to imagine what it would be like to walk in another man's shoes and to wonder how another man's world might be shaken by the patterns he perceived.

Harvey didn't answer the question, as he knew from experience when Sir Ian was wondering aloud, using the Socratic method to probe his own mind for answers.

"Well then," Sir Ian continued, "that demands an answer, but first we'll have to make sure he asks himself this question: What will happen to me when slavery is abolished? Now, it's time to share a confidence: I have my own source of intelligence on Martin McCrary, and I believe he could be a valuable asset in the future. Let me explain."

Adopting the matter-of-fact tone he used when discussing the most serious matters, Sir Ian described how he had been close to the famous abolitionist William Roscoe, when he was a young man. In fact, he had been close to Roscoe's favorite daughter, the beautiful poet Mary Anne, and at one time had hoped to marry her, but a wedding was forbidden by his own father, The McDonald of his day, as the Roscoes were commoners. A few years passed by and Mary Anne was pushed into an arranged marriage with an iron merchant named Jevons, after her father died. Some twenty years ago, in an act of love remembered, Mary Anne had asked Sir Ian to stand as Godfather for her daughter, Jane Jevons. When both of Jane's parents died,

Sir Ian assumed responsibility for her education and upbringing.

"I arranged for my goddaughter, Jane, to encounter Martin at St. George's Hall, during a charitable concert. She's staying with me over at Croxteth Hall, and has much to say." Sir Ian allowed the words to sink in, before continuing his story, without explaining exactly how he had arranged the encounter.

"I should tell you, my goddaughter has a brilliant mind and is blessed with patience and insight far beyond her 20 years. She believes Martin might be susceptible to recruitment, to join our enterprise, under the right circumstances. How would you feel about that, Harvey?"

For a moment, Harvey's head was set spinning, as he overcame his surprise and considered the implications. After pondering the question in silence, a clear path emerged in his mind:

"She may be right, Sir Ian." Harvey admitted, as he rubbed his palms on the tops of his thighs. "It seems to me I should play a role in this endeavor, for example by revealing our brotherhood and perhaps some aspects of my relationship with you."

Sir Ian felt a deep sense of pride in Harvey and never regretted the trust he had placed in him.

"There may be risks," Sir Ian admitted, "if he rejects my approach. If that happens, you won't be able to return to South Carolina."

"I can see that, Sir Ian." Harvey responded, "I would be reluctant to return, on my own account, if not for my mother and sister."

"I know, Harvey—your motivations have always been pure. I make this promise: If Martin rejects my proposal and you are unable to return to Charleston, I will use my private connections to secure freedom for your mother and sister, bringing them to the location of your choice. If Mr. McCrary refuses to sell them, out of spite or any other reason, I shall have them taken in secret and escorted safely to Reverend Coulter, no matter the cost."

"I know you're a man of your word, Sir Ian." Harvey continued, "but before I can take such a risk, I need you to help me understand why you believe Martin is so important."

"Of course, Harvey—you deserve as much."

The conversation continued as Sir Ian provided a concise assessment of the political situation in the United States, based on the unique insights he collected from numerous sources, including men who had fought in Bloody Kansas and others serving in the federal government in the District of Columbia.

"So I believe a civil war between free and slave states is inevitable, as there can be no peaceful solution." Sir Ian concluded. "The influence of the abolitionists will continue to grow, as they struggle to prevent the spread of slavery in the new territories, because their cause is just. Men on both sides of the argument have demonstrated a willingness to fight, in some cases resorting to the murder of innocents in Kansas. The voices arguing for secession grow louder, as does the response of their allies in England, some of whom occupy positions of real power and influence in London. We need men like Martin, with his powerful father and impeccable connections in the South, to be our eyes and ears, to keep us informed as the forces of secession gather for the coming conflict. His potential access to information of value is worth the risk, should armed conflict erupt in the future."

Harvey and Dr. Satterwhite sat and looked at one another for a few minutes, allowing Sir Ian's words to sink in. His words rang true, based on the things they already knew. Michael spoke first:

"Both of us have collected new intelligence that supports your assessment," the physician offered. "During our stay in Hamilton, I met with a man known to you, the ship-owner from Baltimore. He confided that he has been recruited by George Trenholm's associates to transport a large shipment of the latest Enfield rifles to South Carolina, for use by the local militia. Governor Murray in Bermuda stands behind this endeavor, with plans to supply more rifled muskets in the future, should South Carolina and the other slave states secede from the Union. These weapons could provide a decisive advantage on the battlefield, as they are far more accurate than any other muskets available in North America."

"It seems Trenholm has fully committed himself," Sir Ian observed. "I understand Hank McCrary is one of his closest associates in South Carolina."

"That's true, Sir Ian." Harvey interjected. Mr. Trenholm meets frequently with Mr. McCrary in Charleston, and Mr. Trenholm provided funds for Martin's outfitting and onward travel, when we were brought to Bermuda by the Birkenhead."

"As I suspected," Sir Ian responded, "the two men are allied in support of independence for South Carolina, to preserve slavery and the cotton trade. What else did you learn, Harvey?"

With a great deal of pride, Harvey reached into his jacket and presented a hand-written list of George Trenholm's contacts in London, specifically those who promised support from unnamed members of Parliament if the Southern states chose to secede from the Union. He described how he had obtained the list from Trenholm's private room at the American Consulate, while leaving no trace of his intrusion. Sir Ian poured over the list eagerly, mumbling to himself as he recognized many of the names.

"These men tried to be clever, by not providing the names of the specific MPs they represent, but their affiliations are well known to me. You have no idea how valuable this intelligence will be, as I marshal the forces needed to prevent Her Majesty's Government from taking sides in the coming conflict. I should admit, gentlemen, neutrality is the best we can hope for."

Sir Ian didn't mention the fact that one of the men on Harvey's list was a particular friend of Lord Palmerston, the Prime Minister himself. That connection was worrisome, and steeled the old man's determination to take decisive action, behind the scenes. His greatest ally was the institution of slavery itself, which was deeply unpopular in most of England, outside areas such as Liverpool and Manchester, which depended on the cotton trade for their prosperity. His first step would be the placement of a series of articles in English newspapers, highlighting atrocities committed by pro-slavery forces in Bloody Kansas, stretching the truth, if necessary. He also needed to exploit the jealousy of the merchants and bankers of London, who resented the advantage King Cotton gave their competitors in Liverpool

"There's more, Sir Ian." Harvey interjected. "A man who claimed to be a lieutenant in the Royal Navy approached me in Hamilton and requested my assistance, to report on the McCrary family and all things related to South Carolina. He also asked me to keep an eye on Dr. Satterwhite here, seeing as how he accepted the Governor's offer to serve as physician for the Colony." Harvey glanced over at Michael and grinned before continuing: "I acted the simpleton and accepted his proposal, assuming that might be useful to you in some way." Harvey hoped his decision was the correct one.

"Harvey and I compared notes, Sir Ian," Dr. Satterwhite continued, "and it seems likely the officer who approached Harvey is a certain Lieutenant Walter Tisdale. He works directly for Governor Murray and is involved in the arrangement to ship British arms to South Carolina."

The two men had Sir Ian's full attention.

"Michael, do me the favor of preparing a detailed written report on Tisdale, based on what you learned in Hamilton. I need to conduct some inquiries, but it seems safe to assume his sponsors extend well above Governor Murray, perhaps to certain admirals who favor secession for the Southern states. They foolishly see the United States as a competitor on the high seas rather than a potential ally against the other European powers." Sir Ian stopped a moment to ponder.

"Of course, Sir Ian." Dr. Satterwhite responded. "I should tell you, I met the Lieutenant at the Governor's reception and he struck me as no fool. I'll need to deal with him frequently in Bermuda."

"Yes, indeed, Michael. Accepting the Governor's offer was a brilliant move on your part, as Bermuda will likely to play a critical role in supplying arms and provisions to the Southern states."

Turning to Harvey, Sir Ian asked an obvious question:

"Did the lieutenant give you instructions regarding future contact?"

"Yes Sir, he did. I was directed to approach a certain door at the Admiralty office in Liverpool, where I was to ask for a Commander Wallace." Harvey wasn't eager to further entangle himself, but would take the first steps, if Sir Ian asked.

"Commander Wallace. Of course, that makes perfect sense." Sir Ian considered how much he should reveal to his companions, without putting his other contacts at risk. "The Commander is a dangerous opponent, and a trusted representative of that faction in the Admiralty which embraces the notion of a Disunited States of America. It's hard to believe, I know, but some senior officers in the Royal Navy, men older than myself, still resent the Rebellion by the American colonies, resentments that were nurtured when they were midshipmen in the War of 1812. "

Sir Ian took a moment to consider his options. Dr. Satterwhite would return to Hamilton soon, to keep an eye on Governor Murray and Lt. Tisdale. With help from other assets, the physician should be uniquely positioned to frustrate the opposition in Bermuda.

Commander Wallace was another matter.

"Listen, both of you: A double game can be difficult, but the gain may be worth the risk. We have time to make a decision, regarding any contact with Commander Wallace. I'll make some inquiries before our next meeting. In the meantime, we should focus on more pressing matters."

Sir Ian shifted in his chair before continuing:

"First, have you noticed anything unusual in Liverpool, Harvey? Has anyone attempted to follow you? Have you met anyone who seemed overly curious about you or Martin?"

Harvey considered all of the events since his arrival in Liverpool and could only think of one noteworthy incident: His encounter with James Bulloch and the Georgian's connection with the Cromwell Steamship Company and Laird Shipbuilding. He repeated the story for Sir Ian's benefit.

"That's useful information, Harvey. Please do let me know if you learn anything more about Bulloch." Sir Ian made a mental note to learn more about the American's contacts with Laird Shipbuilding, which was known to produce some of the most advanced steamships in the world.

"Now, let's turn to the matter at hand." Sir Ian continued. "I'm deeply grateful for your efforts in Hamilton, Harvey. The results speak for themselves. Still, I have to wonder, what could be accomplished if you and Martin worked together, as brothers?"

Harvey shifted uncomfortably in his chair but nodded for Sir Ian to continue.

"Take a moment to consider: What will happen to the slaves, to your mother and sister, if the Southern states secede and establish an independent nation, more dependent than ever on human bondage? How long would the leaders of such a nation perpetuate slavery? A hundred years or more? What if we could work together to prevent that from happening? Or failing that, to minimize the chances that a slave-owning nation could defeat a free nation in a bloody civil war?"

Sir Ian paused for a moment, before revealing more of his thinking.

"There's something else I must offer, in strictest confidence: I've forged a secret alliance with a group of prominent Americans, Republican men who share our concerns about the future. I plan to share much of the intelligence we acquire with those allies, hopefully to prevent secession and war, but barring that, to insure a Northern victory. Would you like to be a part of that?"

Sir Ian knew Harvey well, so the question was rhetorical. When they first met, Harvey was searching for meaning and purpose in his life, dissatisfied with the trivial pursuit of pleasure and feeling rather worthless. His work with Sir Ian had satisfied that need, and more. Now, he saw the cause was greater than he had imagined, with more at stake. Harvey had heard the talk about secession, listening to the hot-headed young men in Charleston as they prattled on about honor and glory. Until today, he hadn't known such talk should be taken seriously. For Harvey, the choice was easy: He couldn't imagine sitting out the conflict, living somewhere safe and comfortable, while his mother and sister languished in bondage and white men fought for the right to keep them as slaves.

"You know my answer, Sir Ian." Harvey responded, in a quiet voice. "I'm with you."

The Scotsman placed a hand on Harvey's shoulder.

"Then let's do this the right way, and make every move count!" Sir Ian inspired loyalty in the men and women who worked for him, by harnessing their hearts to worthy objectives.

The discussion continued for another hour or so, as the conspirators made arrangements for the approach to Martin, carefully laying the groundwork to improve their chances for success. Harvey felt no guilt, in betraying the son of his former master—or the father they shared in common. He believed a partnership with Martin was in the boy's best interest, to prepare him for the coming chaos and inevitable changes in his life. The longer they talked, the more Harvey believed the plan would work, as he recognized Martin's need to rebel against their tyrannical father. He also considered the influence of Martin's Grandfather, the Reverend Coulter, who had been working secretly with Harvey for years to move slaves along the underground railroad to freedom.

Sgt. Bower held their horses at the ready when Michael and Harvey emerged from the cottage. Sir Ian stood in the doorway and waved goodbye before turning back to his notes and his codes, with a long list of tasks to accomplish before the sun set.

The two companions spoke very little as they rode back to Liverpool, securing their cloaks in an effort to shield themselves from a rising wind. Their horses were nervous and jumpy at first, but settled down after a mile or so. Before

265

parting and going their separate ways in the city, they reviewed plans for future contact, with the physician serving as a cut-out and messenger for Sir Ian.

Harvey's heart was filled with hope and determination as he returned to the Angel Hotel, eager to probe Martin's state of mind during their planned excursion to Lime Street Station later that evening.

CHAPTER 16:
UNEXPECTED DEVELOPMENTS

The world felt rather small, as Harvey listened to Martin's account of his lunch meeting with James Bulloch, the mysterious Georgian.

"Mr. Bulloch was very grateful for your help, Harvey. He asked me to give you a small purse, if I agreed you deserved it."

Martin reached into his pocket, retrieved a small leather pouch and dropped it in Harvey's lap, as they rode in a small black carriage along Hanover Street, in route to Lime Street Station.

"Bulloch's a bit old-fashioned, I suppose. I told him you're a free man and he could have given you the purse himself." After everything they had been through, Martin was more likely to anticipate Harvey's point of view than he had been in the past.

"I'm sure we can find a way to put Mr. Bulloch's money to good use!" Harvey joked, grateful for Martin's courtesy but hoping to learn more about the man, for Sir Ian.

"How did you find him?" Harvey asked, following up with a simple, open-ended question.

"He's a hard character, difficult to read. I attribute that to his years in the Navy. He's well connected locally. In fact, he introduced me to a British Naval officer at lunch, a Commander Wallace. They seemed birds of a feather, those two, polite enough—but serious and purposeful. Bulloch apparently told the Commander about your remarkable action, in coming to his defense."

Martin gazed absentmindedly out the window of the carriage, completely unaware of the reaction his words had caused. If Harvey were white, Martin might have noticed the blood draining from his face.

"Unbelievable!" Harvey thought to himself. Martin met the very man Lieutenant Tisdale asked me to contact when we reached Liverpool. It couldn't be an accident, he decided. Now Commander Wallace knew he was in town—and would expect him to make an appearance.

As Harvey struggled to wrap his mind around the problem, he realized the situation could be worse than he imagined: The Birkenhead was a British packet ship. Packet ships carried mail, both official and private, from British colonies back to England, from Bermuda to Liverpool. What if Lieutenant Tisdale forwarded a letter to Commander Wallace, telling him to expect a visit from Harvey? The

Commander would undoubtedly wonder why Harvey had failed to do what he was told. Consequences were likely.

Harvey realized he would need to contact Dr. Satterwhite, first thing in the morning, to get some advice on how best to handle this unexpected development.

After a few minutes of silence, Martin commented casually:

"I forgot to mention: Upon learning I wished to find certain entertainments this evening, both Bulloch and Wallace recommended an excursion up to Edge Hill. Come on, let's go!"

The coachman dropped Martin and Harvey at the entrance to the Lime Street rail station, another monument to Liverpool's prosperity in the Age of Cotton. The stone facade was topped by a single curved roof made of iron, with a functionality that matched its graceful proportions. The station was relatively quiet at that hour, but still attracted passengers and vendors tending their booths. In fact, it was unnaturally quiet, for a train station—raising questions that were soon answered when Martin and Harvey reached the platform. Passenger cars were lined up on the rails, but no steam engine could be seen or heard, even after a close examination.

"That's the curious thing about this station," Martin explained, repeating what he had learned from Bulloch. "From Lime Street, the cars are pulled up a long tunnel, using ropes secured to a stationary engine installed in a brick building on Edge Hill. Once the cars reach the hill, your typical steam engines are secured to the front of the train, for the journey on to Manchester. On the way back down to the city, brakemen control the descent, relying on the force of gravity to provide locomotion. The tunnel was constructed to avoid tearing up the city when the railroad was first built. Fantastic!"

Harvey shared Martin's fascination with technology and the two men spend a few minutes touring the station, looking up at the ironwork supporting the ceiling and admiring the craftsmanship that went into the construction of such a fine monument to modernity.

"We're supposed to collect our tickets for the night train up to Edge Hill, which apparently returns to Lime Street at midnight. That's curious!"

Working their way over to the ticket counter, where the agent sat reading his newspaper, both men where surprised when the agent seemed to recognize them.

"You must be Mr. McCrary!" The agent said. "A Mr. Bulloch told me to expect a young American, accompanying by his manservant. Your tickets were paid in advance, with his compliments. Best board straight away: She departs in 10 minutes!"

"It seems Mr. Bulloch was more grateful for your service than we realized!" Martin suggested, as they turned and walked back to the platform.

"More likely he wants to make an impression on Hank McCrary's son, in pursuit of his business interests!" Harvey responded, in a typically cynical fashion.

"You're probably right." Martin admitted. "No matter, let's enjoy the ride!"

Harvey was touched by his unwitting younger brother's youthful enthusiasm, reminding him of playful Summer days in the woods and rivers of South Carolina. The memories caused Harvey to feel some regret for the risk he and Sir Ian wanted Martin to take, but he knew the cause was worth it. As Sir Ian had pointed out, Martin's world was about the change, whether he wished it or not.

The conductor was polite but firm when the two men approached the train.

"Your ticket is good for first class, Sir." The conductor remarked, as he spoke directly to Martin. "But your servant will need to ride in third class, the second car from the end." The man sported a huge handlebar mustache which seemed to point in the same direction as his arm, like the minute hand and hour marker on the face of a grandfather clock at precisely 9:45 PM.

"Sorry about that Harvey, looks like you'll have to fend for yourself!" Martin quipped.

"Not to worry, Suh—I'll see you up on the hill!"

Harvey offered a mock salute as he strode down the platform to his assigned car. He climbed up, took a look around and sat down on a rough wooden bench. Two sailors in Royal Navy uniforms sat in the rear of the car, apparently drunk, laughing and talking amongst themselves. Otherwise the car was empty. A few

271

minutes later, the train lurched, with none of the usual warning sounds provided by a huffing steam engine or its spinning wheels. When the train entered the tunnel, the suddenly sober sailors stood up and approached Harvey. Their demeanor was polite and respectful, but uncompromising.

"There's a man who wants to see you, Mr. Harvey." The shorter of the two sailors announced. "He's waiting in the last car. Please follow me."

The sailor gestured with one hand, as his taller partner stood off to one side. Feeling trapped but unwilling to escalate the encounter into a conflict, Harvey stood and did as he was told, his mind racing as he considered the possibilities. The tunnel was pitch black as he was escorted through the rear door of the third class car, stepping over to the last car in the train. Curiously, all of the windows in that car were hung with heavy curtains, offering complete privacy to the occupants. The walls were richly paneled and the seating was comfortably upholstered. Harvey assumed he was standing in a private car of some kind, a car that belonged to the imposing figure seated directly in front of him.

"Commander," the sailor announced, Mr. Harvey delivered as requested, Sir!"

"Thank you, Smyth. You're dismissed, but stand by in the next car until we reach the Hill."

"Aye, Sir!" The sailors turned smartly about and returned to their rough benches in the third class car. Both men were pleased to pull special duty that evening, as the Commander had given them a handful of coins to spend up on the Hill—a rare privilege, indeed.

"Sit down, Mr. Harvey." The Commander ordered, as he cleaned his pipe. "Would you like a cigar?" He pointed toward a wooden box on a small table next to Harvey's chair.

"Don't mind if I do, Suh." Harvey helped himself to a Cuban, striking the match with relish, and wondering what to expect.

"My name is Commander Wallace." The man continued. "I believe you've heard of me."

"Yes Suh. You're a friend of Mister Walter, in Bermuda." Harvey turned his head before sending a smoke ring drifting across the car.

"That's right." The officer said calmly, pulling a draft from his pipe.

"I'm curious and disappointed, Mr. Harvey." The Commander remarked casually, but with an edge of authority in his voice. "Why haven't you come to see me? I've been expecting you."

Harvey placed his cigar in the tray, stood up at a polite distance from the Englishman and assumed the role of a penitent black man begging forgiveness from his master.

"I'm sorry, Suh, but I was afraid, afraid of what might happen. Can't imagine what a nigger like me could do to help a man like you."

Harvey held his hat in his hands and tried not to make eye contact.

"Afraid? I doubt it. For God's sake, sit down, man!" Commander Wallace gestured at the comfortable leather chair by his side.

"You can stop your shuffling and sniffling, Harvey." The Commander demanded. "James Bulloch is a particular friend of mine, and he told me what you did down by the harbor."

"I saw a man who needed help, that's all, Suh." Harvey responded, as he took his seat again, as requested, and reached over to retrieve his cigar.

"Listen up, Harvey, because I'm not going to repeat myself. There's two things I have to say: First, your actions down by the harbor were remarkable and deserved a reward. I understand Bulloch has taken care of that. Second, Bulloch told me about Martin's father, and there' simply no possibility a man like Hank McCrary would allow his only son to travel around the world escorted by a simpleton. So put away the fool and act like your true self, at least when you're meeting with me."

"All right, Suh." Harvey sat back in the chair and puffed on his cigar, trying to relax.

"Now, I'll forgive you for failing to show up, just this once, but from now on, I expect your cooperation, because I'm going to make it worth your while." Commander Wallace looked over at Harvey, pausing for effect as he offered the carrot before the stick. "I'll also make sure the authorities stop looking for the man who stuck a knife in the back of a merchantman's skull, down by the harbor."

The Commander paused again, to allow his words to sink in.

Harvey remained silent, but nodded his head in understanding.

"Now, starting with the assumption that you're no simpleton, tell me what you learned during your voyage from Hamilton to Liverpool."

"Well, Suh, the Lieutenant asked me to stay close to Dr. Satterwhite, as he'll be working as the physician for the colony in Bermuda. I did what he asked and watched him closely." Harvey was on unfamiliar ground and paused to give himself time to reflect before offering any specific information.

"So, what did you learn?" The Commander urged him on.

"Well, Suh, he seems trustworthy to me. He spoke often about his trip to Barbados, with Dr. Snow, and seemed focused on how to improve sanitation for the freed slaves and their families, 'cause that would increase the profits for the owners of those sugar plantations." That should be safe enough, Harvey thought, hoping to avoid tripping himself up by offering false information that could be verified.

"All right, Harvey. What about Mr. Prescond, the black representative from Barbados, and his friend, the abolitionist preacher?" The Commander didn't reveal the fact that he had both men under active surveillance, to identify their friends and associates.

"They were polite with one another, Suh, but not close. I never saw them whispering below decks in private or anything like that. Now, don't get me wrong, the Doctor is opposed to slavery, he told me himself and said he was pleased to learn I'm a free man, but he's no radical, like that preacher. He told me he believes slavery will eventually fade away, on its own, peaceful like. He said free men work harder, increasing profits, and cited Barbados as an example." Harvey left it at that.

"That sounds reasonable, Harvey. After all, Her Majesty's Government has banned slavery everywhere in our territories and the Royal Navy has done as much as anyone to stop the slave trade. That means you're on the right side, if you work for me. Do you understand that, Harvey?"

"Yes Suh, of course Suh. I wish I could see Barbados myself, to find out what my home in South Carolina might be like in the future."

Let the man think I've accepted his arguments, Harvey thought to himself, and will serve him loyally in the future. Although it would have been better to have guidance from Sir Ian, Harvey was committed to a double game, now. He burned with silent anger when he considered the fact that Commander Wallace was part of a group that would stop at nothing, even the dismantling of the United States of America, to preserve the cotton trade that enriched so many great men in England.

"Good man!" Commander Wallace exclaimed, by way of congratulations. "The train will reach Edge Hill soon," He offered, "So we best establish a means of communication."

Much to Harvey's surprise, Commander Wallace told him the doorman at the Angel Hotel was a former sailor, who had worked under his command and served him still.

"If the doorman passes you a message, do what he says. Any message you give him will be passed to me. Before you leave for your voyage back to America, I'll give you instructions on the things I need you to do for me back home in South Carolina, and I'll provide you with a proper way to contact one of my associates at the British Consulate in Charleston. Understand?"

Harvey offered his assurances and stood up. Fully committed now, Harvey shook the Commander's hand and returned to his bench in the third class car, a few minutes before the train stopped at Edge Hill. "One step at a time, one step at a time!" Harvey mumbled to himself, as his head filled with doubts and he resisted a rising sense of panic.

For their part, the sailors seemed to ignore Harvey, as if they had never met.

When Harvey disembarked, he found Martin standing in a jolly crowd of well-dressed Englishmen who had been drinking hard liquor all the way up from the station. Two of the men had their arms around Martin's shoulders and were trying to lead him toward the most reputable of several whorehouses tucked discreetly around Edge Hill. Some enterprising businessmen had established a niche market, using train cars that were otherwise unneeded at night to haul customers up from the city, with their dens of iniquity hidden from the prying eyes of Liverpool's moral watchdogs in the center of the city. Martin managed to excuse himself long enough to have a brief conversation with Harvey.

"Look, Harvey—I'm truly sorry, but they do things differently here in Liverpool. Certain establishments admit certain classes of men, with no exceptions. I imagine you're relieved to be free from escort duty this evening, so enjoy yourself! I'll see you back at the train at Midnight!"

"All right, then—but watch the drink, 'cause I'm not gonna carry you back to Liverpool!" If need be, Harvey would carry Martin on his back, and the younger man knew it, but Harvey enjoyed reminding Martin of a previous escapade in New Orleans, when he passed out in Lucy's arms. Although the same couldn't be said for her, Lucy was Martin's first and he would never forget her.

Harvey shook his head and turned his back after watching Martin rejoin the rowdy young Englishmen. He felt exhausted, after the long ride with Dr. Satterwhite, and went looking for a bath. Scanning the area, he caught a brief glimpse of Commander Wallace's sailors, just before they entered the first in a series of three taverns on the opposite side of the tracks from Martin's classy destination. Harvey decided he would explore the last establishment on the block, the "Merry Goat." Before entering, he paused to admire the artistry of the sign-maker, who had gifted the Billy with a lurid grin and an impressive set of balls. His revere was

278

interrupted by the delightful sound of feminine laughter emerging from a window on the second floor, as the shadow of a half-naked woman scurried past the backlit curtains.

Looks like I'm at the right place! Harvey thought to himself as he opened the front door.

He was greeted by a hulk of a man who appeared to be all belly and no neck. He was sweating profusely on a cool evening, but his eyes suggested he wasn't as stupid as he looked.

"Welcome to the Goat!" He offered, with an Irish accent and a throaty growl. "Sean's the name and whores are my game. What's your pleasure?"

"A bottle of Irish whiskey and a hot bath, to start!" Harvey took an instant liking to the proprietor and appreciated his directness.

"Do you have the coin?" The fat man asked hopefully.

"Indeed I do!" Harvey responded, jiggling Bulloch's leather pouch in his left hand. "Earned it today, plan on spending it tonight!'

"You've come to the right place!" Sean beamed enthusiastically, "Hop on up the stairs and tell the old woman to fix you a bath and I'll send up a bottle. When you've stewed long enough, give us a shout and we'll offer a couple of young ladies to choose from."

The stairs creaked a bit as Harvey climbed up to the second floor, where he found himself facing a gnarly old she-gnome dressed in black, like a witch in a fairy tale.

"Don't bother asking," the old witch muttered, I heard what the fat man said. Follow

279

me down the hall and we'll set you up with a tub."

Harvey found himself longing for the elegance of La Casa de Venus, as he followed the old woman down the unpainted and uncarpeted hallway, ducking as he entered a small room with an even smaller tub.

"Make yourself comfortable!" The witch suggested, "plenty of hot water on the way!"

The room was simply furnished, with a wrought iron bed, a window hung with cheap cotton fabric and a simple tub made of tin, just large enough for a grown man. The tub looked clean enough, Harvey was pleased to see, and was filled half way to the top with cold water. Before he could undress, three boys marched in carrying heavy buckets filled with hot water. They looked exhausted, except for the ginger haired boy, who spoke before shutting the door behind him:

"The ladies are already arguing about who's gonna take the big black man!" The boy exclaimed. "Don't let 'em down, 'cause they're bored with all the rest of 'em this evening!"

Uncharacteristically, Harvey found it difficult to muster any enthusiasm, especially if the whores looked anything like the old shrew.

Looking around for a place to hang his things, Harvey had to settle for a ladder-back chair, which was just sturdy enough to hold his clothes without tipping over, as long as he left his shoes on the seat as a counterbalance. Feeling a chill in the air, Harvey eased himself into the tub, emitting a sigh of relief as he settled in for a soak. His mind drifted as he tried to avoid thinking about everything he had gotten himself into over the past several days. Perhaps he'd be better off if he told Sir Ian he'd made a mistake, that he didn't want to return to South Carolina, that he simply wanted to find a quiet place to settle down?

Harvey's meandering thoughts were interrupted when the old crone reappeared, with a smallish bottle of Irish whiskey and an even smaller glass. She dragged a stool over by the tub, set the glass down on top of the stool and filled the glass for Harvey.

"I doubt a Yank like you has ever tried anything like it," she warned. It's smooth as silk, the Breath of Life we calls it, nothing like your nasty Bourbon or your smoky Scotch. Sip it slowly and savor the best whiskey on God's green earth."

The old woman sounded almost motherly. She mumbled to herself as she shuffled out the door and shut it firmly behind her. Harvey reached over and took the glass in his right hand, shifting it to his left before taking a sip. The old shrew spoke the truth, Harvey thought, as he sipped again. Wonderful stuff! He downed the glass quick as lightening and didn't wait to pour himself another. A few minutes later, he was completely relaxed, with all of his worries banished to a dark corner of his mind, relishing the hot water as he soaked his stiff muscles. As he drifted off into a no-man's land between sleep and waking, his thoughts turned to the beautiful proprietor of La Casa de Venus in Havana. She formed an almost painful vision of beauty in his mind and he longed for her like no woman he had ever known. The more he struggled to reach her, the further she receded in his mind. She turned to tease him, tearing her dress away to reveal her magnificent breasts, only to laugh and skip away when he reached for her.

Moments later, Harvey awoke with a start and discovered his natural impulses were alive and well, ready for an adventure. As if on cue, someone tapped softly at the door.

"Come on in!" Harvey responded lazily, taking another sip of Sean's whiskey as he sunk deeper into the tub with a sigh.

The old woman held the door open as three women walked in. They wore simple cotton dresses, with no face paint and no fake jewelry, so different from the whores he had known in America. All three of the whores looked like farm girls, with strong bones and rosy cheeks. The first two girls were brunettes and could have been sisters, with the same plain but pleasant faces and large, round bottoms. The third was a redhead, with soft blue eyes and a face covered with freckles. She smiled and lowered her eyes when Harvey nodded in her direction. The other girls giggled as they left the room, reaching out to touch the redheaded girl's arm as they passed.

"My name is Anne." The girl said softly, as she reached over with a towel.

"The name's Harvey," he responded as he stood to face the girl, allowing the water to fall off his remarkable physique before accepting the towel and stepping out of the tub.

"Let me help you," the girl offered bravely, as she took the damp towel and dried Harvey's back, admiring the cut of his shoulders and shape of the muscles leading down to his narrow waist. Pleasantly surprised, Harvey stood silently as Anne dried the rest of his body with tender care. When she was done, Anne stood before the finest looking man she had ever seen, in her short life as a woman with no parents, no family and no connections, trying to make her way in a cruel world.

This man is different, a gentle giant, she thought to herself, and I plan to enjoy him.

Neither Harvey nor the girl were disappointed, as he explored every inch of her milky-white skin, making a silent vow to please her before he allowed himself to be pleased. He took her naked body in his arms and laid her gently on the bed, kneeling on the floor as he kissed her breasts, moving slowly down until there was no were else to go, employing all the skills he had acquired with countless women over the years, bringing Anne to the brink and back again until she cried out for joy and mercy. The Merry Goat grew quiet, as most of the girls and their patrons had never heard such a fuss in their lives.

After Anne caught her breath and came to her senses, she took Harvey's head in her hands and pulled him up to the bed.

"Take me, take me now!" She begged, as she pulled him closer.

Harvey complied and took her with real pleasure, with no sense of rush as he savored the experience. Anne freed herself from every restraint, moving rhythmically beneath him. As for Harvey, he lost himself entirely in the moment and joined Anne in a chorus of shouts when they finally came together.

The two strangers held each other like lovers, as long as Anne felt she could.

"I'd better go." she said, with genuine regret. "Sean's not a bad man, given what we do for a living, but he won't tolerate a lingerer."

"Wait!" Harvey said, as he rose to find his things. "You deserve something special."

Harvey stood up and walked over to the ladder-back chair. He reached into the pocket sewn into the waistband of his old woolen trousers and retrieved one of his precious Double Eagles, the last surviving treasure from the Ship of Gold.

"Do you have a place to hide your valuables?" Harvey asked kindly.

"Indeed I do!" Anne answered unhesitatingly. "Sean knows I have plans and hope to set myself up as a seamstress, just as my mother did before she died. He won't go looking."

"All right then." Harvey responded, as he pressed the gold coin in her hands, which had never held anything of such value.

"Oh, thank you!" Anne gasped, as she turned to examine both sides of the coin.

"It was minted in San Francisco." Harvey elaborated, "from California gold."

"You come back and see me anytime," Anne insisted, as she reached up to kiss Harvey on the cheek. She turned and gathered up her skirts as she ducked out the door, leaving Harvey alone in the room.

Feeling merry indeed, Harvey got himself dressed and headed downstairs to settle up with Sean.

"Did you enjoy my whiskey?" Sean asked with a grin, as he slid Harvey's coins into his pocket and nodded toward the stairs.

"Magical stuff!" Harvey exclaimed, "How about a bottle for the road?"

"With pleasure, and gratis!" Sean reached around behind the bar and handed Harvey a small bottle with a picture of the Merry Goat on the label. "Be sure to share the bottle with a friend, and spread the word about our fine establishment!" The Irishman was an enterprising entrepreneur who enjoyed absolute confidence in his product.

Harvey walked out the front door feeling pleased with himself and the Merry Goat. His complicated world seemed just a little bit brighter than it had on the strange train ride up from Lime Street. He resolved to stop worrying, to let each day take care of itself. His soul longed for music, so he ambled in the direction of the only music he could hear: The sound of a woman's voice floated over the tracks, accompanied by an energetic piano. Following his ears like a dog follows its nose, Harvey ambled toward the music, stopping briefly to admire the full moon as it broke through a ring of clouds. He reached up for the halo with his left hand, pondered the mysteries of the universe.

Harvey's mood changed with the music, which shifted to a slow, melancholy air. The voice was clear and pure, with no trace of a vibrato or showy theatricality. She sang in a language unknown to Harvey, but the sense of pain and loss was universal, bringing tears to Harvey's eyes. Blocking out his surroundings, Harvey followed the music until he found himself standing under a large window at the classy establishment Martin had entered earlier that evening. The neighborhood was strangely silent, its revere broken only by the sound of a horse walking slowly up the street, until the rider stopped in his tracks, entranced by the sound of the music. After the angelic voice stopped singing, the silence remained, as the audience was unwilling to break the spell. Moments later, a glass shattered and the magic was lost, as the crowd broke into thunderous applause and drunken cheers of approval.

Feeling inexplicably sad, Harvey sat down on a barrel and waited, thinking of his mother and sister back home in South Carolina. A few minutes later, Martin emerged from the fine house of ill repute, looking unexpectedly sober, like a responsible young member of the clergy.

"There you are, Harvey!" Martin spoke quietly, as he skipped down the stairs. "Come on, let's get back to the train."

To the best of Harvey's knowledge, Martin had never taken a woman without his assistance in making the arrangements. He was curious to learn more about his younger brother's experience over the course of the evening, but something in Martin's demeanor suggested he should wait and listen rather than probe with a disrespectful sense of humor.

"Did you hear the woman singing?" Martin asked, as they walked toward the train, turning up their collars to keep out the chill.

"Brought me to tears." Harvey admitted. "Left me thinking about my mother."

"I know what you mean." Martin acknowledged. "The singer is Welsh—what a strange and wonderful language! By all appearances, she could be Jane Jevon's older sister. You know, the young lady I met with David Small, over at St. George's hall. I saw the woman when we entered the place and couldn't stop thinking about her all night. Jane, I mean."

"You've got it bad, don't you?" Harvey asked sympathetically.

"I couldn't do it, Harvey. I couldn't take a girl tonight. I just sat by the piano, downstairs, and listened to that woman sing. Didn't feel right, doing anything else."

"I've got just the thing, to help with your troubles!" Harvey insisted, as he offered Martin a drink from his precious bottle of whiskey.

"What's that?" Martin asked, as he took a second gulp. "Incredible!"

"It's from the Merry Goat!" Harvey responded, pointing out the balls on the label. "I'll take you there sometime, as you're free to step down to a lower establishment, even if I'm not allowed to step up!"

"I'd like that, at least for the drinking." Martin offered a wry smile as he passed the bottle back to Harvey, who took a swig for himself before securing the precious nectar in his pocket.

Shifting into the familiar role of companion and protector, Harvey glanced over each shoulder, scanning for possible threats. His sense of peace and tranquility was overturned when he realized they were being followed. One of the two men trailing them looked vaguely familiar.

"Looks like we may be in for some trouble." Harvey advised, as he put an arm around Martin's shoulder. We best get over to the train."

Martin looked around and didn't see a thing, but knew better than to contradict Harvey on such matters. They reached the small platform a few minutes later, but no one was around, as the train wasn't scheduled to depart for an hour. At least the area is well lit, Harvey thought to himself, and we can keep our backs to the train. Surely, the crew are close at hand and will return if they hear shouts?

The two strangers were joined by a third man, who walked with the swagger of an experienced fighter. With no where to run, Harvey placed himself between the threat and his younger brother. He didn't brandish his knife, but kept it concealed, at least for the moment. When the men were about 30 yards away, their faces were recognizable in the light around the platform, and Harvey understood the danger: One of the men had participated in the attack on James Bulloch, the one who ran when

Harvey came to rescue Bulloch. The man was easy to recognize because his face was badly pock-marked and his eyes were bunched together above a thin nose.

When the three strangers stopped, the pock-marked man whispered in the ears of his rough-looking companions. The largest of the three, the fighter, stepped forward and spoke:

"You're the nigger who killed our friend, isn't that right? Couldn't believe our luck, when Bertie spotted you over at the Goat."

Turning to his companion, the fighter continued:

"You won't be running this time, will you Bertie?"

The ill-favored merchantman nodded in agreement and brandished an evil-looking knife to illustrate his resolve. The third man drew a club from his left sleeve. The leader pulled back his coat to reveal a pistol tucked in his trousers. That narrowed Harvey's options considerably.

"You best scoot between those trains and make a run for it," Harvey never took his eyes off the threat as he spoke to Martin. "There's no need for you to be involved in this."

Martin's feet wanted to run, but he couldn't leave Harvey to face those men on his own, not after everything they had been through. Defiantly, he stepped forward and stood beside Harvey.

"You men best be off!" Martin ordered, in a strained voice. "We've already seen four hangings in Liverpool this week, and that'll be your fate, if you persist!"

The three merchantmen laughed at the sight of a thin young gentlemen coming to the aid of his big black servant. The aggressor pulled his pistol and stepped closer.

"We'll be persisting, I think." The big man responded definitively. He looked like he knew what he was doing, with no trace of weakness or doubt in his demeanor. He turned briefly to share a word with his companions, who nodded their heads in agreement.

"The best solution will require some compensation, young Master." The man suggested, in a mocking tone. "You give us the nigger and all your money, and we'll let you live. I'll wager you have plenty of niggers, back home, and more money to replace your losses."

Harvey shoved Martin behind him and moved toward the aggressor. If only he could get close enough to seize the pistol, they might have a chance.

The big man was too experienced for that. In one fluid motion, he cocked his weapon and pointed it directly at Harvey.

"The nigger's a dead man, no matter what." The pistol-welding man hissed. "The only question is what's gonna happen to you." The man directed his statement to Martin as he kept Harvey in his sights.

Moments later, the sound of a pistol rang out, with a thunderous cracking noise that ricocheted off the side of the train. Surprisingly, Harvey didn't feel any pain. Frantically, he looked down and searched for the inevitable gut-shot. Nothing. Looking up, he watched the expression on the gunman's face fade from rage to panic, as he dropped to his knees. As the seconds stretched into a lifetime, the gunman tried to raise his pistol again. A second shot rang out, and the right side of the gunman's head flew off, like a bird taking flight. Two more shots rang out, and his companions fell to the ground. The man with the club died quietly; the ill-favored man screamed like a pig at the slaughterhouse.

Before Harvey could step forward to apply the coup de grace, two British sailors emerged from the shadows, the same men who introduced Harvey to Commander Wallace. Both men carried long-barreled Navy revolvers, with smoke rising from their barrels. The larger of the two men winked at Harvey as he approached the screaming pig, muttering with contempt as he blew the man's brains out.

The two sailors checked the dead men's pockets, finding nothing but a handful of coins. As the hurried footsteps of approaching trainmen echoed down the street, the senior man spoke up.

"Sorry for the trouble!" The sailor exclaimed in a matter-of-fact voice, as he knelt by his victim. "No need to worry yourselves, we'll clean up the mess!"

The sailor stood up and holstered his weapon before continuing:

"There's been a rash of robberies on the Hill, so we've been standing by in hopes of collecting the reward. This one here," the sailor said, kicking the dead gunman in the ass. "Is Notorious Ned. He's worth 10 pounds, dead or alive!"

291

Never one to look a gift horse in the mouth, Harvey put his arm around Martin's shoulder and led him over to the first class car, where a porter had finally opened the door. The two companions held back as a crowd gathered around the bodies. Martin was still in a bit of shock, having never seen a man killed in cold blood, nor heads blown off or brains spilled. Harvey slipped the bottle of Sean's whiskey in Martin's pocket and patted him on the back as he helped him climb up to his car.

"See you back at the station!" Harvey offered encouragingly, as the stiff old porter servicing the first class car shooed the black man away, pointing toward the rear of the train.

Both men rode the train in silence, although their cars were filled with chattering drunks discussing the bloody scene back on Edge Hill. They remained silent all the way back to the Angel Hotel, as they scurried along in a somber little carriage. The streets were quiet when they reached their hotel at 1:30 in the morning. The doorman received them without complaint, but asked the companions to tread softly on the stairs, to avoid waking the other guests. They shut the door to their room quietly and went straight to bed, not bothering to wash up. Harvey slept soundly, but Martin was troubled. In his dream, Martin was a little boy, trying to save his mother from a faceless intruder, who kept his back to the child. The boy's tender heart dropped through the floor when the intruder shot his mother through the head, recreating the carnage he had witnessed earlier that evening as one side of her head took flight. The little boy screamed at the back of his mother's killer, who turned to face the boy with a vicious grin.

That murderous face belonged to his father, Hank McCrary.

CHAPTER 17:
THE TELEGRAM

When Martin and Harvey rose the next morning and headed downstairs at the Angel Hotel, they were surprised to find all three of the Small men waiting in the lobby, wearing black suits and grave expressions on their faces. David Small was especially distraught, as he fiddled nervously with his hat and looked away, rather than meet Martin's gaze.

Paul Sr. approached Martin like an usher at a funeral, holding a telegram in his hand.

"What is it?" Martin asked, overwhelmed with a sense of dread.

"I'm truly sorry," Mr. Small began, "but you're mother passed away during your absence. We received a telegram from your grandfather this morning."

With a sense of horror, Martin recalled the images from his lingering nightmare. He flinched, like the boy in the dream, as his mother fell to the floor. He reached for the message with trembling hands.

The telegraph was devastatingly short.

"Dear Martin." The message began. "With deepest regret and a broken heart, it has fallen on me to share the tragic news: Your beloved mother, my only child, has departed this world, only days after learning of your miraculous survival. Her death was unnatural and the authorities in Charleston believe she was murdered. Your father is indisposed. You must return to Charleston immediately, as your presence is required to oversee your family's affairs. I wish there were words I could offer by way of condolences, but I have nothing but prayers to offer. May God protect you on your journey."

The telegraph was signed "The Reverend Matthew Coulter" and was apparently sent to New York on the 7th of October, and then carried to Liverpool aboard a steamer from New York.

Martin crushed the telegraph in his hands and dropped it to the floor as he collapsed in a chair, causing a piece of decorative china hanging on the wall to crash to the floor. Harvey picked up the message, smoothed out the wrinkles and read it for himself, without asking for permission, ignoring the shocked looks on the faces of the Small men, who were unused to such insolence.

'My mother was murdered!?"

Martin uttered the words out loud, with no care for strangers. A group of men on the far side of the lobby began whispering to one another, discomforted by a scene of personal tragedy that should have been kept private. Although his stone-cold heart was thawed by Martin's loss, Paul Sr. was ruled first and foremost by a keen sense of propriety. He looked to his son David, who spoke for the family.

"Martin, we'd like you to come and stay with us, until your ship leaves for New York. We've booked passage on the next available steamer, which leaves in two days."

"All right, then." Martin responded in a daze, as he was helped to his feet and shepherded toward the door by Paul Sr. and David.

Paul Jr. turned to Harvey and issued terse instructions:

"Pack Mr. McCrary's things. We'll send a wagon around to collect you precisely at noon. You'll be accompanying Mr. McCrary on his journey in two days time. In the meantime, we'll find a place for you to stay with our servants. Do you understand?"

The condescending tone infuriated Harvey, but he concealed his anger.

"Of course, Mr. Small, I understand. I'll have Martin's things ready at noon."

Harvey's heart was troubled. Martin's mother had never liked him, because she suspected her husband's relationship with his slave mother, but she had never been cruel and had always been a loving mother to Martin, despite her infirmities.

This will be hard on the boy, Harvey thought to himself. What should I do now? Abandon the plan to bring Martin around to our cause, or move to take advantage of the young man when he's most vulnerable? Harvey sat down on the steps outside the hotel, trying to clear his head. Moments later, it hit him: Why didn't Martin's father, HIS father, send a message? Why did Reverend Coulter describe Hank McCrary as "indisposed?" Why was Martin needed to oversee his family's affairs? Martin's father would never cede control over his personal empire, unless he had no other option.

The shock of realization was almost too much to bear, as Harvey knew from his own mother that Hank McCrary sometimes abused the women in his life. All the more reason to hate him.

The inevitable question formed in Harvey's mind:

What if Hank McCrary murdered his wife?

In that instant, Harvey grasped the truth. Mrs. McCrary lived a sheltered life in her Charleston mansion and never ventured forth without her coachmen and servants, like a fine English lady. In fact, she rarely went out at all, preferring a quiet, private life. Harvey remembered a conversation he once had with a card-playing police inspector in New Orleans, who said married woman were always murdered by their husbands or a lover and only prostitutes and the destitute were murdered by strangers.

The telegram was strange, in other ways. What would prevent Hank McCrary from communicating with Martin, his only acknowledged son and heir? Either the man had come unhinged, when his wife was murdered, or he had been charged with the murder himself. Harvey knew the latter option was most likely, as husband and wife were not close, and the Old Man and never shown any signs of mental illness. And there was another thing: The house-slaves said their master hadn't slept with his wife in over 10 years. That came as no surprise, as Harvey knew McCrary had taken many lovers over the years, and slept with high class prostitutes at every opportunity.

Harvey had also witnessed the old man's volcanic temper, which erupted when he was drunk.

No, it seemed unlikely the old man would lose his wits over this.

Harvey's heart was filled with resolve. Hank McCrary kept his mother and sister as slaves, and used them as leverage to keep him in bondage. Harvey's status as a "freedman" was a farce, in so many ways. The old man had beaten Martin's mother, Harvey's mother and who knows how many other women over the years. If he was capable of killing Mrs. McCrary, that was all the more reason to destroy him, and other men like him. Harvey decided he would do what he could to bring Martin around to Sir Ian's side, even if that meant he might have to remain behind in England, should the attempt fail. He would have to trust Sir Ian to secure freedom for his family, if it came to that.

Putting his doubts aside, Harvey hurried over to the George hostel. With hat in hand, he informed the clerk he had an urgent message for Dr. Satterwhite that could only be delivered in person, holding out the telegram by way of evidence. As it was still morning and the physician had not yet emerged from his room, the clerk escorted Harvey upstairs and knocked on his door.

"Yes, who is it?"

The voice on the other side of the door was instantly recognizable to Harvey, who was relieved to find his friend was in his lodgings.

"It's William, Sir, the desk clerk. There's a man here with an urgent message."

The door opened immediately and Dr. Satterwhite emerged, in a loose shirt and stocking feet.

"Thank you, William, Mr. Harvey is known to me—you may go!"

The clerk nodded stiffly and retreated to the lobby, as Harvey entered Michael's small but comfortable accommodations.

"What is it, Harvey?" The physician asked, noting the look of concern on his friend's face. "I know it must be urgent, as we both agreed it's far too risky to meet at either of our hotels."

"It couldn't be helped, Michael." Harvey began, as he presented the telegram. Dr. Satterwhite scanned the message quickly and looked up at Harvey.

"Her death was unnatural?" Dr. Satterwhite repeated, "they're investigating her murder? This is shocking, indeed!"

Harvey got straight to the point.

"I believe Mrs. McCrary was killed by her own husband, Martin's father. My father."

Michael remained silent as he eyes read the telegraph again, and again.

"Yes, I see what you mean. I assume Martin has received no message from his father?"

Despite the unpleasant circumstances, Harvey was impressed by the physician's ability to size up a situation quickly.

"That's right. It must have taken some time for the news to reach Reverend Coulter up in the mountains, and even more time for him to travel to Charleston. Any message from Hank McCrary should have reached Martin well before the telegram from his Grandfather." It all seemed clear to Harvey.

Dr. Satterwhite paced around the room, to get his blood flowing and his brain working.

"You're close to Reverend Coulter, aren't you?" Michael asked.

"Yes. As you know, I've helped him smuggle quite a few slaves to freedom over the past four years. We've shared the same risk of a hanging." In Harvey's mind, you couldn't get any closer than that.

"Do you think the Reverend was trying to send you a coded message, without revealing the entire truth?" Michael held up the wrinkled telegram in his right hand.

"I do," Harvey explained, "if Hank McCrary murdered his wife, Mr. Coulter may have felt the news would be too much for Martin to handle."

"Do you believe we should proceed with the plan?" Michael asked.

"There's no better option, as far as I'm concerned," Harvey asserted, "Martin must accept Sir Ian's proposal before we leave for New York in two days."

"I agree, despite the risk." Dr. Satterwhite circled the small room as he considered their options.

"All right, then. We don't have much time. We'll set the stage for a private conversation before the two of you leave. I'll be off to see Sir Ian immediately. He's staying at his townhouse in the city, by the way, and I should be able to meet him within the hour."

"I'm very glad to hear that!" Harvey exclaimed, with genuine relief. His mind was racing but he remembered to share other critical information:

"I should mention, we're leaving the hotel and moving over to the Small residence, on Duke Street. I don't remember the exact address, but expect they'll be putting me up in the carriage house. I should be able to sneak over to the Nelson monument this evening. I'll wait there until you find me, and I'll return just after sunrise if we miss one another."

From experience, Harvey knew things could get complicated if they missed their first contact.

"Agreed, that'll do. Sir Ian will have to work some magic, to make all the necessary arrangements, but I've seen him do far more with less time." Michael wasn't as confident in his own abilities, as a spy, but he wouldn't let his friends down.

"There's more I have to tell, before your meeting with Sir Ian." As succinctly as possible, Harvey retold the story of the unexpected approach by Commander Wallace, at Lime Street station, and their rescue by the Commander's men, up on Edge Hill.

"Good God!" The physician interjected, "could this affair possibly get more complicated?"

Pacing the room as he struggled to suppress a growing sense of alarm, Michael took a deep breath and responded in a calmer fashion:

"I'll share the news with Sir Ian, deferring to his judgment on how best to proceed. I'll see you at the Nelson monument between 8 and 9 this evening, or the first hour after sunrise in the morning."

No less worried than his physician friend, Harvey offered one final detail:

"That's wise, as the salty doorman at our hotel works for Commander Wallace and he'll undoubtedly rely the news of our departure. The Commander strikes me as the sort who will come looking for me if I fail to contact him again."

"Damnation! The enemy has eyes everywhere!" Dr. Satterwhite had experienced a great deal of stress in his medical practice, but preferred not to rush when dealing with espionage, as he knew better than anyone he was still an amateur in that field of endeavor. He decided to focus on what he knew, rather than worrying about what he couldn't control.

"Whatever you do, Harvey, don't come back here. I'll change accommodations later today, to minimize our vulnerabilities. If we miss one another at the Nelson monument, I'll send a messenger to look for you at the Small house. Keep your eyes and ears open, until we meet this evening!"

The two men embraced as friends before Harvey excused himself, exiting via the servant's entrance at the back of the hostel, ignoring the protests of a scullery maid as he pushed through the door. A scruffy looking tom-cat hissed with frustration, as the noise had enabled his prey to escape. A plump looking mouse paused at the entrance to its bolt-hole, as if he wised to thank Harvey for the favor.

When Harvey reached the Angel Hotel, the doorman extended his right hand and passed a small note, in a discreet fashion. The doorman didn't speak as he turned to face the street and stood with his hands behind his back, in the military style.

"Curse my luck!" Harvey thought, as he pocketed the note until he was safely behind doors in Martin's room. He opened the small slip of paper and read it carefully:

"Meet me outside St. Thomas Church on Park Lane at 6 this evening. We must prepare for your journey. W."

"Damn! Commander Wallace already knows we're leaving Liverpool in two days. If I don't show up for the meeting," Harvey realized, "he'll simply pick me up off the street at his leisure!"

Harvey paced around the room, gathering his wits.

"I can handle this!" He decided. "Stay calm and meet each challenge as it comes. First the meeting with the Commander at the Cathedral, then over to the Nelson monument to see Michael. I'll hear what the Commander has to say, then I'll pass it on to Michael."

"See, that's not so complicated!" Harvey assured himself.

While a plan fixed in his mind, Harvey packed all of Martin's belongings and hauled his trunks downstairs. A wagon dispatched by Small and Sons arrived at noon, and a cheerful driver by the name of Ed helped Martin with the trunks.

The Small family home was even more impressive than Harvey remembered, from his last trip to Liverpool, as the compound had enjoyed the kind of expensive renovations that reflected the family's growing prosperity. The Georgian architecture was gracious, with a clean facade reaching up three floors. The house was graced with a wrought iron staircase leading up to the main entrance, one floor above street level. Two men carried Martin's trunks up to his guest room and Harvey was escorted around back, to the carriage house. By way of acknowledging his gratitude for the driver's assistance, Harvey helped the man move a few boxes and tools, enjoying the distraction of honest work.

"The original owner was a tobacco merchant.' Ed observed. "Now cotton is King, but the house seems a bit Small-er, with the current occupants!" Puns exploiting the surname of their employers were popular with the servants, as Mr. and Mrs. Small were humorless task masters.

After the work was done, the two men sat down on a pair of barrels to enjoy a lunch of bread and pork sausage, washed down with a watery ale whose flavor was inexplicably enhanced by the smell of fresh hay. The men exchanged a few jokes and, dusting off the crumbs, marched up a pair of rough wooden stairs to the loft above. The driver showed Harvey where he could rest his legs and suggested a friendly game of cards. Harvey let the man win a few pennies, which only seemed fair.

"Best get back to work!' Ed said, as he stood and stretched by the window. "I have to pick up some new furniture for Mrs. Small over on Jamaica Street—would you like to join me?"

"Sure, why not?" Harvey responded, standing up and walking over to join his new friend as they looked down on a beautiful courtyard with a small English garden.

"Isn't that your man, Mr. McCrary, sitting there by the fountain?"

"That would be him!' Harvey agreed, surprised to see his younger brother reading a Bible.

"And who's that?" Harvey asked, as a beautiful young Englishwoman with brown hair emerged from a rear entrance, accompanied by David Small. "Do the Smalls have a daughter?"

"Sure enough," Ed responded, but she's a homely little lady and looks nothing like that beauty!

Both men paused to admire the heavenly apparition for a moment before exchanging appreciative glances and stomping off to work.

The Small family had respected Martin's desire to spend some time alone in the garden, grieving for his mother. David offered the American his personal copy of the Bible, which hadn't seen much use. Martin found little consolation, and the tears began to fall when he remembered how his mother had dreamed he might become a pastor, like her father. Her dreams had been dashed by the ambitions of Martin's father and his desire to groom a suitable heir for the fortune he had struggled to build.

Martin's eyes were still moist when Jane Jevons approached down the garden path, escorted by David Small. His heart leaped with joy, followed by pangs of guilt. "How was a man supposed to feel, when he lost his mother?" He asked himself. "Why do I feel joy at the sight of a woman I barely know, when I've lost the mother I've known all my life?" Shaking his head in confusion, Martin stood up and put on the best face he could manage.

"Ms. Jevons! I didn't expect to see you again!" Martin cursed himself, as the words seemed to reveal a secret hope.

"I came as soon as I heard about your terrible loss. I hope you don't mind?" Jane stood politely by the fountain, with a look of genuine concern on her face. David decided to speak up:

"Ms. Rebecca stopped by this morning, with her mother. They were most distressed and I'm afraid Rebecca ran straight away to find Ms. Jevons. I thought you could use the company. Forgive me if I've erred," David said quietly.

"No, not at all!" Martin assured, moved by David's kind gesture. "I'm very pleased to see Ms. Jevons and only regret I must leave Liverpool in two days."

"I'll leave the two of you alone for a while, then."

David smiled kindly as he turned and deserted the garden. Martin stood silently for a moment, gathering his wits, before offering Jane a seat on the marble bench.

"I'm so sorry for your loss, Martin." Jane began. "I believe I can understand as well as anyone, as my mother died when I was young and my father passed away two years ago."

A wave of emotions cascaded through Martin's heart, as he beheld the beautiful girl sitting next to him. How could he feel the way he did, on the day he received such terrible news? Was he that shallow? But here was a young woman who had suffered more, and she cared enough to share her condolences with a near stranger. Remarkable.

Somehow Martin found his voice, rising from a heart filled with the kind of empathy that can only grow in grief-stricken soil.

"I'm truly touched by your concern, Jane, especially coming from a person who has lost more than I, at a younger age. Please tell me about your mother."

Jane smiled gently before responding: "I think of her everyday. She was a great woman, an educated person and a poet of some stature, but the strain of giving birth to 11 children was too much."

She didn't mention the fact that two of her youngest siblings died, when they were infants.

"Tell me about your mother," Jane asked softly.

"She would have liked you," He began. "She loved poetry and attended excellent schools in Charleston and Philadelphia. I was her only child." He couldn't bring himself to mention the three miscarriages his mother suffered when he was a boy, followed by endless bouts of depression.

"With your parents gone, who is your guardian?" Martin couldn't suppress his burning desire to learn more about Jane, even if the timing was wrong, as he had no time to spare.

Jane was secretly relieved, when Martin provided the opening she needed. She was genuinely fond of the American, but that only made it more painful to manipulate him, even if her cause was just.

"That would be my Godfather, Sir Ian McDonald. He was a Presbyterian pastor and a Professor at St. Andrews College, before he came into his inheritance."

St. Andrews? The most highly esteemed college in the Reformed world, at least the English-speaking part. Incredible, Martin thought silently. The thought made him feel a bit insecure.

"Then we share something else in common," Martin offered. "My Grandfather is Reverend Matthew Coulter. He's a graduate of Davidson College and Princeton seminary, where he taught for several years. He's a bit of a recluse, now."

Jane took advantage of the opening:

"Yes, I remember you mentioned him at St. Georges Hall, the abolitionist. I'd love to meet him!"

"I'm sure you would!" Martin responded, with a touch of pain in his voice.

Jane was a sensitive woman and heard every note:

"Please forgive me for being so rude the other night at the St. George's Hall. I told Sir Ian about you and he chided me for being un-Christian."

She realized the conversation was reaching a delicate stage. Tread carefully! She reminded herself.

Martin responded sincerely:

"There's nothing to forgive, as my Grandfather says the same things about slavery, every time I see him. His views are so strong, he was exiled from Charleston and forced to take refuge in the mountains of North Carolina, to avoid a beating or worse."

"You miss him, don't you?" Jane asked, kindly.

"Indeed I do. My mother's death will be very hard on him, as she was his only child. My grandmother died in childbirth, trying to bring a second daughter into the world." Martin's heart filled with love and respect for his Grandfather, which caused him to worry even more about the troubling telegram he had received from him earlier that morning. Where was his father? Why hadn't he heard from him? What did his Grandfather mean, when he said his father was "indisposed?"

The young couple sat quietly for a few minutes, watching a pair of sparrows scoot around the garden before disappearing over a stone wall. Growing bolder, Jane placed a hand on top of Martin's.

"David told me you'll be leaving soon. My Godfather and I would be honored if you could join us for dinner this evening. He sounds so much like your Grandfather. He's truly the wisest man I know, and you may be comforted by his presence."

"Yes, of course, thank you Jane." Martin's heart was thrilled by the touch of her hand, which he dared clasp in both of his. "I'm sure David's family will understand."

"This does my heart good, Martin." Jane responded with genuine affection, tempered by feelings of guilt. "We'll send a carriage around to collect you at six."

Feeling a bit awkward and ashamed, while steeling herself with a reminder of the just cause for which she fought, Jane stood and brushed her skirt with both hands.

"Take care of yourself, Martin. I look forward to seeing you this evening!" Jane looked Martin directly in the eyes as she spoke. He was sure she could read every corner of his mind. Her eyes were remarkably kind, but wise beyond her years. A mystery deserving further exploration.

"I can't tell you what a pleasure it was to see you again." For the first time in his life, when speaking to a woman, Martin absolutely meant it.

After reaching over to squeeze Martin's hand again, Jane turned and walked back to the house, leaving a marvelous scent in her wake and a lingering pain in a young man's heart.

Chapter 18:
A Double Life

After unloading Mrs. Small's furniture and helping Ed put away his horses and wagon, Harvey excused himself and set off on foot from the house on Duke Street. No one seemed to notice, as Martin was closely sheltered by the Small family and his servant wasn't welcome in the house. That was fine, as far as Harvey was concerned, as he had much to do.

The sun had already set by the time Harvey neared St. Thomas Church on Park Lane, as the days were growing shorter, especially in the northern latitudes. Blessed with the night vision of a predator, Harvey watched the church from a distance, only emerging from the shadows after the bells rang the hour. He wasn't surprised when a voice called out as he ambled past a sturdy black carriage hitched to a pair of restless horses. One of the sailors from the shooting on Edge Hill offered a friendly greeting, from his lofty perch next to the coachman, and invited Harvey to climb aboard. The carriage moved out smartly as soon as the door closed shut behind him.

Harvey found himself siting on an upholstered bench inside a comfortable coach hung with dark curtains. Commander Wallace sat on the bench directly across from him.

The British officer was expected. The man sitting next to him was not.

"Good evening, Harvey." Commander Wallace began with a sly smile. "I believe the two of you are already acquainted?" The Commander nodded to his right as he spoke.

"Mr. Bulloch." Harvey responded politely, determined to play the role the Commander wanted him to play, to learn what he could for Michael and Sir Ian.

"Seeing as how you're both returning to America on the same ship, and Mr. Bulloch is in need of your assistance, it only seemed natural the two of you should meet again!" The Commander turned and looked at the man sitting next to him, inviting him to speak.

"Evening, Harvey. I understand the Commander's men where very useful, during that little incident up on Edge Hill." Bulloch planned to take full advantage of Harvey's indebtedness to the Commander.

"Thought I was a dead man, for sure." Harvey admitted. "One of 'em had a pistol and he planned to use it. When the first shot ran out, I figured it was meant for me."

314

"That was fortunate." The Commander agreed. "You can thank my men later, if you like. For now, there's important business to discuss."

"Here's my problem." James Bulloch began, shifting in his seat. "I work out of Savannah. Sure, I get around often enough, but I have things that need taking care of in Charleston, on a regular basis. It's simple, really. I need you to pick up and deliver messages at certain places around town, to connect my people with the Commander's people. From time to time, you may be asked to knock a man around, if he fails to follow my instructions. Do you think you could handle that?"

"Yes Sir, that sounds simple enough, as long as I can avoid attracting attention from Mr. McCrary. He won't take it kindly if I neglect my duties."

The two white men looked over at one another and smiled grimly before Bulloch pulled a damp-looking newspaper out of his heavy leather briefcase.

"Martin is the only McCrary you have to worry about, now. Read this."

The Georgian passed the newspaper over to Harvey. Bulloch and Commander Wallace sat quietly as the black man read the front page of the Savannah Courier, dated 10 October 1857.

"Hank McCrary arraigned for the murder of his wife. Son missing and presumed lost at sea."

The article offered few details, but the meaning was clear, just as Harvey had surmised. It was still shocking, unbelievable. "I best act

315

that way!" The reluctant double agent thought to himself.

"Oh, Lord!" Harvey exclaimed. "We just learned this morning that Mrs. McCrary was murdered. That's why me and Martin are staying over with the Small family."

"Were you fond of Mr. McCrary, Harvey?"

James Bulloch had an agenda and he intended to press forward.

"Well, Sir," Harvey began carefully, "he freed me four years ago, so I'm in his debt."

"I'm sorry for what's happened to Hank McCrary and his wife, but there's a new reality in Charleston, now. Martin McCrary is likely to inherit one of the greatest fortunes in America, and he trusts you. My men told me how you put yourself between Martin and that killer, up on Edge Hill. Why, when you consider what you did for Martin and what you did for me, I'd say you're one remarkable nigger!"

For a man like James Bulloch, that passed for a gracious compliment.

"It's seems to me," Commander Wallace picked up the thread, "your talents have been wasted, so I'd like to groom you for something greater. A man like you could earn himself a considerable fortune, enough to set himself up in a place like Bermuda. Imagine, living in a British colony, where slavery is outlawed and black men are allowed to own property and run their own businesses. I might be able to arrange that, after a few years of good service on your part. What do you think about that?"

316

Harvey sat quietly for a moment, trying to decide if he should mention his mother and sister, or the fact that he was Hank McCrary's bastard son. He saw no advantage and concluded it would be difficult for the two men to uncover his secrets on their own. Harvey felt a sense of pride in knowing he didn't need Commander Wallace, that he couldn't be bought at any price. He knew he'd have to work hard to conceal his true loyalties, but decided it was worth the risk.

"I'm willing to do most anything you want, Commander Wallace, if you could set me up in Bermuda!" Harvey's former life as a slave and the bastard son of a planter had prepared him well for those occasions when he needed to lie convincingly.

"Good man! Now here's what we need you to do."

The two white men provided simple instructions for establishing a secure link between the British Naval Attaché working at the Consulate and James Bulloch's personal network in Charleston. They briefed him on the location of a safe house and described two separate dead letter drops, where notes could be exchanged without the need to meet a contact in person. Harvey was told all of the messages would be sealed and written in a code he couldn't read: His job was to serve as the middle man, moving the messages from one point of the city to another. Bulloch assured Harvey some coins would be left with every message, to compensate him for his time and trouble. Additional instructions and funds would be provided during monthly meetings at the safe house, assuming his service was satisfactory.

"My associate has only been at the Consulate for three months," Commander Wallace revealed, "so he needs a reliable local man like you to serve as his eyes and ears, to carry his messages and to do whatever else he requires. I'll let him introduce himself at the safe house, when the time comes. Mr. Bulloch will give you more information on his contacts during your voyage to New York."

Harvey didn't know the exact purpose of the partnership between Commander Wallace and James Bulloch, but he guessed it must have something to do with the planned shipment of British rifles to South Carolina. Was there more to that story? He decided to press his luck.

"Mr. Bulloch, you know better than anyone I have to be careful. A black man sneaking around Charleston all hours of the day and night could get himself killed quicker than a cat in a dog fight!"

Hoping to put Harvey at ease, Bulloch revealed more than he intended.

"I'll get you a pass, from the Governor himself, certifying that you are engaged in official business on his behalf. You'll be immune from harassment by the local authorities. Would that suit you?"

"Why, that's a relief, Mr. Bulloch!"

Harvey had heard of such things, before, and the bearers of such passes were usually engaged in some sort of officially sanctioned smuggling. He knew he was involved in a very dangerous game and only hoped he could produce results that justified the risk.

Before dropping Harvey off along the Strand, Bulloch provided arrangements for remaining in contact during the voyage to New York, without attracting unwanted attention. Commander Wallace gain Harvey a handful of shillings and promised more in the future.

The sailor disguised as a coachman tipped his hat when Harvey climbed down from the carriage. It was almost seven in the evening, and he had to check himself thoroughly before making his next meeting with Dr. Satterwhite. Given the latest developments, he didn't want to miss their rendezvous.

As Harvey weaved his way through the streets and lanes of Liverpool, Martin was sitting down to a private dinner with Jane Jevons and her guardian, Sir Ian McDonald. He was delighted to sit across the table from Jane, although she seemed a bit downcast that evening. She made an effort to smile, when she noticed Martin glancing in her direction, but was mostly content to listen as the two men spoke.

"Did your mother have many relations?" Sir Ian asked politely.

"No Sir, my grandfather is her only surviving family. She was an only child, like me, and my Grandfather couldn't bring himself to remarry, after my grandmother died." For some reason, Martin felt comfortable discussing his family in front of Jane and her kind-hearted guardian.

"Your Grandfather and I have much in common, as I never remarried after my wife passed away. Your grandmother must have been a remarkable woman." A master of elicitation, Sir Ian asked for more without asking at all.

"Indeed she was! They met when my grandfather was attending the Seminary at Princeton. I believe her family was from Philadelphia—yes, that's right—her father was pastor at Chambers Church." Martin recalled, while pushing some food around on his plate absentmindedly. "Grandpa told me she was blessed with an intellect and a will superior to his own, which she used to disabuse him of his foolish notions about slavery. According to Grandpa, she opened his eyes by using cogent arguments to shred the usual rationalizations and biblical justification. She was dear friends with the Grimke sisters. You may have heard of them?"

"Of course, Martin." Jane spoke up: "They wrote 'The Testimony of a Thousand Witnesses'—that book was an inspiration to every abolitionist in Britain, including my mother. They were from South Carolina, the daughters of a wealthy planter—very much like you."

Jane paused for a moment and looked over at her guardian, who nodded in silent agreement. It was time to press on.

"Martin, some day you will inherit thousands of slaves and the wealth they created for your father. How do you feel about that?"

Jane spoke softly, but with a bit of an edge to her voice.

"I imagine I feel a great deal like my grandfather must have felt, when he first met my grandmother!" Martin smiled at Jane, hoping she wouldn't be offended by his boldness.

Sir Ian had always regarded a keen sense of humor as a sure mark of character and intelligence, especially when the humor was intended to disarm, rather than hurt others. He was impressed with Martin's reaction to Jane's provocative question and rewarded him with hearty laugh that began deep in his belly and continued without restraint. Jane joined in, pleased to see her guardian in good spirits. Martin felt he might die from happiness, as the sound of her laughter was pure joy to his ears.

After the three of them had settled down and enjoyed another sip of wine, Sir Ian followed with a more direct question of his own:

"Martin, I've been a student of your country all my life and taught courses on North American history, at St. Andrews University. I've followed the most recent political developments with intense interest and have corresponded with many imminent scholars throughout the United States. As you will be returning home soon, would you like to hear some of the conclusions I've reached?"

"Of course, Sir Ian. I'll remember what I can and share it with my Grandfather." Martin's curiosity was awakened and he was honored such a prominent scholar would take the time to educate him.

321

Sir Ian liked to gesture with his hands, so he pushed his plate away from the table and leaned forward, focusing all of his attention on Martin.

"I believe the armed conflict in Kansas and Missouri is about to spread and will eventually engulf your entire nation in a great Civil War, on an unimaginable scale. The opposing sides have dug in their heals and have already demonstrated their willingness to fight. In some cases, both sides have resorted to murdering innocents in the new territories. Where you aware of that?" Sir Ian wanted to keep Martin engaged as he lead him down a chain of logic, step by step.

"Well, Sir, I've heard the usual stories, but Kansas seems so far away from South Carolina." Martin was feeling uncomfortable, as he preferred not to think about the future, which he imagined would require several decades of service to a domineering father before he would be allowed to think for himself.

"It's true, your nation is vast, but the distances are shrinking quickly, thanks to the railroad and the telegraph. Men are flooded into Kansas and Nebraska, from as far away as Florida and Maine, some fighting to spread slavery and some to stop it."

Sir Ian paused for a moment before continuing:

"If I'm right about the coming Civil War, which side will prevail?" The old man clasped his hands on top of the table and waited patiently for Martin to respond.

"I honestly don't know, Sir. I imagine the Southern states, because they have cotton, which generates more money, especially given the financial crisis up North." Martin was out of his depth and he knew it, but he felt a sense of loyalty to his home state.

"If the Southern States prevail, how long to you believe they would sustain the institution of slavery, when it has already been abandoned by almost every other nation in the world?" The Scotsman's thinking on the issue was clear, but he knew Martin's thoughts were muddled.

"Once again, I just don't know. Everyone seems to agree we'll eventually have to give it up, but no one seems to know when that might be." Martin was pleased the old man seemed to take his opinion seriously, but that only caused him to question Sir Ian's judgment, as he didn't feel he deserved that kind of respect.

"That's exactly right!" Sir Ian exclaimed. "The great men who founded your Republic knew slavery would have to end some day, but the Institution became more entrenched as it spread to new lands in Alabama, Mississippi, Louisiana, Arkansas and Missouri over the past 50 years. Now your country has millions more slaves than it did in 1776 and the Southern States depend utterly on slavery to sustain their way of life. New territories have opened in Kansas and Nebraska, and men are already killing each other over the issue. The political process has broken down and both sides are using whatever means necessary to control the legislature in

Kansas, with fraudulent elections organized by both sides."

Sir Ian shook his head sadly, as if was sharing tragic news with a friend.

"No, it can't last, not for much longer. All of the wisest men I know agree on this fundamental issue: The question that has plagued your nation since its founding is coming to a boil and civil war is inevitable. The South cannot win that war, as the North enjoys an overwhelming advantage in population and industry. War has become an industrial enterprise, Martin, and the side with the strongest industry will have the weapons needed to win the war. Once the war is over, slavery will be abolished and the Southern states will lie in ruins."

"My Godfather and I have been discussing this all afternoon, before your arrived, Martin." Jane interjected. "We're both wondering if you've considered what will happen to your family and your fortune, when slavery is abolished, as it inevitably will be."

Martin squirmed in his chair before responding:

"I've never given it much thought," Martin admitted, "as I've always regarded it as my father's fortune, not my own."

Jane looked over at Sir Ian and they both wore kind but mournful expressions.

"There's something you need to know." Sir Ian began carefully. "I wish it could be otherwise, but the latest news from Charleston is distressing." Sir Ian stood and walked around the table next to Martin and placed a copy of the same newspaper Commander Wallace had shown Harvey an hour earlier.

"I'll leave the two of you alone for a while. I hope you'll join me in the library when you're ready."

Martin's hands shook as he read the text of the article. Jane moved around the table and sat next to the troubled young man, offering words of sympathy and a comforting presence.

As Martin and Jane sat alone in the dining room of Sir Ian's Liverpool townhouse, pondering the terrible allegation that his mother was murdered by his father, Harvey found Dr. Satterwhite waiting for him as at the Nelson monument, looking deeply worried.

"Hells Bells!" The physician exclaimed as he shook hands with Harvey. "I was afraid you might not make it—there's so much that needs doing! Come, a coach is waiting just around the next corner!"

The two men moved quickly, waiting to catch up on the latest news until after they reached the carriage. Dr. Satterwhite began by outlining Sir Ian's plan, which required Harvey's participation that very evening. Harvey followed, with a concise description of his most recent encounter with Commander Wallace and James Bulloch.

"I'm out of my depth," The physician admitted, "but Sir Ian seems confident you can handle the Commander. Where I see obstacles, the two of you see opportunity. I suppose that's one of the reasons why he admires you so much!"

Dr. Satterwhite's compliment wasn't idyll, and his respect for Harvey grew with every encounter.

"We best put that aside for now." Harvey suggested, as they approached Sir Ian's townhouse.

"You're right, we can talk about the Commander tomorrow." Dr. Satterwhite paused for a moment, before continuing:

"Sir Ian believes I should stay in the background, in the event Martin rejects his offer. There's still much I could do in Bermuda, if it comes to that, so there's no point in revealing my role to Martin."

"I understand completely, Michael. Until tomorrow, then!" Harvey shook Dr. Satterwhite's hand before climbing down from the carriage. He waited until the rig disappeared in the darkness before rapping quietly on the door.

Sgt. Bowler unlatched the heavy door immediately and ushered Harvey up to the library, where Sir Ian was sitting alone by the fire, nursing a cup of tea.

"Harvey, I'm very pleased to see you!" Sir Ian rose on aging knees, using a cane for leverage.

"Likewise, Sir! Where do things stand?" Harvey asked.

"He's in the dining room with my goddaughter, Jane. Did Michael share the news about your father?"

"Indeed he did, but not until after I heard the news from Commander Wallace and his friend, James Bulloch." As succinctly as possible,

Harvey described the latest chapter in his unavoidable double life. Sir Ian's reaction was inspiring:

"That's wonderful news, Harvey! If we proceed with care, we should be in a position to frustrate the enemy's every move. Still, everything depends on the last piece of the puzzle. I'm counting on you to bring Martin over to our cause. Are you ready?"

Sir Ian placed a hand on Harvey's right shoulder and offered a wry smile in reaction to the look of genuine surprise on the big man's face.

"I thought I was only here to support your efforts!" Harvey responded.

"No, I've given it much thought and it seems obvious now: It's all up to you. He needs to know you're his half brother. He needs to know about your mother and sister, the way your father freed you but has used them to keep you on a short leash. Both of you need to talk about the fact that your father murdered Martin's mother. I want you to tell him we've been working together for years, that you've risked your life to bring an end to slavery. You also need to tell him about his Grandfather and his role in the struggle. Tell him you need his help, that's the world is about the change, whether he helps you or not. If he waivers, make sure he understands you won't be going home, that he'll be alone in Charleston without you, without his mother or his father, when slavery falls down around him."

Harvey paced around the room as he absorbed the challenge Sir Ian had offered.

"I'll do it!" He proclaimed. "I'll find a way to help him make the choice for himself."

"Come, come, sit by the fire!" Sir Ian gestured toward a pair of comfortable chairs. "They may be a few minutes yet."

Harvey took a seat by the fire and leaned in close as he compared notes with Sir Ian, gathering his wits for the critical moment.

As the quiet conversation continued in the library, Jane did her best to comfort Martin. It was a terrible thing, to lose one's mother, only to learn your father may have been her murderer. She couldn't imagine how she would handle such terrible news, herself.

The act of empathizing with Martin caused Jane to recall painful memories of loss, when she was a child. She was lucky, in a way, as she had been surrounded by a large, loving family. When she took a quick inventory, she realized Martin only had his Grandfather, and Harvey. He might lose both of them, too, if he rebuffed Sir Ian's proposal.

Martin didn't reject Jane's attention when she placed both of her hands in his. He appreciated the silent sympathy, the way she listened patiently and didn't attempt to console him with platitudes.

If I had a woman like her, Martin thought to himself, I would never hurt her. The thought of someone harming any woman he loved caused the young man to feel incredibly angry toward his father, the man who had bullied and finally murdered his mother. He felt ashamed of himself for ignoring one or two incidents when his mother appeared with a bruise or a limp, which she had explained away as the result of clumsy accidents. He had overheard the house slaves talking about the "Master's" terrible temper, a temper he had witnessed himself.

"I should have known this would happen, some day!" Martin muttered, as he looked up at Jane. "It shames me to admit my father is not a decent man. He's always treated my mother terribly, and she's always been so frail. I should never have left her alone with him."

"Martin, you aren't responsible for anything your father may have done, you mustn't blame yourself!" Jane decided to reveal something about her own family.

"When my mother died, my father took the blame on himself, for asking too much of her, for giving her too many children and for being away from home when she was critically ill. He turned to drink, railed against God and wallowed in misery. If not for Sir Ian, I'm sure he would have drunk himself to death." There was more to the story, but Jane hesitated.

"Was Sir Ian close to your father?" Martin asked, grateful to talk about anything other than what might have happened to his mother.

"Not as close as he was to my mother." Jane decided to unburden herself, to hold nothing back. "You see, my mother and Sir Ian where once in love and hoped to marry, when they were about our age. Many years later, she

329

asked Sir Ian to stand as my Godfather, in memory of their lost love."

"What happened?" Martin asked quietly, while looking at Jane. He was secretly in love himself and wondered what his fate might be. Would their story also end in tragedy?

"Sir Ian wanted to marry my mother, but his parents rejected the match, as my family are commoners and his family are very proud. My father, Thomas Jevons, was a good and decent man, but he could never fill the hole in my mother's heart. You can see it in her poetry." Jane sat calmly and did not look away when Martin looked deep into her eyes. She understood that look and felt genuine affection herself, which gave way to a feeling of shame as she considered her role in advancing the evening's agenda.

"Sir Ian is genuinely concerned about you, Martin, as am I." Jane continued, truthfully. "He's a wise and wonderful man, with great experience in the ways of the world. Why don't we join him in the library?" Jane stood up and offered her hand. Martin accepted the gesture and accompanied her down the hall, regretting the need to release her hand before entering the room.

Jane stood to one side, allowing Martin a clear view. He was shocked to find Harvey sitting by the fire, looking serious and purposeful.

"Harvey, what on earth or you doing here?" Martin was more surprised than angry.

"I heard what happened to your mother back in Charleston, Martin, and figured I should

330

look after you." Harvey stood up and strode across the room. "Aren't you going to introduce me?" He asked politely, gesturing toward the fine looking woman he had first seen from a distance the day before.

"What? Oh, of course. Jane, this is John Harvey, from South Carolina. We grew up together and he serves me still."

"Mr. Harvey, I've heard much about you." For her part, Jane thought Harvey looked like an ebony statue of an ancient Greek God. His eyes were alive with intelligence and purpose. She didn't object when he stepped forward to kiss her hand, despite his nominal status as a servant, as she knew he was Martin's older brother and a valuable partner of her godfather.

Sir Ian inserted himself: "Jane, why don't the two of us leave Martin and Harvey alone for awhile. They have much to talk about."

"Martin," the Scotsman continued, to head off any objections. "Mr. Harvey is much more than he seems, an able man I hold in very high esteem. I hope you listen carefully to what he has to say." Taking Jane by the arm, the old man escorted his beloved goddaughter back to dining room, where they poured another glass of wine and waited.

"What's going on, Harvey?" Martin asked, wondering how Sir Ian seemed to know him so well.

"There's something important I need to tell you, given the terrible news from Charleston." Harvey hesitated for a moment, trying to frame his words carefully.

"Well, out with it!" Martin demanded impatiently, irritated by the unexpected interruption of his evening with Jane.

"I'm gonna take a seat and suggest you do the same!" Harvey insisted and Martin complied, his sense of irritation held in check by growing curiosity.

Harvey plunged in, head first: "I know it's a terrible thing to learn, that your father may have murdered your mother. He's my father, too."

Martin was thunderstruck. He could feel the blood rushing in his ears and his head began to spin. He felt nauseous and sat back in his chair, trying to understand the words, then it all made sense.

He felt angry, betrayed.

"Why didn't you tell me before?" He muttered through clenched teeth.

"Because the Old Man keeps my mother and sister as slaves, and he threatened to sell them to a stranger if I told you." Harvey knew he needed to remain patient, although his brother's initial reaction was galling. His patience was rewarded.

"That sounds like him." Martin admitted, redirecting his anger at his murderous father. "So that's why he always knew you wouldn't run?"

"Partly that. Plus I've known you were my brother since you were five years old." Harvey allowed the idea to sink in as he waited patiently for Martin to speak.

"So, that day when you saved me from breaking my neck, when I almost fell out of that old oak tree, you already knew we shared the same father?" Martin was incredulous. He could still remember dangling by one arm, as Harvey grasped his wrist and refused to let go, despite the risk to himself.

"That's right, little brother. Otherwise I might have let you fall!" Harvey's dark sense of humor always seemed to surface in tense situations.

Martin had to stand up and move about the room. It was too much to take in.

"Oh, my God!" Martin exclaimed, as his mind worked through the implications. "Is your little sister my sister, too?"

"That's right. Sarah is just as much your sister as I'm your brother. She looks even more like your father than you do, if you could see past the color of her skin." Harvey suggested.

Martin sat down again, his head spinning. He felt guilty for the way he had treated Harvey in the past, especially when his father first freed him. "What a petty, despicable brat I must have been," he thought to himself. Martin tried to set those feelings aside, as he had so many questions to ask:

"Does Grandpa Coulter know?" Martin needed to know the answer to that question because his grandfather was the man he most admired in the world.

"Yes, he does." Harvey admitted. "He's known ever since I was born. He knows our father's character, as well as anyone. It broke his heart when the heathen bastard married his only daughter, although he's grateful for you. Your Grandpa must be in a bad way now."

Harvey's words helped Martin realize the story wasn't just about him. His father, Harvey's father, had murdered his own wife. His mother was also Grandpa Coulter's only child. Everything began to make sense, as he considered the impact of the crime on everyone involved.

"Was father behind Grandpa being exiled up to the mountains? Did he use someone else to rattle the cages, to stir up trouble with his congregation over his abolitionist views?" Martin was beginning to see the world more clearly as the scales were lifted from his eyes.

"You're not as stupid as I thought!" Harvey conceded. "Sure, our Daddy was behind the whole scheme. In fact, he almost got your Grandfather lynched. But don't you worry, Reverend Coulter found a way to get even with Hank. It still makes me laugh, every time I think about it!"

"What are you talking about?" Martin asked, wondering why he always seemed to be the last one to learn anything important about his own family.

"Why, Reverend Coulter has smuggled dozens of slaves to freedom over the years, with help from yours truly." After allowing this words to sink in, Harvey made a deliberate effort to slow the pace, to allow every revelation to stand on its own, leading to the outcome he desired.

"You did what?" Martin stood up, agitated beyond belief: "You could have gotten yourselves killed!" Martin stood directly in front of Harvey, shaking his fist over his head.

"We're both grown men and we both agreed to take the risk." Harvey responded, with a hint of anger in his voice. I could have left with the first batch slaves and run away to Ohio. But I stayed, because I had a duty to my mother, my sister and my brother, though a fool and an ingrate he may be."

The last remark had the desired effect and Martin tried his best to calm down before asking the obvious question:

"Why didn't you just take your mother and sister and leave, years ago?"

"Surely you know Hank keeps them under lock and key, up on the plantation?" It was hard for Harvey to avoid scoffing at his half-brother's naiveté. "He watches them close and would turn the world upside down looking for us, if we ran. The bastard feels like he owns my sister and I even more than the rest of his slaves, seeing as how he lay with our mother and brought us both into the world."

Harvey looked over at Martin, to make sure he was getting a better grip on reality.

"I didn't know, John." Martin offered by way of apology, using his brother's first name. "I don't get over to the plantation very often and haven't seen your mother or sister in years."

"Do you wonder why I'm filled with hate, why I didn't kill the bastard years ago? I've had plenty of chances!" Harvey challenged Martin to

335

slip into a black man's shoes, if only for a moment.

"I hope you don't hate me." Martin responded. "You've got plenty of cause."

"There's many things I learned from your Grandfather, but the most important lesson was simple: All children are born innocent. They share no blame for the crimes of their fathers. He helped me understand that. I don't have to be like our father, and neither do you." Harvey paused, to give Martin a chance to ponder the revelation before continuing.

"The second most important thing I learned from your Grandfather, who knows I'm not a good Christian, is also simple: Even a sinner like me can do some good in this world, if I choose. He helped me find a purpose for my life, and that purpose eventually led me to Sir Ian." Harvey gathered his thoughts as the conversation reached its climax.

"I don't understand, John." Martin replied. "What does Sir Ian have to do with my grandfather?"

"Why, they've dedicated themselves to ending slavery in America! My work smuggling runaways up to your Grandfather in the mountains is only half the story. I've also been working for Sir Ian for the last five years." There it was, the stage was set.

"Working for Sir Ian? I'm completely lost, Harvey. You've been on the road with me since early last Summer and you were working directly for Father, our father, before that. What could you possibly be doing to help Sir Ian?" Martin was genuinely confused.

Time to lay it all out, Harvey decided: "I've been spying on our father, and every other slave owning bastard back in South Carolina, ever since my first trip to Liverpool. I've done everything I can to help him keep track of all of those bastards plotting to dismantle the United States of America, so they can preserve King Cotton and keep the money flowing. I'm doing my part to bring the whole damn thing to an end and I'm willing to die for the cause!"

Overwhelmed, Martin sat down again. He listened carefully as his only brother continued to speak in calm, measured tones. Harvey asked Martin to join him, to join his Grandfather in the fight. He challenged Martin to give his life real meaning, to consider his future, to help shape it rather than passively riding the waves of chaos and war that were sure to come. He pleaded with Martin to consider the fates of the thousands of human beings owned by their father, including Harvey's mother and sister. He asked Martin to help him bring a measure of justice to the man who killed his mother.

As the conversation continued, Martin began asking Harvey to explain how they would work together, rather than asking why. Recognizing the significance of that critical moment, Harvey stopped and embraced his brother as true brother for the first time in their lives. Leaving Martin waiting by the fire, Harvey disappeared for a moment and returned with Sir Ian. The three men sat facing each other and continued to speak quietly, with the younger men looking to the Scotsman for guidance. It was a moment Martin would never forget, as he made a deliberate decision to leave his childhood behind, to live for something greater than himself, to take responsibility for the future, to be a man.

For her part, Jane laid awake in her bedroom upstairs, wondering what would happen to Martin, if she would see him again, if he could forgive her. Jane was an even greater presence in Martin's mind, as he asked himself the same questions and wondered if he could persuade her to be his wife some day. He knew she would ever marry a man who lived off the backs of human chattel. All the more reason to bring the evil to an end, he decided.

CHAPTER 19:
HOMEWARD BOUND

Martin woke the next morning to the sound of a
crow rapping on the windowsill of his room at the
Small house on Duke Street. He felt refreshed
and relished the fading images of a pleasant
dream before the thoughts and memories of the
previous day crowded around him. His
confidence teetered on the brink of indecision as
he considered the risks he was taking and the
solemn commitments he had made. Most of all,
he thought about his half-brother, Harvey, and
his mother and sister, who faced a terrible fate if
he was caught spying on the secessionists. "She's
my sister, too!" Martin reminded himself, trying
to recall her face. The thought was painful and
caused him to jump out of bed and stride across
the room. He splashed cold water on his face and
looked into the mirror above the washbasin,
gathering his resolve. For the first time in his

life, he knew exactly what he had to do and believed he could do it. He was pleased to find that conviction still clung to his heart, after a long night of second guessing.

The young American made his excuses in a brief conversation with Mrs. Small downstairs, declining the offer of breakfast while claiming the need to attend family business before boarding the steamer to New York the following morning. He found Harvey waiting for him out on the street, leaning casually against a brick wall as he sheltered himself from a soft rain under a small awning. The moment of truth had arrived and Harvey was uncharacteristically silent. Martin fell in beside him as they set off for St. Thomas Church on Park Lane, for a secret rendezvous with Commander Wallace. Things could go very well or they could go badly. There was only one way to find out.

After walking in silence for a block or two, Harvey spoke first:

"Would you like to review Sir Ian's plan?" He asked gently, still wondering if Martin was capable of pulling it off.

"There's no point, my role is simple enough, for now. Things will be more complicated when we get home, that's for sure."

Martin turned and stopped to face Harvey:

"Are you sure you need to come with me? If my father, OUR father is convicted of murder, I'll inherit the estate. I could free your mother and sister, OUR sister, and send them to join you here." Martin spoke earnestly and had made the same argument the previous evening.

Harvey continued walking for a few moments before stopping and turning to respond, placing his hands on both of his younger brother's shoulders:

"You've changed, Martin, really changed since we survived that shipwreck. I can't tell you how much it means to me, to have you worrying about other folks, the fate of my mother and sister, when you've just lost your own mother. But you know as well as me, there's just too many ifs stacked up in a row for me to stay here in Liverpool. We don't know if the Old Man murdered your mother. Even if he did, we don't know if a rich man like him will be convicted in a place like Charleston: His friends could easily find a scapegoat, I've seen it done before. I can't stay here and wait to see what happens to my family, my slave family. If your father is innocent, or if he is found not guilty, he will be free to do as he pleases, and he has sworn to take revenge of my mother and sister if I don't come home, or if anything happens to you. So please, stop asking me to stay behind. I won't do it."

Martin was looking down at the ground as he listened carefully to Harvey, sensing the truth in his words. He looked up and grinned:

"All right then, John, we're partners, for better or worse!"

"For better or worse!" Harvey agreed as he crushed Martin in a bear hug and lead him on toward their fateful encounter with a potentially dangerous man.

The black carriage was waiting near the main entrance to St. Thomas church, as expected, but this time Commander Wallace emerged from the coach before Harvey and Martin approached. He walked up and stopped directly in front of the half-brothers, sizing up Martin for a moment before allowing Harvey to introduce them. He removed his gloves before shaking hands, and said simply: "Follow me."

The two Americans followed the Commander, who was wearing a long waxed overcoat and a low, wide-brimmed hat, as he led them to a small garden gate behind the rectory.

"Come in!" He invited, "The Rector is a particular friend of mine. We'll have the place to ourselves until noon."

Martin didn't notice when a pair of sailors in plain clothes took up positions across the street from the rectory, to insure their Commander wasn't interrupted, but Harvey did.

The rector's library was sparsely furnished. The Commander took a seat in a large leather armchair and offered Martin a place in the chair next to him. Stepping into his role as the loyal servant of a wealthy South Carolinian, Harvey stood behind his master.

"I have to admit, I was surprised when Harvey suggested a meeting."

Like other successful men in his profession, the Commander often sought advantage by inviting others to speak before committing himself.

For his part, Martin had been coached on the need to project confidence, to behave like a man of his station:

"Imagine my surprise when I learned my personal man-servant was approached by representatives of Her Majesty's government without my permission."

Like any spy-master, Commander Wallace didn't enjoy being caught red-handed. In such situations, he found it useful to focus on common interests, to avoid focusing on unpleasant facts that might otherwise derail a potentially useful relationship.

"My apologies, Mr. McCrary. Given your age, I felt it would be inappropriate to approach you without your father's permission, but Harvey tells me you're just the man we should be talking to, especially given the tragic developments back in South Carolina. Please accept my condolences on the death of your mother."

There it was, the whole can of worms. The Commander was curious to see how Martin would behave: Would he speak rashly, like a hot-headed young blood, or would he control his emotions and seize the opportunity in front of him?

Martin nodded his head solemnly and looked over at the Commander with ice cold eyes. "I have no doubt my father murdered my mother and I hope he burns in hell."

"I see." The Commander began, "So it's safe to assume you will inherit your family's fortune, and your father's position in Society?"

"My father has no other heir. He has brought shame on our family's honor, which I plan to restore. It won't be easy, but I should be able to turn things around, with help from friends like George Trenholm." Sir Ian had coached Martin to bring up his connections with Mr. Trenholm, knowing he was a key player in the conspiracy to lead South Carolina down the road toward Secession.

The remark had its desired effect, but Commander Wallace was too experienced to give anything away, at least not until he learned more about Martin.

"I see you're man of character, Mr. McCrary, with the courage and fortitude needed to deal with such a tragic loss." The Commander waited for a reaction and was impressed when he discovered Martin was unmoved by casual flattery. Most men his age would glow with pride in response to such a compliment. Time to move the conversation along.

"I'm curious, Mr. McCrary, why did your man Harvey show such remarkable loyalty, acting against his own interests, in reporting his conversations with Lt. Tisdale and myself?" The Commander smiled dangerously as he glanced up at Harvey. "I asked him the same question, but he wouldn't say."

Sir Ian had prepared Martin with the appropriate response:

"It's simple, really. We grew up together, and he's my half brother. I should also mention his mother and sister are still held as slaves, on one of our plantations back in South Carolina.

My father may be an adulterer and a murderer, but he isn't stupid. He taught me never to trust anyone without considering their motivations."

Martin played his role convincingly, portraying a cold-hearted aristocrat raised to rule other men. As Sir Ian had intended, a switch flipped in Commander Wallace's mind and he decided, at that moment, to forge an alliance with the precocious young American.

"That's good, very good. How do you perceive my motivations? Do you believe we can find the common ground needed to build a relationship based on mutual trust and respect?"

Martin responded with confidence:

"That's simple enough, really. The prosperity of my my state depends on the cotton trade, as does the prosperity of your nation. The cotton trade depends on slavery. If slavery is abolished in the South, my family will be ruined—and the British Empire will be weakened. Therefore we must work together to preserve slavery, even if that means Secession for South Carolina and the other cotton states. That sounds like the basis for a trustworthy relationship, to me."

The Commander stood and walked over to a small table, where he poured two cups of tea, offering one of the cups to Martin before taking his seat again.

"Then we understand each other perfectly." The Commander paused before framing his next words carefully. "I can assure you, personally, as I have assured others, that Her Majesty's government will be prepared to support South Carolina, should she decide to secede from the Union, to protect your livelihood and your way of life."

"That's exactly what I wanted to hear." Martin responded. "How can I help?"

"As you said, it's simple, really: Assume your station in Charleston. Say nothing to anyone about our secret alliance, as that would only fuel the anger and determination of the abolitionists in New England. Seek out like minded men and keep me informed of the situation in Charleston, so that I might provide the right support at the right time. Speak to your congressman and senators and demand they do whatever it takes to preserve the cotton trade, the foundation of our mutual prosperity."

Commander Wallace had no intention of asking Martin to undertake more sensitive tasks until he had learned what the young man was capable of doing.

"I would do all of that, in the absence of an alliance with you, but how will I keep you informed, living on the opposite side of the Atlantic?"

Martin leaned forward in his chair, an eager student at the feet of a master, only the Commander didn't know a true master was pulling the strings, behind the scenes.

Wallace tapped his cup nervously before taking the next step: Establishing clandestine communications with an agent of influence in another country. He felt reluctant, for reasons that were unclear to him at the time, but dismissed his concerns as undue caution in the face of a great opportunity.

"I'll leave that to another ally, someone you need to meet."

The Commander rose and walked over to a dark mahogany door and rapped twice. A serious looking man with a military bearing emerged from the hallway.

"I believe you've already met Mr. James Bulloch, of Savannah."

Martin rose and shook hands with the intimidating Georgian.

"Well, Mr. Bulloch, I'll leave you alone with Mr. McCrary. I'm sure you have much to discuss, and it would be best if I left you alone. The Rector won't return until noon. Mr. McCrary, I hope to see you again during your next trip to Liverpool—bon voyage!"

The Commander distanced himself, both physically and professionally, from a private conversation between two Americans, adding a layer of security to the conspiracy. He trusted Bulloch completely and could afford to remain patient as his capable American partner took the reigns in hand.

"Please, call me James," Bulloch insisted, while gesturing toward a pair of waiting chairs. "May I call you Martin? I detest British formality."

Martin accepted the gesture and pretended to relax, but felt more nervous than he had with Commander Wallace. Instinctively, Bulloch seemed the more dangerous of the two.

Hoping to forge a productive partnership with a fellow American, Bulloch charged ahead:

"Commander Wallace and I have known each other for years and I trust him to protect our purpose and our identities, but he is a British Officer, after all. Although it's true many prominent British men are deeply concerned about the viability of the cotton trade, their way of life isn't under threat from the abolitionists: Ours is. It's really up to us to do something about it, before it's too late."

"I agree, my father has been saying the same thing for years." A pained look crossed Martin's face as his mind turned to his family's troubles.

Stepping gingerly, Bulloch felt compelled to speak:

"I met your mother once, at a dinner party in Charleston some 15 years ago. I was a young Naval Officer, at the time, and she was the proud mother of a five year old boy. She played the piano beautifully and sang like an angel. Truly a gentle soul."

Martin was genuinely touched and smiled in gratitude.

"I'll miss her singing," He admitted.

After pausing for a moment, in respect, Bulloch continued:

"I wish we had more time to get acquainted, but we have much to discuss in this private venue, before we meet again in public. First, we must work together to insure the secrecy of our work, to conceal our intentions from prying eyes. Do you think you can do that?"

"Of course," Martin responded, "if you teach me how."

"We'll take it step by step," Bulloch assured him. "First, we should be seen together in public as little as possible, to conceal our friendship from the enemy. We'll do that by using your man Harvey here as a cut-out, to pass messages between us—with your permission, of course."

"He seems well suited for the task, and has certainly proved himself trustworthy," Martin remarked, while glancing casually over his shoulder.

For his part, Harvey could barely conceal his amazement at his brother's magnificent performance—exactly what Sir Ian had hoped for.

"I agree, truly remarkable! If it's acceptable to you, I will use Harvey as my personal courier with certain individuals working at the British Consulate in Charleston, and with other allies in the city. For your protection, none of them will know of you role in our affairs, and they will receive the same courtesy from you. Later, when the time is right, a political movement will emerge and we'll all stand together to defend our rights, but for now our critically important business must be handled in private."

"I accept your conditions wholeheartedly, James, but will need your advice when I get back home to Charleston." A natural actor, Martin allowed a bit of genuine uncertainty to emerge in the tone of his voice, to lull Bulloch into believing he was in control of the situation.

"And you shall have it!" Bulloch assured Martin, as both men stood to shake hands and seal the bargain. The Americans spent the next hour reviewing a simple contact plan that would enable them to remain in touch, without showing their hand.

When all of the details had been discussed and reviewed again, Bulloch invited Martin and Harvey to leave the rectory, first, reminding Martin to maintain some distance aboard ship during their voyage to New York. They found themselves walking on a nearly-empty street, as they worked their way toward Exchange Flags, for a final business meeting at Small and Sons before their next journey began.

Harvey wasn't surprised when he discovered Commander Wallace's sailors trailing them at a distance, as the British spymaster was curious to know where they might go following the meeting. He said nothing to Martin, for the moment, as he might reveal his awareness by looking over his shoulder. Sir Ian had prepared a contingency for such an eventuality, and the success of their venture did not depend on any additional personal meetings before they boarded the steamer. Harvey had only to leave a scarf hanging in his window above the Small family's carriage house, to signal the successful outcome of their conversation with Wallace and Bulloch. All future contact with Sir Ian and Dr. Satterwhite would be impersonal in nature, until

Martin and Harvey were able to travel to Liverpool or Bermuda.

Later that evening, Sir Ian's man-at-arms, Sgt. Bowler, walked past the Small house on Duke Street and made note of the scarf hanging in the loft window above the carriage house. An hour later he found the Scotsman resting by the fire, nursing a cup of tea. The news was thrilling, warming his heart and, inspiring him to take a stroll in the garden. His heart soared as he gazed up at the stars on a clear October evening, feeling young again as he enjoyed a rare moment of private celebration. With help from his American friends, he had penetrated the heart of a grand conspiracy to dismantle the United States of America, by encouraging Secession in the Southern states. Given the great wealth generated by the cotton trade, on both sides of the Atlantic, he knew the odds were against them: Secession and Civil War might be inevitable, but at least they had a chance to influence the outcome of such a war, God willing.

About the Author:

Phillip O. Otts is a veteran of the CIA's Clandestine Service. He retired in 2006 to pursue a life-long interest in writing. A native of Alabama, he was born in a small town with a Confederate memorial in front of the courthouse and a monument to a Confederate ancestor dominating the family graveyard. After spending much of his adult life overseas, Mr. Otts developed a deep appreciation for those remarkable individuals with the courage and integrity to overcome the limitations of their tribal echo chambers, like the rare German who spied against the Nazis, or the brave Russian who defected from the Soviet Union—or the handful of Southerners who recognized the evils of slavery and took tangible steps to end it. This insight was the driving force behind *The Storm Before the War*, the first in a series of novels set in the Civil War era.

Previous published works: *The Sword of the Prophet*, a terrorist thriller set in the early years of the Obama administration.

More Great Historical Fiction from Bygone Era Books:

And the Wind Whispered by Dan Jorgensen

Bittersweet Tavern by S. Copperstone

Divine Vengeance by D. W. Koons

Girl in the River by Patricia Kullberg

The Harlot Saint by Susan McGregor

Immortal Betrayal by Daniel A. Willis
Immortal Duplicity by Daniel A. Willis
Immortal Revelation by Daniel A. Willis

Into the Hidden Valley by Stuart Blackburn

Kilpara by Patricia Hopper

Nazi Love by Michael Phayer

The Other Side of Courage by Robert Nordmeyer

Primitive Passions by John N. Cahill

The Prince of Prigs by Anthony Anglorus

The Sands of Kedar by Diana Khalil

Whispers of Liberty by Heidi Sprouse